Praise *for* the writing of bestselling author Cindi Myers

"Charming. The protagonists' chemistry and Lucy's spunk keep this fluffy novel grounded."
—*Publishers Weekly* on *Life According to Lucy*

"Delightful and delicious…Cindi Myers always satisfies!"
—*USA TODAY* bestselling author Julie Ortolon

"Cindi Myers provides a mature perspective in *What Phoebe Wants*, somehow balancing outrageous situations with real heart."
—*Romantic Times*

"Chick lit fans will enjoy this amusing contemporary romance."
—*The Best Reviews* on *Life According to Lucy*

Cindi Myers

Cindi Myers became one of the most popular people in eighth grade when she and her best friend wrote a torrid historical romance and circulated it among their peers. Fame was short-lived, however; the English teacher confiscated the manuscript and advised her to concentrate on learning to properly diagram a sentence. From this humbling beginning, she went on to write nonfiction for national and regional publications ranging from *Ladies' Home Journal* to *Popular Mechanics*, but she never got rid of the fiction bug. Her first novel was published in 1999 and she's been steadily writing fiction ever since. Blessed with an appreciation for everyday humor and a complete lack of a physical sense of direction, Cindi Myers has devoted herself to taking the scenic route through life. She lives with her husband, dogs and a demanding parrot in the mountains of Colorado.

THE Next NOVEL™

My Backwards Life

Cindi Myers

MY BACKWARDS LIFE

copyright © 2005 Cynthia Myers

i s b n 0 3 7 3 2 3 0 4 2 7

This edition published by arrangement with Harlequin Books S.A.

® and TM are trademarks of the publisher. Trademarks indicated with
® are registered in the United States Patent and Trademark Office, the
Canadian Trade Marks Office and in other countries.

TheNextNovel.com

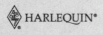 HARLEQUIN®

PRINTED IN U.S.A.

From the Author

Dear Reader,

Like most people, I lead a pretty conventional life. But I have a secret: I am a rebel at heart. I've never staged a protest, lived in a commune, hitchhiked cross-country or climbed Mt. Everest, but I imagine what those things would be like.

Unlike my heroine, Grace, who thinks her life is unconventional and longs for a more traditional lifestyle, I admire people who are a little bit outside the curve of conventionality. I suppose my ideal would actually be to live more like Grace's friend, Myrtle, whose life has been filled with exciting experiences.

In the end, however, it doesn't matter what kind of job we have, where we've traveled, whether we're married or unmarried, wealthy or of more modest means. What matters is the relationships we build along the way. Whether they're in traditional roles, like the mother-daughter bond Grace shares with Trudy, or the different kind of love she and Gil have for each other, each one is important and special.

My Backwards Life is a celebration of all those wonderful relationships of friendship, love and family. I hope you enjoy reading this story as much as I enjoyed creating it.

I love to hear from my readers. You can visit my Web site at www.CindiMyers.com, e-mail me at Cindi@cindimyers.com or write me at P.O. Box 991, Bailey, CO 80421.

Happy reading,

Cindi

In memory of
Michael D. Healy
1957–2002

CHAPTER 1

In high school driver's ed, I earned the distinction of being able to drive backwards better than anyone else in my class. Not that there is a lot of call for this particular skill, but you have to work with what you have, and I have been going about life in Reverse ever since.

Which is to say that, while other women were going to college, finding careers, marrying and having babies, I dropped out of college, had a baby, got married, got divorced and got a job. And then, at the ripe old age of thirty-five, I decided to go back to college. I figured with a diploma in my hand I could literally turn my life around and start heading forward again.

"Moving forward is good," my friend Gil said as he poured me a second cup of coffee. He cocked one eyebrow in his best Rhett Butler impersonation, which used to make me weak at the knees, but now just makes me think I was too easily impressed. "Any particular reason you decided to do this *now?*"

I traced my finger around the rim of my coffee cup. We were sitting in the kitchen of his duplex, located off Enfield Road in Austin's Tarrytown neighborhood. I'd come over to balance his checkbook, which I do every month, though I always say I'm going to stop doing it. "Remember I told you that vice president's position came open at the bank?"

"Ye-es." He drawled out the word, watching me expectantly.

"I applied for the job. Since I've been head teller for three years now, and since I've been at the bank longer than anyone else, I thought I had a good shot."

"And?"

"And I didn't get the job." I cleared my throat, determined to appear blasé about this, though inside I was seething. "Mr. Addleson said the position required a college degree. Apparently all my years of experience don't count as much as a diploma."

"So you decided to go back to school." He nodded. "It makes sense."

Did it? I wasn't even sure I *wanted* the vice president's job, but the money had sounded too good to pass up. When I didn't get the job, the rejection felt personal. Grace Greenleigh, who dropped out of college after three semesters, doesn't have what it takes to get ahead in life. I felt stuck. Stagnant.

You know how when you buy a red minivan and suddenly, everywhere you look you see red minivans? Suddenly, everywhere I looked, I saw people making exciting changes in their lives. My father announced he was taking early retirement from his job. My daughter started high school. My best friend was divorcing her jerkwad husband and was starting over.

And there I was, running in place like a hamster on a wheel, wearing myself out going nowhere. Signing up for classes at St. Edward's University felt like a good way to jump-start my life again.

"What are you going to study?" Gil asked.

"I guess business. That's what I was studying before. Except a lot of my credits didn't transfer, so it's almost like starting over."

"Don't worry. You'll do great."

Gil is my best friend. He's also my ex-husband and the father of my daughter. He'd be the perfect man for me except for one small detail.

He's gay.

What can I say? We were very young when we got together. Those early college years are enough of an identity crisis without adding sexual confusion into it. You might say our relationship was an experiment that failed, except of course for our daughter, Trudy. I was just beginning my sophomore year at Southwest Texas State when I found out I was pregnant, and Gil did the right thing and married me.

Talk about a way to ruin a good friendship. Before that terrible two years were over, we were hating ourselves, hating each other and feeling pretty hostile toward random strangers who had the misfortune to cross our paths.

Now that we're divorced, we're good friends again. We have joint custody of Trudy, who seems cool with the situation, in that remarkably flexible way children have of dealing with the bizarre. Gil is in a committed relationship with Mark, an artist who makes collages out of "found objects," which is a fancy way of saying things he digs out of the trash.

"A lot of people wait until they're older to go back to school," Gil said. "It makes sense you'd learn more when you're settled in life."

I sipped my coffee and made a face. I was trying to learn to drink it black, since that was less fattening, but I hated the taste. "That's just the point. My life is not settled. At least, not the way I want it to be."

Gil smiled and nodded. "Ah, I see."

I should mention that Gil has this annoying belief that he knows me better than any other person on earth. That he can "read" me, as if I were some kind of roadside sign. "You don't see anything," I snapped. "There's nothing to see."

He closed his lips over his teeth, but the smile was still there, a smug grin. "You're hanging on to the old 'husband and three kids and a house in the suburbs' thing, aren't you?" he said.

"No." I shoved my cup away, sloshing coffee onto the tabletop. I'll admit that at one time I had certain…*expectations* for my life. And that may have included a husband and more than one child. Maybe even a house in the suburbs. But that didn't mean I expected any of that at this late date. I dabbed furiously at the spreading coffee stain with a paper napkin. "I just want a better job. Something more fulfilling. Something to provide a future for Trudy and me."

"You never know. You might meet someone at St. Ed's."

I lifted my head and glared at him. "I don't need a man to make me happy."

His smug smile was gone, replaced by a searching look that made me halfway believe he *could* see inside me, to some secret place I didn't even know about. He reached out and covered my hand with his own. "Gracie, everybody needs somebody. There's no shame in that."

I pulled my hand away and forced a laugh. "Please! You make it sound like I'm some old woman living in a garage apartment with fifteen cats. I have friends. I have Trudy. And you."

He sat back and studied me over the rim of his coffee cup. "You know what I mean. When was the last time you had sex?"

"Gil!" I could feel myself blushing and that made me madder still. At thirty-five, you ought to be past blushing. "That's none of your business."

"That's okay. I already know the answer. It's been too long."

I picked up his bank statement and pretended to be engrossed in it. The truth was, it had been so long since I'd had sex that I couldn't even remember it. But that had nothing to do with my decision to go back to college. I really did intend to get my life straightened out and headed in the right direction. "This is a mess, Gil. I can't find half these checks in your register."

He grinned again. "Why don't you just tell me to shut up instead of changing the subject?"

"All right then, shut up."

"No. I'm not the silent type. You know that." He stood and came around to peer at the bank statement over my shoulder. "Don't tell me I've screwed this up worse than anyone else who comes into the bank."

I grimaced. "Not worse. But at least as bad." I work at the Tarrytown Branch of Merchant's Bank. My official capacity is head teller, but all that title gets me is a lot of headaches for very little money. I laid the bank statement aside. "Maybe I won't stick with the business major. Maybe I should go into teaching or something."

He picked up the bank statement and frowned at it. "You hated school. Didn't you tell me that in high school you were voted 'girl most likely to blow up the building'?"

I shifted in my chair. "I was going through a rebellious period. And all I did was set off a smoke bomb in the women's restroom."

He patted my shoulder. "My junior anarchist. Don't you know that little incident is on your permanent record? Might make it hard to find a teaching position."

Of course, I know that whole "permanent record" thing is a bunch of hooey.

Isn't it?

"I'm just thinking I need a job where I can be, I don't know…nurturing."

He considered this. "How about a nurse?"

"I faint at the sight of blood."

"Day care?"

"That pays worse than banking."

"You could always have another baby."

I swiveled around to face him. "Are you volunteering to be the father?"

It was his turn to look embarrassed. Just a little pink around the cheeks. "Uh…no," he muttered.

I laughed. "Don't worry. I doubt if Mark wants to share."

"Share what?" Mark, dressed in shorts and a vintage *Mary Hartman, Mary Hartman* T-shirt, shuffled into the kitchen from his workshop/garage. His black hair stood up in back as if he'd repeatedly run his hands through it and he had a jeweler's loupe attached to his forehead like a third eye.

"Gil thinks I should have another baby," I said. "I asked him if he wanted to be the father."

Mark opened the drawer next to the sink and began searching through its contents. "No sharing. I'm not into that kinky shit. We got any corks around here?"

"Gracie's going to be a college girl," Gil said.

"No shit?" Mark fished a cork from the drawer and pulled the jeweler's loupe down over his eye. "Stay away from those sorority sisters. They'll have you ratting your hair and wearing little sweater sets and all that shit."

"You've been watching too many *Gidget* movies on cable." Gil carried our cups to the sink. "And stop saying that word all the time. Trudy's liable to pick it up."

Mark moved the loupe back to his forehead and frowned. "Stop saying what word? 'Ratted?'"

"Stop saying shit. Can't you think of something else?"

Mark shrugged. "Sorry, man. Guess it's just a bad habit."

"Well think of something else." Gil nodded toward the cork in Mark's hand. "What are you going to do with that?"

Mark grinned. "It's for a new piece I'm working on. A single cork floating on a sea of nuts and bolts and all this heavy metal sh—uh, stuff." He held up the cork. "Sort of a statement about one person's ability to rise above all the heavy sh—*things* in life."

"Sounds interesting," I said. This is the safest comment for Mark's artwork, much of which I don't even pretend to understand.

He nodded. "I've been bustin' A coming up with ideas for new pieces, getting ready for a big show next month."

"You have a show? Congratulations!" I tried to hide my shock. Obviously, other people appreciated Mark's "creations" more than I did. "Where is it?"

"Sud Your Duds, over on east Sixth."

"Sud Your Duds?" I frowned. "Isn't that a Laundromat?"

"Yeah, cool, huh? It's the latest thing—showing artwork

in a utilitarian atmosphere. The show itself kind of makes a statement that way."

"Uh-huh."

I caught Gil's eye. He shrugged and clapped his hand on Mark's shoulder. "What can I say? The man's a genius."

I looked away. Moments like this were always a little awkward. Seeing the two of them together always caused a certain tightness around my heart, an old ache I'd gotten used to suppressing. I mean, I truly like Mark, and I was happy that Gil was happy with him. But I hated that he had a part of Gil that I still wanted—the part of his heart and soul that it wasn't in Gil's nature to be able to give to me.

I stood and hooked my purse over my shoulder. "I'll have to finish your bank statement later, Gil. I have to pick up Trudy, then get over to the campus bookstore before it closes."

"You know if you need us to watch her any while you're in class, we will," he said, walking me to the door. He put his hand on my shoulder and stopped me as I opened the door. "And hey, I know you'll be a success, whichever direction you decide to go."

"Thanks." I stood on tiptoe and kissed his cheek. Every woman should have a Gil in her life.

Who am I kidding? I'd settle for a straight man who remembered to pick up the dry cleaning occasionally.

As my Mom always told me, I'm entirely too picky when it comes to the opposite sex.

* * *

I pulled into the drive of Reagan High School just as Trudy came out of the side door to the band hall, flute case in hand. Trudy is fourteen and going through what my mother always called a "phase." She does this periodically, like a crab moving out of one shell and into another, searching for the right fit. There was the imaginary friend phase, where we had to set a place at the table every meal for "Marlena" and the ballerina phase, where she wore a leotard and walked on her tiptoes for months. Later came the Victorian novel phase, during which she wore her hair in a crocheted snood and dusted her face with white powder in an attempt to achieve a pale, consumptive look. The current phase involves dying her hair jet-black, wearing a studded dog collar and reciting painfully bad poetry which rhymes words such as "suicide" and "betide."

"Mom, I need a bar of Ivory soap and a turkey baster for school," she announced as she slid into the front seat.

"Good afternoon, Trudy. I'm fine, thank you."

She rolled her eyes at me and fastened her seat belt. "I need a bar of Ivory soap and a turkey baster."

"I heard you the first time." I put the car in gear and drove away. "But why?"

She shrugged. "Some kind of science experiment."

A number of experiments involving turkey basters and Ivory soap came to mind, none of them appropriate for the classroom. "What—" I shook my head. Why would I want to explore that topic further? I turned the car onto Riverside. "We have to go to the campus bookstore first."

"Why?" She leaned forward and examined her face in the visor mirror, turning this way and that, searching for every flaw. Not that there are any, of course. When I was Trudy's age, I had acne and my nose was too big for my face. Trudy takes after her father—the same flawless skin, thick hair and sea-blue eyes.

"So I can buy the books for my classes."

She tore herself away from her reflection and stared at me. "So you really did it? You really signed up for college?"

"I really did it. Starting next week, I'll be a student at St. Edward's University." That had a nice sound to it. A student. A scholar. Someone devoted to improving her mind.

"What about work?"

"I'll work the drive-through afternoons and Saturdays. That way we'll still have insurance. With the money I've saved and money from your father, we should be all right." It wasn't as if we'd ever had all that much money anyway.

Apparently satisfied that I'd still be able to keep her in mascara and pizza, she dug in her backpack and extracted a tube of lipstick. Mouth open wide, she carefully colored her lips vampire-red.

At the campus bookstore, Trudy rifled through the CD bins while I searched the shelves for the required reading for my classes. Is there some unwritten rule that says college texts must weigh ten pounds each and cost fifty bucks? Thank goodness I had a scholarship to help pay the bill.

While I was searching for the right books, I cast a few sideways glances at my fellow shoppers. A tall girl with blond dreadlocks stared morosely at a shelf of philosophy texts while further down, a stocky young man in cut-off jeans and a sweatshirt emblazoned with the name of a band I'd never heard of scowled at the chemistry section. Dismay settled in my stomach like bad potato salad. I was easily the only person in the place over the age of thirty. Where were all the "experienced" students the brochure had talked about?

I struggled to carry a tower of hefty tomes to the counter where Trudy was waiting with a tall, thin boy who wore an alarming amount of jewelry pinned to various portions of his anatomy.

"I really dig your hair," the boy was saying when I arrived.

Trudy fluffed her dead-black locks while I resisted the urge to shout "She's fourteen!" After all, I had been her age once, so eager to impress. To be grown-up.

Yes, and look what had happened to me. I smiled my most "adoring parent" smile. "There you are, dear. We'd better hurry and get home and bake those cookies for your Girl Scout troop."

The look Trudy gave me told me I'd pay for that later.

"So this is your mom? Cool." The boy, whose name tag identified him as "Daveed" plucked a book off the top of my pile. "*Introduction to Economics.*" He grinned. "So you're a freshman, huh?"

"Not exactly." To my dismay, only about half the credits I'd earned in my previous try at college had transferred. "I'm more of a junior-sophomore."

He dragged the book over the scanner and reached for the next one. "Well, don't worry. We get a lot of older students in here." He said the word "older" as if it were a synonym for "ancient."

Trudy burst out laughing and I felt my face heat to an unbecoming red. God, what was I getting myself into?

Trudy took the books from me and carried them to the car. "After all, we don't want you to strain your back or anything," she said. "We read in health class that older women are prone to back problems from osteoporosis."

I made a face at her. "I suppose I deserved that."

"What was that crack about Girl Scout cookies?" She waited while I unlocked the car. "I was just talking to the dude. Don't you trust me?"

"Oh, I trust you. But I don't trust him."

"You don't trust men." She dropped the books in the back seat, then climbed into the front. "Maybe if you dated more, you wouldn't be so suspicious."

Are there many things more humiliating than having your daughter tell you you don't date enough? It's not as if I purposely avoided men. At least five times in the twelve years since my divorce I'd made a serious effort to "get back out there," as my mother so helpfully put it. But "out there" was a scary place and after a while meeting strange men and sitting through awkward dinners didn't seem to be worth the trouble. "I don't have time to date," I said. "I have a job and now school. Not to mention a daughter to raise."

She laughed. "Maybe you'll meet some cool dude at school. Then you'll be too busy to worry so much about me."

"I've got news for you, dear. Worrying is a mother's job."

"And you're really good at it."

"You give me lots of practice."

She stuck her tongue out at me and I laughed. What would I do without Trudy? Some days she drives me insane, but most of the time, she's the main reason I hang on to any sanity at all in my crazy, mixed-up life.

By the time we picked up the soap and baster at the grocery store, it was six-thirty and the thought of going home and cooking anything made me want to weep, so I drove to Taco Bell for dinner. As we pulled into the parking lot, Trudy made a face. "What are we doing here?"

"Dinner. My treat." I reached for my purse.

She shook her head. "They serve meat here."

I opened my wallet and checked my meager supply of cash. "What do you want? Burrito supreme? Or Nachos Bell Grande?"

She stuck her nose in the air. "I can't eat meat. I'm a vegetarian."

I stared at her, feeling another "phase" coming on. "Since when?"

"Since lunch today. I took one look at the cafeteria's mystery meat special and knew I could never eat flesh again."

That's my daughter, the drama queen. I've learned the best approach is to pretend everything is perfectly normal. "Then you can have a bean and cheese taco." I opened the car door. "Now come on. I'm hungry."

A burrito supreme, three bean tacos, an order of nachos and a package of cinna-twists later, we pulled into the drive of the little bungalow we rent on a side street off Exposition Boulevard. It's a fairly modest house, a two-bedroom stucco built in the fifties, with small rooms and squeaky wooden floors. But it has a giant pecan tree in the front yard, and a backyard large enough for a big flower garden, my one extravagance in an otherwise frugal life. The rent's cheap and it's close to the bank and Trudy's school. I only hoped the landlord wouldn't one day decide to renovate and sell out to the many high-tech millionaires who are invading all of Austin's old hippie neighborhoods.

"Why are Joyce and her boys standing in their front yard?"

I wondered the same thing as I pulled the car into our driveway and watched my best friend and next-door neighbor, Joyce Dilly, head toward me. With her mass of dark brown curls and upturned nose, Joyce looks like one of those fancy bride dolls I always wanted as a kid. She teaches fourth grade and all the little boys in her class are in love with her. All the little girls want to *be* her.

"Grace, do you think I'll ever have another day in my life when things don't go wrong?" she asked as I climbed out of the car.

"What's happened?" I asked.

"Kevin's football is stuck in the shoe tree."

The football wasn't stuck in a closet accessory, but in an actual tree in the front yard. The previous resident of the house, a performance artist who went by the name of Raynaldo, had decorated the tree with fifteen pairs of shoes suspended from the branches. The ensemble included fuchsia stilettos, tiger-print platforms and a pair of orange high-top sneakers.

"If Peter was here it wouldn't be any big deal, but what am I supposed to do?" Her voice had an edge of hysteria and her eyes glistened with unshed tears.

Peter was Joyce's soon-to-be-ex, a spineless snake who hadn't even had the decency to tell her face-to-face that he was leaving her. Instead, six months previously he'd left a note on the kitchen table for her to find when she came home from work.

"It's okay." I put my arm around her and we walked toward the tree. "You can get through this."

"Some days I wonder." She took a shaky breath. "If it wasn't for the boys I think I'd probably fall apart."

"You're doing great." I squeezed her shoulders, then directed a smile to the boys, eleven-year-old Kevin and ten-year-old Kyle, both of whom were red-haired, freckle-faced little clones of their no-good father. I wondered sometimes if this didn't make it that much harder on Joyce. After all, she was reminded of Peter every time she looked at her sons.

The boys were standing with Trudy under the shoe tree. "Hey boys," I said. "How did your football end up in the shoe tree?"

"Kevin bet me he could knock the Doc Martens off that branch." Kyle pointed to the chunky black boots that hung by the laces from a limb to the left of the stranded football.

"I almost did it," Kevin said, his lower lip jutted out in a pout.

"Mom, how are we going to get it down?" Kyle's voice rose in a whine.

"I could climb up there and get it," Kevin said.

"Absolutely not." Joyce put her arm around him. "You could fall and break a leg."

"Then you climb up there." Kevin glared at her.

Joyce shot me a pleading look. "I'm afraid of heights. Grace, could you get it?"

"Me?" I shook my head. "I stopped climbing trees the day Ronald Millwood told me my butt looked twice as big when seen from the ground."

"I promise I won't make any comments about your butt. I won't even look at your butt." She chewed her lower lip,

23

then played her trump card. "If you won't help me, I'll have to call General Edison."

General Edison is our mutual landlord. A very old, very cranky retired military man who believes the best renter is a silent renter. He operates on a philosophy similar to my father's. When we were children and my dad suspected we were up to anything, he'd yell up the stairs, "You girls don't want me to have to come up there!"

This girl certainly didn't want General Edison to have to come out here. Especially not over a stupid football stuck in a tree. One look at the ball up there amidst all those shoes and the General would be calling up his real estate agent and driving For Sale signs into our front yards.

I handed Trudy my purse. "Hold this."

"You're going up there to get it?" Kevin asked. "Cool!"

"You won't think it's so cool if I fall and break my neck."

Joyce grinned. "I promise to sign your cast."

I jumped up and grabbed hold of the lowest limb of the tree, the one where a black Mary Jane hung. After I pulled myself up, it wasn't too difficult to scale the branches, past the fuchsia heels and orange high-tops, on up to where a pair of red sandals dangled beside size nine men's wingtips.

The football was wedged in a small forking branch just above the Doc Martens. I stopped underneath them to catch my breath and contemplated what I should do next.

"You're doing great, Mom!" Trudy called up to me.

"You're making me nervous," Joyce countered.

I glanced down at the quartet watching me. "I'm the one who's nervous," I shouted down.

"You're almost there," Kyle said. "You can almost reach the ball."

I turned my back on them and looked out over the neighborhood. The late summer dusk bathed everything in a smoky light, softening the landscape into shades of green and gold and erasing the faded paint and scarred woodwork of the rows of rent houses so that they looked new again. Ready to welcome soldiers home from Korea and their brides. The couples would raise families in these houses, celebrate birthdays and anniversaries, play cards and hold cookouts, and everyone would live happily ever after.

The picture looked romantically rosy from here. Sensible. Uncomplicated. Completely opposite my own life. Gil had accused me of *hanging on to the old "husband and three kids and a house in the suburbs" thing,* and maybe he was right. Was that so bad? Wanting a more traditional kind of life as a wife and mother?

"Mom! Are you going to sit up there all night?"

I blinked. In the gray dusk the houses looked old and run-down again. The man at the end of the block roared into his driveway on his Harley, while a woman in tie-dyed overalls sat on her steps, smoking a cigarette.

I looked up at the football. Still there. Sighing, I pulled myself another foot up into the branches. From here I could lean over and grab hold of the limb in which the ball was imprisoned. I shook it as hard as I dared and was rewarded by the ball plunking down on top of my head on its way to the ground.

"Yea!" Kevin and Kyle cheered and raced to catch the ball while Trudy leaned against the tree trunk and giggled.

I glanced back out at the darkening street. Lights were coming on now. I could hear air conditioners humming and the sound of traffic over on MoPac Expressway. Two doors down, Ronald Jackson came out on his porch and began to play the saxophone. I laughed. My fairy-tale vision had been interesting, but this was more like it. A funky neighborhood of shoe trees and psychics, hippies and slackers. A place where someone like me could feel right at home.

Of course, about that time, the newspaper photographer showed up.

CHAPTER 2

There's nothing like having your picture on the cover of the local newsrag to make you famous. Or maybe I should say notorious. Nobody lays out the red carpet when you arrive, but people do point and stare when you pop into the corner market for a carton of milk.

Was it my fault that reporter was working on a story on yard art when he spotted me sitting in the shoe tree? Or that I couldn't climb fast enough to get down before he snapped that picture? Or that he cornered Joyce and the boys and somehow turned me into a big hero for retrieving a lousy football?

When I arrived at work at the bank the morning the paper appeared, I found a copy of the article displayed prominently. "Grace! You're a celebrity." My boss, Dwayne Addleson, came marching across the lobby toward me.

"Um, not exactly." I stuffed my purse in a drawer and tried not to look as embarrassed as I felt. "It's no big deal."

Mr. Addleson regarded the picture of me in the tree. "Whatever possessed you to hang your shoes outside like that? I mean, isn't it awfully inconvenient when you want to wear them?"

Through long practice, I refrained from rolling my eyes. I know Addleson does not say these things to be intentionally funny. "I don't wear them. And they're not my shoes. It's not even my tree. It's in the yard next door."

"Oh." He looked disappointed. "Then I suppose you won't be showing up for work in those leopard-skin platforms."

I shook my head. "Not a chance."

"Oh." He rested his folded hands on his chest and continued to stare at me.

"Is there something else you wanted to talk to me about?"

"Yes. I noticed on the schedule you're only working in the afternoons next week. Why is that?"

It took a lot of effort to hold back the groan that was already forming in my throat. Mr. Addleson is a very intelligent man, but he "forgets" things that might inconvenience him, such as vacation requests, promises of pay raises and changes in work schedules. "I'm starting college next week," I said. "I talked to you about it. When you told me the vice president's job required a diploma, I decided to go back to school to finish my degree."

"But the vice president's job has been filled." He frowned. "You didn't think we'd hold it open until you graduated, did you?"

I sometimes wonder if Addleson is as dense as he appears, or if he merely gets his jollies jerking my chain. "You're not?" I widened my eyes, miming innocence. "Then I guess I'll just have to hope another job comes open by the time I get my diploma."

He frowned. The veins stood out alarmingly on his balding head. "Then you won't be able to come in early Monday?"

"Nope. That's my first day of class."

"I was really hoping you could help train our new girl."

The "girl" in question was fifty-two years old, but Mr. Addleson belongs to the generation of men to whom all female employees are girls. "Opal is going to train Muriel," I said. "We've got it all worked out."

"All right then, if you're sure you won't reconsider. I mean, have you thought about night school?"

I somehow managed to hold back a sigh. "I'll be in Monday afternoon, Mr. Addleson. Everything will be fine. You'll see."

At least, I *hoped* it would be fine. If not fine, at least tolerable. Anything less than disastrous is a plus on some days.

I'd just settled in at my desk when yet another copy of the offending picture loomed into view. I stared at the color image of myself up in the tree. Ronald Millwood had been right—from that angle, my butt looked enormous. I glanced up at the person holding the picture and automatically sat a little straighter in my chair. "Mom! What a nice surprise."

At fifty-five, my mother is still a very attractive woman, with platinum hair, porcelain skin and bright blue eyes. Too bad I took after my dad, who is a melancholy mix of Irish and German. From him, I inherited my freckles and auburn hair that refuses to be styled. My parents have been married thirty-six years and each has a defined role: my dad is the strong, silent supporter and my mother is the flighty, talkative worrier. Mostly what she worries about is me.

"Why didn't you tell me you were going to be in the paper?" she said now, rattling the pages.

"I wasn't sure about it myself." Secretly, I'd been hoping they wouldn't use the picture, even though the reporter had assured me the shot was "perfect" for the story he was writing.

"You can't imagine how embarrassed I was when Sarah Milligan called to tell me about it." Mom sank into the chair in front of my desk. "I had to run out right away and buy twenty copies for the relatives."

Oh great. Another one for the scrapbook. "Most embarrassing moments in Grace's life." "Mom, you shouldn't have gone to all that trouble." Believe me, I meant that.

"It's no trouble. I'm sure Aunt Polly will be thrilled."

Aunt Polly is ninety-six and living in a nursing home in New Orleans. The last time I saw her, some twenty years ago, she kept calling me "Elaine" and couldn't remember how we were related. Yeah, I'm sure my picture in the paper is going to make her day.

Mom folded the paper and put it in her purse. "How are you doing? How is Trudy?"

"We're both fine. I'm starting college next week."

It was a really big decision for me to decide to go back to school and frankly, I was hoping for a pat on the back from my mom. I mean, if she can brag about my getting stuck in a tree full of footwear, you'd think she'd be thrilled with the idea of me furthering my education, wouldn't you?

And you'd be wrong. Mom pursed her lips and studied me. "I've been thinking a lot about that, dear, and are you sure that's such a good idea? I mean, it's a lot of expense and work and well…you aren't getting any younger."

"Exactly why I'm doing it now. I've waited long enough." I leaned toward her and lowered my voice. "I want a better life for myself and Trudy. A better job. Getting a degree will help me do that."

"Yes, dear, but maybe instead of an education, you'd be better off finding a husband. One who already has an established career, who can support you and Trudy in the style you deserve."

I sat back. This is a familiar refrain of my mom's. Maybe it's because she comes from the generation where women are trained from birth that their highest goal is to be a wife and mother. (Who am I kidding? *I* grew up with the expectation that I'd marry and raise a family just like my mom and her sisters did. The fact that I hadn't achieved this sometimes bothered me, but not as much as it bothered my mother.) "Oh sure, Mom. Men are lining up to marry me. Rich men with great careers who are thrilled at the idea of helping to raise somebody else's teenager."

The corners of Mom's perfectly lipsticked mouth turned down. "You make Trudy sound like a liability."

"I think she's the world's greatest kid, but to a man looking for a woman to date, a teenager in the house isn't considered a plus. Not to mention all the younger, prettier, richer single women out there competing for Mr. Rich-and-Good-Looking's attention."

"You're a very attractive woman. And if you'd spend a little more time on your appearance…"

"Right now, I want to spend more time on my education. I think that's a better investment in the future."

"Are you even trying to find someone? Do you date at all?"

I bit back a groan. As if we hadn't had this conversation a hundred zillion times already. "I don't have time to date. I have a job to do and a daughter to raise. Besides, I *like* being single. Nobody to answer to. Nobody else to have to please."

She narrowed her eyes and fixed me with the look she'd given me back in junior high, when I'd been caught toilet papering Frankie Winslow's yard. "When was the last time you had a date?"

I shifted in my chair. "Uh, it's been a while."

"How long?"

My mother ought to hire herself out to interrogate

criminals. I dare anyone to lie to her. "A few years. Well, maybe more than a few." Try three. Okay, maybe five. But honestly, I didn't have any desire to date. And it's such a tremendous hassle to get gussied up like a prize heifer at the fair, endure hours of small talk, and then suffer through awkward groping at the door. Most of the time, I'd rather stay home with a good movie and order in pizza.

Mom reached across the desk and patted my hand. "Just because things didn't work out with Gil doesn't mean there's not someone out there for you."

I pulled away from her. "Gil has nothing to do with it." Not much, anyway.

Okay, so maybe I *had* spent some time early on comparing other guys to him. And maybe it was true that I was still closer to him than I'd ever been to any man. But I was over that. Mostly. "If I met someone interesting, I might start dating again, but that's not my focus right now." I pulled a stack of file folders toward me. "Now if you don't mind, I really have to get to work."

She smiled and stood. "All right, dear. I've got to get to the post office. Everyone is going to be so pleased to see your picture. Though I hope next time you make the paper, it's an engagement announcement."

"Mom!"

"You may have given up, but I certainly haven't. Your father and I would worry less if we knew you had a man you could depend on when we're not around."

Sure Mom. Mr. Right is just around the corner. And with my luck, he's about to step out into traffic and be hit by a truck.

At thirty-five with a daughter and a job and all those things that supposedly make a person an adult, I like to think that I've reached a certain level of maturity. Then something happens to remind me that, deep down inside, I'm the same awkward child I was when I was ten. Mom always said I was a late bloomer, but this is ridiculous!

Which explains why Monday morning at 7:00 a.m., my bedroom looked like a bomb had exploded in Macy's. Clothes tangled with belts tangled with shoes knotted with underwear twined with scarves. Trudy's eyes widened when she poked her head into the room. "Mo-om! What's going on?"

I hugged my arms to my chest and surveyed the chaos around me. "I don't have anything to wear."

Trudy picked her way through a tangle of jeans and plucked a tie-dyed sarong from the end of the bed. "What's this?"

"Ummm…fashion mistake?"

Eyebrows raised, she scanned the room. "From here, your whole wardrobe looks like a fashion mistake." She grabbed a pair of jeans off the pillow and tossed them to me. "Just wear these, and some kind of shirt."

I threaded my fingers through a hole in the knee of the jeans. "I can't wear these to the first day of school. It's college, not junior high."

"The college dudes I've seen dress pretty *cazh*." She shrugged. "You know, it's all about attitude. Nobody wants to look as if they care about anything as shallow as clothing."

"But I *do* care." I grabbed a pair of khakis from the pile at my feet and tried to smooth out the wrinkles. "And since when do you know any 'college dudes'?"

She rolled her eyes. "Like I don't notice the guys walking around campus or over on the Drag? Austin *is* a college town, you know?"

I pulled on the khakis and added a black and khaki blouse in a geometric print. "How's this?"

She put one finger to her chin and studied me critically. "I guess that'll have to do. After all, you are older than most students."

"Don't remind me." I hunted through the piles at my feet until I found a pair of brown sandals. "Are you ready to go? We're going to be late."

For the first time that morning, I really looked at my daughter. She was dressed in her usual mourning garb—black cargo pants, black shirt, black boots, lots of black eyeliner. My eyes narrowed. "What is that thing in the middle of your forehead?" It looked like a dot of red paint.

"That's a *bindi*. Hindu women wear them."

"You are not a Hindu woman."

"It's a symbol of my solidarity with oppressed women around the world."

I had to stifle a sigh. I reminded myself that it could be

worse. Much worse. She could be hanging out with motorcycle gangs or running away from home. Put into perspective, a spot of red paint in the middle of her forehead was nothing.

A cup of coffee in one hand, my backpack in the other, I followed Trudy out the door. So far, we were only fifteen minutes behind schedule. If I avoided traffic jams and ran all the yellow lights, we might just make it.

Joyce, dressed in a denim jumper with apples on the pocket, was headed up the walk with her morning paper. "Good luck, Grace!" she called. "Have a great first day of school."

"Thanks. I'm really excited."

"Why would anybody be excited about school?" Kevin stood in the doorway, still in his Batman pajamas, a giant bowl of cereal in his hands.

"Kevin, you go get dressed right now," Joyce ordered. "You're going to be late." She looked over her shoulder at me and rolled her eyes. "Boys!"

When I reached the car, Trudy was standing by the driver's side door. "Can I drive?"

"No. Now come on, we don't have time to fool around."

She shrugged and made her way to the passenger side. "In two years, you'll have to let me drive."

"I'm your mother and I don't have to let you do anything." I checked my mirrors, then pulled away from the curb. "Besides, two years is a long time from now. They might raise the driving age before then."

"Mo-om!" Her horrified tones suggested this was too awful to contemplate.

While Trudy searched for a radio station we could both tolerate, I ran through my mental list of things to do. I had to drop Trudy off, get to campus, find a place to park, find my classes, find the right books in my pack and try to figure out what the hell I was doing going back to school at this point in my life. Was I crazy?

Yes. Certifiable. But I was going to do it anyway.

"So what classes do you have today?" Trudy asked.

"Uh, economics, horticulture and English."

She made a face. "They all sound boring. Why don't you take something interesting, like scuba diving?"

"I don't think there are many job opportunities in scuba diving for women my age."

"Mom, you talk like you're ancient."

Maybe that's because this morning I felt ancient. The lone middle-ager in a crowd of adolescents. "You, yourself, pointed out this morning that I'm considerably older than the average college student."

"Not 'considerably.'" She tilted her head and studied me. "You look younger than your age. If you don't act like an old lady, no one will even know."

"Oh? And what do you consider acting like an old lady?"

"You need to quit talking about how old you are, for one thing. That is so not cool. And don't talk about me all the time. If you tell people you're the mother of a teenager, they'll think you're really old."

I nodded. "On the verge of senility."

"You know I'm right. And it wouldn't hurt if you'd listen to some cool music, and maybe do your hair in some mod style."

"I don't think Mr. Addleson would go for that." As befitting a banker, conservative is his middle name.

"Don't worry. You'll do okay, Mom. Everybody's nervous the first day."

"What makes you think I'm nervous?"

"You just missed our turn."

"Shit! No, you did not hear me say that." I swung into the left-turn lane and signaled for a U-turn. "Why didn't you say anything?"

"You're always telling me not to back seat drive." She gave me an angelic smile. "Besides, I don't mind being late. That way I get to make a dramatic entrance."

I made a growling sound under my breath and swung the car around. So much for trying to stay young. I could practically hear the gray hairs popping out all over my head.

A half hour later, I found a parking spot in the commuter lot at St. Ed's. Number one on my list of things to do today was get a parking permit. In the meantime, I crossed my fingers and prayed I wouldn't get towed.

I consulted the map in the student guide and began trudging toward a distant building labeled "Adm." Five minutes later, I was standing in a quadrangle surrounded by imposing sandstone buildings. I stared up at the soaring towers and rows of polished glass windows and felt sick to my stomach. I had expected to be awed by my introduction to academia. To be impressed by the weightiness of the task ahead of me. Instead, what I mainly felt was lost, with a large side order of impending panic.

I stared at the map again. The artist must have majored in abstract expressionism, because as far as I could determine, this collection of lines and squiggles had no basis in reality. Or maybe this was the map they gave to new students like me, a sort of hazing ritual.

I was fighting the urge to run home and crawl under the covers when a tall young man in jeans and a Galveston sweatshirt approached me. "Can I help you?" he asked. "You look a little lost."

"I am lost." I held out the map. "I'm trying to find the Administration Building. I have to get a parking permit."

"I'm headed that way myself. We can walk together." He offered his hand. "Josh Campbell."

"Grace Greenleigh. I'm new here." I suppressed the compulsion to giggle. Apparently an end to sustained panic can reduce a person to silliness. Or maybe I was temporarily dazed by the brilliance of Josh's smile. Perfect white teeth gleamed in his tanned face, and brown eyes studied me from beneath a shock of surfer blond hair. The sleeves of the sweatshirt had been ripped off, apparently to show off his considerable biceps. The overall effect was breathtaking.

"I'm a senior. I'll be glad to show you the ropes." We started across the quadrangle toward the elusive Administration Building. "I know how overwhelming it can be, coming back to school when you're older."

So much for the momentary thrill of being singled out by the campus hunk. "Is it that obvious?"

He laughed. "I just meant that I started college later too. After I got out of the Navy."

I looked at him again. Now that I thought about it, he did look a *little* older than the average student. Maybe it was the few fine lines around his eyes. Or the lack of zits. "How old are you?"

"Twenty-six."

Sorry, but twenty-six is not "older" from a thirty-five-year-old's perspective. I couldn't think of anything else to say until we reached the door of the Administration Building. "Well, uh, thanks for helping me out."

"The permit office is down here." He took my elbow and steered me down a dark hall. "I'll wait and help you find your first class."

"Oh. Well, that would be nice." Very nice, actually. Was everyone here going to be so helpful, or had I merely lucked out?

I stood in line ten minutes to get the parking permit. When I came out in the hall again, I didn't really expect to find Josh there. But he was leaning against the wall, long legs stretched out in front of him.

He straightened at my approach. "Did you get your permit?"

I held up the green and black sticker. "Forty-five bucks. But I guess it's cheaper than a towing fee."

We started down the hallway side by side. "What's your first class?" he asked.

"Um, Economics 2301. In the Business Administration Building."

"Dr. Hauser?"

I glanced at him. "What was that?"

"Is Dr. Hauser teaching that class?"

I fumbled with my schedule, dropping the parking permit in the process. Josh retrieved it, then took the schedule from my hand. "See, here it is—Econ. 2301. Hauser." He took my arm. "Come on. If we hurry, we won't be too late."

I thought he was just going to show me the classroom, but he walked in after me. "Are you in this class too?" I asked.

He grinned. "I flunked it my freshman year and I'm just now getting around to making it up." He settled his backpack on the floor beside a desk. "My real major is sociology. What about you? What are you studying?"

I sat in the desk across from him. "Business. I'm finishing a degree I started a few years ago."

Okay, more than a few, but he didn't have to know that.

He dazzled me with that smile again. "Maybe we could have coffee later. Talk about it some more."

I was still a little stunned as I turned my attention to the front of the room. Was it possible a twenty-six-year-old stud was actually interested in me? I shook my head. The bigger question was, was I interested in him?

I smiled to myself. Why not? After all, this whole college thing was all about new experiences and a fresh start in life, right?

The door opened and a thin man in a tweed sport coat walked in. He was balding on top, with a neatly trimmed goatee tinged with gray. Exactly what I'd imagined an economics professor would look like. Nice to know some of my expectations would be met.

"I'm Dr. Hauser and this is Economics 2301. Microeconomic Principles." He laid a briefcase on the desk and looked out at the rows of students. "I'll begin by explaining the requirements of this course. We will cover a chapter of the text each week. There will be a test every other week, covering two chapters. These test scores will account for forty percent of your grade. A midterm exam will account for another thirty percent, with the final exam making up the final thirty percent."

I slid down a little lower in my chair and stifled a groan. A chapter a week? Tests every other week? That was a lot of work, and a lot of studying I wasn't sure I had time for.

Dr. Hauser put his hands behind his back, looking quite pleased with himself. He studied us for a moment while we squirmed in our chairs and avoided his gaze, then said, "Now you know what I expect from you, I'd like to find out a little more about you. I want each of you to introduce yourself and state why you're here today." He perched on the edge of the desk. "You already know my name, and I'm here because the university administration takes the somewhat narrow-minded view that they don't have to pay me if I don't show up."

Nervous laughter. A slave-driving economics professor with a sense of humor. That was an interesting twist.

Most of my fellow students, however, were not that interesting. As they introduced themselves, it quickly became apparent that I was surrounded by fellow business majors taking the course because it was a requirement for their degree. One of the exceptions was Josh, who said he'd always wanted to be a fantasy novelist and thought economics would be a good start, since it didn't appear to be based on any kind of reality.

This earned him a scowl from Dr. Hauser, who apparently didn't appreciate a smart-ass. Having earned my own degree as a wise-acre, I thought Josh was pretty clever.

The other person who stood out in that sea of drones was a short dumpling of a woman swathed in Kinte cloth. She rose out of her chair by the door and stalked to the front of the class, the beads in her iron-gray braids clacking in time to her movements. All my fears about being the oldest in the class evaporated. This woman was really old. Grandma old. Orthopedic shoes and wrinkles old. "My name is Myrtle Busby and I'm eighty years old," she declared in a clear voice heavily laced with a Texas twang. "I'm taking this class because I'm tired of my snot-nosed broker talking to me like a midget brain. He thinks if he dazzles me with all his talk about 'supply side' and 'economic indicators' I'll take some dud of a stock off his hands. I'm here to show him he's got another think coming." She turned and shot a look at Dr. Hauser that dared him to even try any of that double-talk on her.

"Um, yes. Well, we're glad to have you with us, Ms. Busby." Dr. Hauser scanned the room once more and his gaze zeroed in on me. "What about you, miss? I don't believe you've introduced yourself and told us why you're here."

I'd been pretending I was invisible, hoping to avoid being put on the spot like that. The truth was, I had no idea why I was here. I was playing this whole college thing by ear. Kind of the way I lived my life.

As Dr. Hauser's gaze remained locked on me, I sighed and stood up. Who was I kidding? That invisible act didn't work in eighth grade either.

"I'm Grace Greenleigh and I'm here because I'm trying to decide what I want to be when I grow up."

I sat down quickly, not sure whether to be relieved or upset by the twitters of laughter around me. Something like a smirk—or maybe it was just a smile, it was hard to tell—formed on Dr. Hauser's face. "What you want to be when you grow up," he repeated. "I might make some remark about your appearing to be fully grown, but I wouldn't want you to think I was a sexist."

More laughter, not as pleasant this time. I glowered at the professor. I had a feeling economics was *not* going to be my favorite subject.

* * *

Horticulture was my favorite class, but then, gardening was my hobby, so I'd expected to enjoy learning more about it. English also wasn't bad, made better when Myrtle Busby slid into the chair next to mine. She frowned at the graduate student who'd introduced herself as our teacher. Ms. Alexander had long dark hair, long tan legs and a figure that had the male half of the class drooling into their dictionaries. "I was teaching English in the Peace Corps when her mother was a baby," Myrtle said.

"You were in the Peace Corps?"

She nodded. "In South America. Rode donkeys up into the mountains of Peru to open a school for llama herders' children." Her eyes twinkled. "Met my second husband there. A handsome young Yankee who thought I was some country girl he could have a fling with. But he found out soon enough I'm not the kind of woman a man gives up."

My heart beat faster, just listening to her; at the same time I felt a kind of sinking feeling in my stomach. Here was a woman who had done something with her life. She had lived and loved, had adventures, questioned authority and was still ready for more. She hadn't wasted her youth behind a teller's cage in a bank. And what man would ever say I was a woman he couldn't give up?

Between these gloomy thoughts and the hectic pace of the day, I was exhausted and overwhelmed by the time I pulled into my parking space at the drive-through at two o'clock. I had two hundred pages in various textbooks to read by Wednesday and an essay to write for English on my opinion of American literature. When was the last time I'd read literature? Did *Oprah* books and romance novels count?

I lugged my backpack into the bank with me. Afternoons were sometimes slow, and with any luck, I could read in between customers.

I'd just cracked open the first textbook, however, when someone tapped on the door behind me. I got up and peered through the security peephole at a little old man in aviator glasses.

"Mr. Bob, what can I do for you?" I asked as I opened the door. Mr. Bob had owned a barbershop in Tarrytown for many years. He's retired now and someone else owns the shop, but he still goes down there and sits all morning, reading the newspapers and drinking coffee. In the afternoons, he stops by the bank for the cookies we put out. He winds up the day at the grocery store, working his way through the free samples. I sometimes wonder if he ever bothers to cook at all.

"Addleson sent me over," Mr. Bob said. He held up a zippered bank pouch. "He said you would straighten everything out about my pennies."

"Your pennies?" I felt a little woozy for a minute there. Maybe this was Mr. Addleson's idea of a joke. He didn't strike me as a prankster, but you never really know people, do you? "Is something wrong with them?"

Mr. Bob shook the bank pouch. I heard the unmistakable rattle of change. "My sister, Louise, has been after me to get a hobby, so I decided to start a coin collection."

I nodded, polite smile still pasted in place. "That's nice." *And what does this have to do with me?*

"Well see, I always think it's good to specialize. For instance, when I was a barber, I always specialized in good, short haircuts for men. None of this ducktail or styling crap. Just a good flat-top, or a basic man's cut."

I nodded. My uncle Mel had been a customer of Mr. Bob's for many years. He'd always come from the barbershop with every short hair on his head standing at attention, walking in a cloud of butch wax.

"So you've decided to specialize in certain types of coins?" I prompted. If I hurried this along, maybe I'd have time to read the first chapter in my economics text before closing.

"Yes. I'm going to collect pennies. Not just any pennies, mind you. I'm collecting wheat pennies."

My smile was genuine this time. Wheat pennies were made between 1909 and 1958, before the government decided to put the Lincoln Memorial on the reverse of the coin. When I was a kid, I'd been fascinated by that design of flanking wheat sheaves. It was special precisely because it was different. "Those are some of my favorites, too."

Mr. Bob smiled, revealing big yellow teeth. "Then Addleson sent me to the right place."

"What is it, exactly, that I'm supposed to do?"

"I thought I'd start by collecting all your wheat pennies."

There was that woozy feeling again. I steadied myself on the doorjamb. "Mr. Bob, I can't give you all our wheat pennies."

"Why not?" He fished a dollar bill from his pocket. "I'll pay you for them. I figure since they're kind of rare, you're not likely to have more than a hundred or so on any given day."

"But Mr. Bob, all our pennies come to us prewrapped. I can't know what they look like until I open a roll."

"You got one of them change machines to reroll them, don't you? We can just open all the rolls into there, sort through them and pick out the wheat pennies, then reroll them. I'll help."

He pushed past me, into the drive-in. "Doesn't look like you're very busy in here, young lady. And I don't have to be anywhere until HEB puts out the fresh cheese samples at five o'clock."

I tried to call Mr. Addleson, but he was conveniently away from his office. I pictured him hiding behind the oleanders out front, laughing himself silly as Mr. Bob and I cracked open five hundred rolls of pennies.

Actually, it wasn't five hundred rolls. More like thirty. That was all we had in the drive-through at the time. I know—I'm a patsy. But how could I say no to a man whose idea of big excitement was free ice cream day at the local Sun Harvest?

In the end, Mr. Bob added eighteen wheat pennies to his collection and I read exactly zero pages in my economics text. Not to worry, I told myself as I locked up the drive-through for the night. I had a half hour to kill waiting for Trudy to come out of band practice. I could do the reading in the car then.

To quote my daughter—*As if!* I had no sooner pushed back the car seat and opened the textbook to the introduction when someone tapped on my window.

I looked up into a pair of puppy dog eyes belonging to a young man I vaguely remembered as Cal somebody or another. A classmate of Trudy's. I rolled down the window. "Hello Cal. Is something wrong?"

"Uh, no. Not really." Cal took off his ballcap, then replaced it on his head, backwards this time. "I just thought maybe I could talk to you."

I sighed and closed the economics text. "About anything in particular?"

"Oh! About Trudy."

Of course, what other subject would we have in common? "What about Trudy?"

"Well, uh, I, uh, think she's really fly. I mean, uh, you know. Pretty." Cal's cheeks glowed pink.

I nodded, suppressing a smile. Is there anything sweeter than a young man with a crush? I looked at him more closely. He wore baggy khaki shorts, a striped T-shirt and boat-sized basketball shoes, as well as the aforementioned cap. He was clean, with short hair and no visible tattoos or piercings. A nice-looking, clean-cut boy.

Which meant Trudy probably didn't give him the time of day. I sighed, remembering myself at that age. If he wasn't older, dark and dangerous, I wasn't interested. Which probably explains why my parents were so relieved when I said I wanted to marry Gil. He was so unlike my previous boyfriends, they figured he was the answer to their prayers.

Which just goes to show parents don't know everything.

"Cal, is there something *specific* you wanted to ask me about Trudy?"

He shuffled his feet and tugged at his hat, then managed to drag his gaze up to my level. "Do you think she'd go out with me?"

"Trudy's only fourteen. She's not allowed to date."

"Well, it wouldn't be a date, exactly, just a bunch of us are going to Dave and Buster's on Saturday to eat pizza and play games and stuff and I thought maybe she could go."

I nodded. "Have you asked her?"

His eyes widened. "No! I mean, well, I thought maybe you could…I mean…"

I couldn't hold back the smile any longer. "Believe me, Cal, it would not be a good idea for me to ask Trudy for you. I'm her mother, remember. Totally uncool."

He stared at his feet again. All I could see were the tips of his ears and they were beet red. "Uh, guess not."

"But you go ahead and ask her," I said. "It sounds like a fun day."

Just then, the doors burst open and a crowd of students rushed out, juggling book bags and instruments cases. "If you want, I'll wait while you talk to Trudy," I said, turning back to Cal.

I wasn't surprised to find him gone. It's probably hard enough asking a girl for a date without doing it in front of her mom. The door opened and Trudy tossed her backpack and flute case into the back seat. Then she climbed in beside me.

"How was school?"

We grinned at each other as we both asked the familiar question. "You first," Trudy said.

"It was okay," I said. "Lots of homework." I glanced at the still-unread economics text on the dash.

"Did you meet any cute guys?"

"School is not about meeting cute guys," I protested, even as I thought of Josh. He would definitely qualify as a cute guy in any female's book.

"Maybe not in an all-girls' school." Trudy took out a hairbrush and began smoothing her hair. "What would you think if I shaved my head?"

I ignored the question. Trudy likes to ask these things to see if she can shock me. After fourteen years, I like to think of myself as unshockable. "I was talking to a boy from your class when you came out. A cute blonde. Cal somebody or other."

"Cal Maxwell. Why were you talking to him?"

"Just passing the time. He's kind of cute."

She shrugged. "I guess. Kind of dorky, if you ask me."

"Dorky can be nice. Your father was dorky in college."

"Dad was *gay!*"

There is that. A fact of our lives that we don't talk about much. I mean, Trudy has known Gil is different since she was a tiny baby, and of course, Mark has been part of the picture for quite a few years now. Having a father who's gay has always been the way things were for her, and if she wonders about it, she never says anything to me. I cleared my throat. "I don't think Cal is gay."

She studied her reflection in the visor mirror. "I don't think so. I mean, Dad says you can't always tell, but I don't think so." She shrugged. "Not that it makes any difference to me."

She flipped down the cover on the mirror and turned to me. "You know, Mom, I think a straight man would probably find you attractive, if you'd just give one a chance."

By some miracle, I avoided running the car up onto the sidewalk. Heart pounding, I risked a glance at Trudy. She looked perfectly calm. "What are you talking about?"

"I mean, just because you made a mistake with Dad

doesn't mean you can't trust your judgment with men or that you're scarred for life or anything."

"What brought this up?" I asked, struggling to calm down.

"We're studying the effects of trauma in psychology class. It's pretty interesting stuff."

"I do not consider my relationship with your father traumatic." *And I cannot believe I'm having this conversation with my fourteen-year-old daughter.*

"I would. I figure it probably made you question your whole identity as a woman and everything."

I pulled the car to the curb in front of our house and switched off the engine. Trudy started to get out, but I pressed down the lock button. "Trudy, look at me," I said.

She did, eyes wide and innocent, but I knew her well enough to see a spark of fear behind the bravado. "First of all, what happened between your father and me is our business. All you need to know is that we are still good friends and that we love you. Got that?"

She nodded.

"Second, I am not scarred or traumatized, or any other label you care to pull out of that psychology text. The only reason I haven't been dating is because I have too many other things going on in my life right now. And besides, a woman does not need a man to complete her life. I'm very happy being single. Not that it's any of your business. Got it?"

She nodded. "Can I get out of the car now?"

I released the lock. "Okay. And remember, after dinner, we both have to study."

She started to open the door, then stopped. "Mom?"

I reached into the back seat for my backpack and stuffed the economics text inside. "What is it?"

"Who is that man on our front steps? He's really cute."

CHAPTER 3

Do you think it's possible for a person's whole body to blush? I think mine did when I looked up and saw Josh Campbell leaning against my front door. I thought at first maybe I was hallucinating, but when I closed my eyes and opened them again, he was still there. "Josh! What are you doing here?" I didn't mean for the words to sound so accusing, but in my everyday reality handsome young men do not stand on my front porch.

"Mom, could you try to act just a *little* cool?" Trudy muttered under her breath.

I shut the car door and led the way up the walk. Josh leaned against the porch post, hands in the pockets of his jeans, ankles crossed. He looked like an ad for some expensive men's cologne. "I thought maybe you'd need this." He held up a familiar green and black parking pass. "In all the confusion over finding your class, I guess I ended up with it."

I accepted the parking pass. "And you came all the way out here to return it? That's so thoughtful."

55

"Geez, Mom, do you have to sound so much like a *mom?*" Trudy hissed in my ear.

I kept an inane grin plastered to my face and tried to give my interfering daughter a swift kick in the shins, which isn't easy to do. It's a wonder we didn't both end up sprawled across the walk.

"How did you know where she lived?" Trudy asked.

I blinked. How *did* Josh know? "I don't remember mentioning my address."

He grinned. "I know this chick who works in the registrar's office. She helped me out."

I'll just bet she did. One flash of that devilish smile, a muscle or two flexed, and the "chick" in the registrar's office probably melted right there. "Aren't you resourceful," I said, as Trudy did more eye-rolling.

"It wasn't that far." Josh nodded toward MoPac. "I work at a bike shop over on Sixth."

Now I could see the purple racing bike leaning against the wall next to him. Somehow, I made it up the steps and took the parking pass from him. "Thanks so much. I'd have panicked later when I couldn't find it."

"No problem." He grinned at Trudy. I could tell he had the same dazzling effect on her. "Who is this?"

"This is my—"

"Sister." Trudy held out her hand. "I'm Trudy. So you and Grace have classes together?"

I'll admit, for about ten seconds, I was tempted. I mean, Trudy may think I don't date by choice, but the truth is, a woman my age with a teenager is the Typhoid Mary of the dating scene. Men trip over themselves running in the other direction.

I've never been a very good liar, though, and this had the potential to be one of those lies that grew larger and more complicated at every turn. "Trudy thinks she's doing me a favor by pretending to be my sister," I said. "But the truth is, she's my daughter."

I'll give the man credit. He didn't turn pale. He didn't swear. His eyes glazed over for maybe half a second and his smile got a little tight around the edges, but otherwise, he hid his emotions well. "You're kidding?"

I shook my head and slipped my arm around Trudy's shoulders. "Would I kid about a kid like this?"

Josh laughed. "You must have had her when you were about twelve."

Maybe he was laying it on a little thick, but did I care? Of course not. I gave him my biggest, most genuine smile. "Would you like to come in and have a glass of tea or something?"

"Can I take a raincheck? The bike shop's open until nine on Mondays and I have to get back to work."

"Sure. Thanks again for dropping off my parking pass."

"No problem. See you Wednesday."

"See you Wednesday."

I was still grinning as I watched him mount his bike and ride off down the street. Trudy showed remarkable restraint, waiting until Josh was out of sight before she spoke. "Mom, you are such a dork!"

Reluctantly, I turned around and went into the house. "Why? Because I told the truth?"

"Because he is a major babe and all you did was stand there grinning like an idiot."

"I invited him in for tea. What else was I supposed to do?"

"You could have flirted with him."

"Flirted?" I looked down my nose at her. "Since when are you an expert on flirting?"

She raised her chin. "I've been studying up. Watching older girls and movies and stuff. I mean, I'll be dating before you know it."

"And meanwhile, you think you can advise me?"

"Mom, you need it. Admit it, you are totally out of your league here."

I laughed. "You're right. I *am* out of my league. Besides, Josh is nine years younger than me. I doubt he's really interested. He probably did stop by just to return my parking pass." The more I thought about it, the more it made sense.

"Mo-om! You are so clueless. Of course he's interested. I'll bet he took that parking pass on purpose, so he'd have an excuse to stop by later."

"Do you think so?" The idea sent a flutter through my stomach. It had been a long time since a man had gone out of his way to see me. "But he's so much younger—"

"Nine years is nothing." Trudy dismissed the idea with a wave of her hand. "Why should men always be the ones to date younger women?"

"Would you date a kindergartner?"

"Mom, this is completely different and you know it. You're both adults. And I think he really likes you. You should go for it."

I was afraid to ask what "it" was. There are some things I wasn't ready to acknowledge my daughter knew about. "Why are you so interested in hooking me up with someone all of a sudden?" I asked.

"My friend Alice Watson's grandmother just moved in with them."

I blinked. "What does that have to do with anything? Stop trying to change the subject."

"I'm not changing the subject. Alice's grandfather died when her mother was a little girl and Alice's grandmother never remarried. Now she's old and alone and doesn't have anywhere to go, so she's moving in with Alice and her mother. Alice had to give up her room and move into the dining room. She says it really sucks."

I studied Trudy to see if she was pulling my leg, but her eyes looked absolutely serious. "So you want me to find someone so I won't have to move in with you when I'm old?"

She nodded. "Dad has Mark, but you don't have anybody but me. I worry about you."

I had to look away then, afraid she'd see the sudden

tears that welled in my eyes. What had I done to deserve a child with such a tender heart?

I was dabbing at my eyes with a tissue when Trudy came up and put her arms around me. "Don't worry, Mom. The right man for you is out there somewhere. We just have to find him."

"Isn't that my line?" I sniffed and stuffed the tissue into my pocket.

"I haven't had my heart broke yet, so you'll just have to save it for later."

"My heart's not broken."

Trudy was wise enough not to answer that one. Okay, so maybe my heart was a little dented around the edges. Love will do that to a person, I guess.

I was mixing up Hamburger Helper for supper when the phone rang. "Grace, honey! Where have you been? I called the bank this morning and they said you weren't there. You're not ill, are you?"

I turned down the flame under the frying pan and sighed into the phone. "I started classes today, Mom. Remember?"

"Oh, that's right! You're a college girl now. So how was it? Any good-looking men on campus?"

Hadn't I had this conversation once today? "I'm going to school to learn, not to find a man."

"There's no law that says you can't do both, now is there?"

"I'm not sure. There might be."

"I don't know where you get that smart mouth of yours, young lady. It certainly wasn't from me."

"Was there something in particular you needed, Mom?"

"I called to ask you to lunch next Monday. My garden club cancelled and I thought if I planned this far ahead, I might actually get to see you for a change."

Do you think when a baby pops out of you, your body automatically starts producing a guilt organ? Something that equips you to induce guilt in your children? From time to time, I catch myself saying things to Trudy that I know, even as I utter them, did not come from the brain I had before she was born. My mother, being older and more experienced than I, has the whole guilt thing down cold. "I'd love to have lunch with you, Mom," I said as I dumped the Hamburger Helper into a bowl. "I get out of class at one. Where should we meet?"

"Oh, come to my house. I'll fix tuna salad." Mom never wants me to take her to a restaurant. I used to think it was because she was concerned about me spending money I didn't have. Now I believe it's because she likes to have the home field advantage.

"All right, Mom. I'll see you then." And I'd come prepared. I wasn't going to let her make me feel guilty because I was still single. I had big plans for my future, whether or not I remarried. Despite Trudy's fears, I didn't intend to have to move in with her.

After supper, I put the dishes to soak and made a space

at one end of the table for myself and my books. At last, a chance to do my homework. I'd never been particularly fond of homework as a child, but now a little zing of anticipation ran through me. I was beginning a new adventure. Entering an exciting new world that might lead to great things for me.

Brrring! Brrrring!

I wonder if the astronauts ever have to postpone a countdown while someone answers the phone? "Hello?"

"Hi, Gracie. I called to see how things went for you today."

I smiled and relaxed against the wall. "Hi, Gil. Everything went fine. I had three classes and they all look pretty interesting."

"What are you taking?"

We talked a few minutes about my courses, and about work, which led to brief discussions of his own daily grind as a salesman, and Mark's latest venture. "I was wondering if you'd be able to come by one day in a couple of weeks and help hang Mark's exhibit at Sud Your Duds?" he asked. "We only have one night to get it up and we could use your help."

"Sure, I'll be there." If nothing else, it would be interesting to see what Mark had come up with in his quest for artistic expression. "Do you want to talk to Trudy?"

"Yes, put her on."

I was halfway through Chapter One, "Introduction to

Microeconomic Theory," when Trudy came hurtling from the back of the house. "Mom!" she shouted.

I put my hands over my ears. "I'm not deaf."

She slipped off a pair of stereo headphones. "Sorry." She held out a pair of black cargo pants. "I just remembered, I need these for tomorrow."

I looked at the pants. They looked like half the pants in her closet. "That particular pair?"

"Uh-huh. But they have a rip." She poked her finger through the place where a back seam had separated.

It would have been tempting to point out that perhaps her expanding backside had strained the seam, but that would have been cruel, wouldn't it? That's how girls develop complexes that haunt them when they're women. Besides, while Trudy was a typical growing girl, she was certainly not fat.

"Would you sew them, please?" she pleaded.

"Why don't you sew them?" I turned back to my book.

"I don't know how." She danced around in front of me. "Mom, *please*." She drew the word out until it sounded like fingernails on a chalkboard.

With a martyred sigh I grabbed the pair of pants and trudged toward the closet where I kept the portable sewing machine my mother had given me as a wedding present. At the time, I'd thought it was a pretty dumb gift. I'd wanted a new stereo or a pair of beanbag chairs for our living room.

Hundreds of baby clothes, pajamas, short sets, recital

dresses and kitchen curtains later, the machine hummed along. I'm pretty sure that an eight-track player and bean-bag chairs would have been donated to Goodwill eons ago.

"Don't they teach you this stuff in home economics?" I asked as I set up the sewing machine at the opposite end of the table from my books.

"It's not home economics anymore. It's life sciences. And we learn cool stuff, like decorating and clothes design and menu planning."

"But no actual cooking and sewing?"

"That's the advanced class."

Maybe that was where I messed up. I went straight to the advanced class in life, skipping over all the "cool stuff."

I still don't know much about economics, but I'm pretty sure I've discovered a cure for insomnia. By the time I finished sewing Trudy's jeans, got our lunches ready for the next day, cleaned the kitchen and did a load of laundry, it was almost midnight, and two pages of "Introduction to Microeconomic Theory" were all I needed to put me out like a light.

I'd just have to carry the book around with me all day and read when I could. Maybe the knowledge would soak through my backpack and into my skin.

First class on Tuesdays and Thursdays was Government and Politics, a course I'd chosen because I thought it might help me become better informed. I reasoned an adult ought to know something about politics, and despite the fact that Austin is the Texas state capital and therefore, a political town, I'd managed to stay woefully ignorant of such things for thirty-five years.

Five minutes before class began, Myrtle Busby slid into the seat next to mine and handed me a muffin. "You look like one of those young women who never eat breakfast," she said.

I laughed. "Does coffee count?"

She pulled a thermos from her shopping bag and filled a paper cup with steaming coffee. "There you go. Now eat up. I made the muffins myself."

I bit into the walnut-studded banana muffin. "It's still warm."

"Just pulled them out of the oven."

"Thanks, Myrtle. You're amazing."

She waved away the compliment. "At my age, you don't sleep much. So I get up and bake." She grinned. "I used to play guitar, but the neighbors complained. Said I turned the amp up too high."

On this astonishing note, the professor walked in, followed by Josh. He grinned and slid into the desk on the other side of me. "Thanks for saving me a seat," he said.

"I didn't save that for you." My face felt hot, and I looked away. Why was I blushing like a high school girl? I came back to college to get the education I'd missed, not to relive my adolescence. God no! I'd rather have a daily bikini wax than go through that torture again.

"I'll bet you didn't eat breakfast either." Myrtle passed him a muffin.

"Thanks!" Half the muffin disappeared in a single bite.

"I hate to break up this little coffee klatch, but we have a class to begin." The professor, a pudgy man in an ill-fitting suit, loomed over our desks.

"Good morning." Myrtle beamed and handed him a napkin on which rested two perfect muffins. "These are for you. I made them myself."

The professor's frown vanished. "Why, thank you." He beamed. "They look delicious."

He headed back toward his desk. "How did you do that?" Josh whispered.

"It's the Little Old Lady factor. I remind everyone of their grandmother. You wouldn't talk back to your grandmother, would you?"

"Myrtle, I want to be like you when I grow up," I blurted.

Still smiling, she looked me up and down. "Better to be just like yourself, dear. You seem to be coming along just fine."

I had a break before my next class and Myrtle and Josh and I headed over to the student union for more coffee. "Did you know the coffee bushes in Colombia produce year-round?" Myrtle said. "So there's always work to be done in the coffee fields. And almost all the fields are owned by family groups. Everyone in the family, even small children, help take care of the coffee plants."

"Were you there with the Peace Corps?" Josh asked. He added two packets of sugar to his coffee and stirred.

"Yes. I volunteered at a medical clinic there. But then my daughter got sick and I had to come home."

"You had your daughter with you?"

"No, dear, this was after my children were grown. My daughter was forty-two and discovered she had breast cancer. I came home to look after her and to help with my grandchildren."

Josh and I exchanged glances over the table. Of course, we both wanted to know what happened.

"She died a year later and my two grandchildren came to live with me." Myrtle stirred creamer into her cup. "It's quite an adventure raising teenagers when you're in your sixties, let me tell you."

"Your whole life sounds like an adventure," I said.

She smiled serenely. "Life always is, if you're willing to look at it that way. Now tell me about Grace Greenleigh."

There I went with that blushing thing again. Honestly, how aggravating. Do other people do this, or is it just me? I can talk about all kinds of things, but ask me about myself and I turn to mush. Not that I'm *embarrassed*, exactly, but my life is somewhat *unconventional*, or at least, different from anyone else's life I know. "I want to hear about Josh first." I smiled brightly at him.

The man knew how to take a cue, bless him. He tipped

his chair back until it was balanced on two legs. "You know most of it already. I got out of the Navy three years ago and decided to go back to school. I'm majoring in sociology and want to go into research."

"So what do you want to research?" Myrtle asked.

"People. Relationships. Society." He lowered the chair until it rested flat on the floor again. "My plan is to write a really killer senior paper and get it published. Then I'll have my pick of grad fellowships. A few more years and I'll be at a top university, writing my bestseller. Scientists are a hot commodity these days."

Myrtle smiled at him. "Sounds like you've got your life all planned out." She turned to me again. "What about you, Grace? What are your plans?"

Um, to make it through the day without losing my mind or my car keys? I shrugged. "I'm not much of a planner."

Myrtle nodded. "There's something to be said for taking life as it comes. Why did you decide to go back to school?"

I picked at the loose Formica on the table's edge. "I work at a bank and I was told I needed a degree to get promoted, so I decided to come back to school and finish my studies."

"She has a teenage daughter who could pass for her sister."

Coffee sloshed onto my hand as I jerked around to look at Josh. He grinned at me. "I think it's cool. But you must have had her when you were pretty young."

"I was twenty-one," I said, gaze focused on the table-top. Okay, so maybe young motherhood isn't that big a deal, but it had felt like a big deal to me at the time, and part of me was still embarrassed about the circumstances surrounding Trudy's birth.

"I was sixteen when I had my first," Myrtle said. "My boyfriend at the time was thirty and the hired hand on my father's farm. When my daddy found out, he came after Mason—that was my boyfriend—with a shotgun and marched us both right down to the justice of the peace." She shook her head. "Mason packed up and left when Bobby was four and Mason Jr. was two."

"Did you raise Trudy on your own?" I wasn't looking at Josh when he asked the question, but I could feel his eyes on me.

"No, her father and I got married." I smiled at Myrtle. "Gil and I ended up divorced, too. But we're still friends."

"How good friends are you?"

You have to admire a man who's upfront, don't you? I turned and smiled at Josh. "Gil and I are friends, but we'll never be anything more. Besides, he's in a committed relationship with someone else." I left out that the someone else was another man. I really liked this guy, and he still seemed interested despite the fact that he already knew more about my life than most of the men I'd dated. No point overwhelming him with all the details.

Anxious to shift the focus of the conversation away

from me, I turned to Myrtle. "It sounds like you've led a really adventurous life."

"Ha!"

The force of her exclamation surprised me. She leaned over and patted my knee. "Life in general is an adventure to me. Every damn day of it."

The adventure that was my life took another sharp turn that afternoon when I arrived at school to pick up Trudy. I was congratulating myself on having managed to read a whole chapter in my economics text without falling asleep when Trudy emerged from the band hall hand in hand with a tall, dreadlocked young man with a number of tiny gold rings attached to his body—some of them in his ears.

I consider myself to be a "cool" mom. I do not overreact when my daughter decides she wants to dye her hair black or wear a dog collar. If she wants to experiment with vegetarianism, I will happily cook tofu and sprouts. I remember what it was like to be a teenager, trying to figure out what life is all about, and I promised myself that I would not be a smothering, overprotective, combative mother. I would strive to understand my daughter and to help her through this passage in her life with love and compassion.

This is what I told myself, but all the talk in the world does not prepare you to see your *little girl* hand in hand with some freaky-looking *boy*. It was as if someone opened a trap door in my brain and swept every reasonable attitude out into space. Before I even knew what was happening, I was out of the car, glaring at that young man like he was a grasshopper devouring my prize roses.

"Uh, Mom? Are you okay?" Trudy stopped a few feet from the car and frowned at me.

"Of course. I'm fine." I stared at their clasped hands. If I had had laser vision, they'd have been sliced in two.

Mom-vision worked pretty good though. Trudy dropped the boy's hand. "Mom, this is Simon."

"Hello, Simon." I tried to smile, but my face was frozen in an expression of menace. The best I could do was to try not to sound as horrified as I felt.

"Simon plays the clarinet."

The clarinet is such an ordinary instrument. Shouldn't a boy who looked like this play something more bizarre—like bongos? "That's nice," I murmured. I was beginning to feel pretty ridiculous. I mean, up close the kid had zits and braces. Behind all the window dressing, he was just an ordinary boy.

"Simon and I are working on a duet for the concert next month."

Just when I was beginning to feel safe… My mother's voice echoed in my head, *That better be all you're working on.* I coughed, choking on words I refused to let pass my lips.

"Mom, are you sure you're okay?" A deep vee forms between Trudy's eyebrows when she frowns hard, the way she was doing now. Gil does that, too.

"I…I'm fine." I grabbed her hand and pulled her toward the car. "Nice meeting you, Simon."

Trudy waited until we were out of the parking lot before she spoke. "What was that all about?"

"What was what all about?" I pretended to concentrate on traffic, but out of the corner of my eye, I watched her. She sat pressed up against the passenger door, arms hugged tightly across her chest.

"The way you acted with Simon back there. You were so rude."

"I was not rude. I was perfectly civil."

"Yeah, if you call *glaring* at someone civil. What was wrong with him?"

"You mean besides the fact that he has more holes in his head than Swiss cheese?" I gripped the steering wheel, white-knuckled. I was definitely channeling my mother now, but I couldn't stop myself.

"Mom! I can't believe you said that. What happened to all those speeches about tolerance and diversity? Besides, Mark has piercings."

"We aren't talking about Mark. We're talking about a young man who was holding your hand."

"Oh, so that's it!" Trudy sat forward, her voice pitched higher than normal. "What's wrong with him holding my hand?"

Nothing. That's the answer I should have given her. The answer the rational side of my brain knew was right. Trudy was fourteen, still innocent, and holding a boy's hand after class really meant nothing.

But that other part of my brain, the wild, irrational, fearful part, reminded me of every way I'd screwed up my life. I'd started out holding a boy's hand and a few years later I'd been sitting in the Planned Parenthood office, crying big fat tears and watching my dreams of college graduation and the life I'd always expected to have washing away.

"I just think you're too young to get serious about a boy," I said.

She laughed. "So that's what this is all about?"

I got the feeling she'd skipped ahead in the conversation. "Trudy, you're fourteen," I said. "I know you think you're all grown-up, but you still have a ways to go."

The smile she gave me was more of a smirk. "Mom, Simon and I are not having sex."

Deep breath, Grace. Concentrate on holding the car on the road. Did I even know what sex was at fourteen? I must have. Or at least, I thought I knew. Say something. She's waiting for you to say something. "That's good to know," I managed to squeeze out in a thin, shaky voice. "I hope you'll wait a long while yet."

"And when I do, I'll practice safe sex and birth control and all that." She nodded her head. "I won't make the same mistake you did, Mom."

I felt weak all over. Really, do these conversations have to take place in the car? It's dangerous. I pulled into the parking lot of a 7-Eleven and switched off the engine. Then I took a deep breath and turned to my daughter.

"Trudy, you were not a mistake," I said. "Maybe I didn't plan on having you, but once you were here, I wouldn't have sent you back for all the gold in Africa."

She squirmed. "I know that. But if you hadn't had me, you would have graduated college like a normal person."

Only she said "normal" as if it were some sort of disease. "God forbid, I ever be *normal!*" I laughed and pulled her to me. "I'm your mother, hon. I want you to grow up, but it's hard to watch sometimes. So go easy on me, okay? I'll try to do the same for you."

"Okay, Mom." She struggled out of my grasp. "Can I have a Slurpee?"

"Sure thing." I reached into the back seat for my wallet.

"And while we're here, maybe we can look for condoms."

She was already out of the car by the time I looked up to find her standing there, doubled over with laughter. "Just kidding!" she cried. "Oh Mom, if you could see your face!"

Note to self: practice stoic expression. With almost four more years of high school to go, I was going to need it.

CHAPTER 4

Trudy was due to spend the weekend with Gil and Mark. Normally I dread those long days in my empty house. I usually fill the time puttering around the yard or doing laundry. Now I actually looked forward to having hours by myself to study. Why didn't I remember that college was so much work? Maybe because the first time around I'd majored in partying instead of academics. I was certainly paying for the sins of my youth now, as I struggled to remember everything I'd supposedly learned before about composing essays and memorizing facts and figures.

But I was scarcely in the door after dropping Trudy off at her dad's that Friday when my phone rang. "Thank God you're home," Joyce said. "Can I come over?"

"Of course." She sounded desperate. Governments and economic order would have to wait.

In less than five minutes, Joyce was at my door, a bottle of wine in each hand. "I need to get drunk, and I don't like to do it alone," she said, moving past me and heading toward the kitchen.

"What happened? Did Peter do something?"

"Yeah, he did something. He finally signed the papers." She pulled two glasses from the cabinet and began searching through the utensil drawer. "Where's your corkscrew?"

I retrieved the corkscrew from a different drawer and handed it to her. "The divorce papers? I thought he was refusing to sign." Not that Peter didn't want a divorce—he just didn't want to have to pay for it.

She nodded. "I think his attorney convinced him that he was liable to come out of this a lot worse if he continued to fight it." She yanked out the cork and tossed it into the sink. "It doesn't matter how much he has to pay, though. It'll never be enough." She filled both glasses, then held one up. "I guess we should toast. I'm officially single again."

Then she burst into tears. I got the glass out of her hand before she dropped it, and gathered her into my arms. "I'm sorry," she kept saying. "I'm sorry."

"What are you apologizing for?" I led her to the living room and sat her on the sofa. "You didn't do anything wrong."

"I just…I'm sick of crying all the time. I thought I would handle this better, but I'm just…not."

"It's okay." I set a box of tissues in front of her. "If it makes you feel any better, I cried when my divorce was final, too. Even though I knew Gil and I were both better off because of it."

"You did?" She blew her nose and looked at me, bleary-eyed.

"Sure I did. It's a very emotional thing to go through."

"And you loved him. The way I still love Peter. The bastard." She dissolved into sobs again.

I patted her shoulder, not sure what to say. Yes, I'd still loved Gil when we split up, but not the way a woman should love her husband. Not really. It was more complicated than that. I'd been young and had an infant daughter and mostly I was…scared. Which was probably what Joyce was feeling right now, too.

I put my arm around her and rested her head on my shoulder, the way I'd comfort Trudy when she was upset. "It's hard," I said. "Things haven't worked out the way you thought they would. But you'll get through this."

She shook her head. "I don't know. Some days I think I won't."

"You will." I lifted her chin and looked into her eyes, my voice firm. "You'll do it for your boys, and you'll do it because you deserve a better life. And you have me and Trudy to help you."

She nodded and sniffed, then blew her nose. "God, I'm such a wreck. Where is that wine?"

"Coming right up." I went into the kitchen and returned with the wine and our glasses. "Drink up. You can spend the night if you want."

"Trudy's at Gil's?"

I nodded and took a long drink of wine. It went down smooth. It had been a long time since I'd really tied one on.

"The boys are with Peter. They wanted to go." She brushed invisible crumbs from her lap. "They miss him."

She didn't add that she missed him, too, but I knew she did. When you love someone so much and then realize they don't love you it takes a while to sink in. Months. Maybe even years.

"So what are you going to do with yourself now that you're a single woman again?" I asked. "Nobody around to tell you whether or not you can spend money or to complain about what you wear or what you cook for dinner."

"Nobody to hog the TV remote."

"Nobody taking all the covers in bed."

"Nobody keeping me awake with his snoring."

"Nobody taking up half your closet."

She refilled our glasses. "Of course, nobody to mow the lawn or change the oil in the car, either."

"You can do those things," I said.

"Yes, but why would I want to?" She took another drink and stared out my front window. "I think I'm going to start dating again."

"Why? So you can find a man to mow your lawn and change your oil?"

She made a face at me. "No, I just think it's sort of like that advice you always hear about climbing back on a horse that bucks you off. I don't want this bad experience with Peter to sour me on men. I want to get out there and prove to myself that there *are* nice guys available."

"It would be easier to hire a lawn service and make an appointment at the Quickie Lube place."

"Just because *you* haven't met the right man doesn't mean he isn't out there."

"Who says I've been looking for Mr. Right—or any other man?" I sipped more wine. "I *like* being single."

"Yeah, but don't you get lonely? And what about sex?"

There was that. I'd sort of gotten used to being celibate, but sometimes… "You don't have to marry a man to have sex with him," I said, with more bravado than I felt. Like I knew anything about that.

"Right. So all I need is to find a man who will mow the lawn, change the oil in the car *and* have sex with me. Should be easy." She drained her glass and held it out for a refill.

I emptied the first bottle, then went into the kitchen for the second. Already I could feel a pleasant buzz. This was definitely better than spending the evening alone with a textbook. When I returned to the living room, Joyce was flipping through the photo album I kept on the coffee table.

"I love this one of you and Gil at your wedding," she said, pointing to a snapshot my mother had taken of us standing in front of the church. Gil was very sharp-looking in a custom-tailored suit, while my A-line dress did little to hide my bloated state.

"My feet hurt, I had to go to the bathroom and I was mad at my mother for making me stand there while she fussed with the camera." I topped off our glasses and lowered myself to the floor on the other side of the coffee table.

Joyce flipped through a few more pages: shots of Trudy as a baby, with Gil, with me, with my parents, by herself. "Can I ask you a personal question?" she asked after a moment.

"I guess." I looked into my glass. "Give me enough of this wine and I'll answer anything."

"When did you know your marriage was over? I mean, for certain?"

I set my glass aside and stared at the floor, as if the answer was down there in the carpet fibers somewhere. "It's hard to say. I mean, part of the problem is that we never should have gotten married in the first place."

"But you stayed together two years. So at least in the beginning you tried to make it work. When did that stop?"

Did it stop the day I watched another man flirt with my husband at a restaurant? The day I realized we hadn't had sex in nine months? Or the day I looked into Gil's eyes and saw the same misery I felt? "I don't think there was a single moment when things changed for us. It was more a gradual realization that this wasn't the right situation for either one of us." I smiled, remembering the bittersweetness of those final days together. "Once we both admitted that and decided to split up, it was a lot easier. Not so much tension. We went back to being friends again. I've always been grateful we didn't stay together so long we became enemies."

"Right now I can't imagine ever being friends with Peter again." She set her empty glass on the table. "It's all I can do to be civil when he picks up and drops off the boys."

"Nobody said you have to be friends with him."

"He probably tells his girlfriend I'm a shrew anyway. I might as well live up to my reputation."

"Give her time. She'll find out what a snake he is. You ought to send her a thank-you card for taking him off your hands."

"That's why I want to start dating again. I deserve someone better and I intend to find him."

"Hear, hear." We clinked our glasses in a toast.

I hoped Joyce *did* find the kind of man she deserved, if that's what made her happy. As for me, I just wanted a passing grade in all my classes and a chance to make a better life for myself and Trudy. As for men—I wouldn't say no to a great guy, but I wasn't putting my life on hold while I waited for one to come along, either.

Three bottles of wine, one ice pack, a handful of aspirin and a heck of a hangover later, I reported for work at the bank drive-through. Though I would have preferred to crawl under the counter and take a nap, Saturdays were invariably busy. I suffered in silence through deposits, withdrawals and payments, mumbling rote greetings into the microphone with all the enthusiasm of an airport security screener faced with holiday traffic.

Fortunately, the drive-through closes at noon on Saturdays. Only a few hours left and I could retreat to my bed and the luxury of moaning out loud without frightening the customers.

I was counting down the minutes when a familiar figure approached the walk-up window. "Hey, Grace." Josh grinned at me from the other side of the glass.

"Josh! What are you doing here?"

"I remembered you said you worked at a bank. I thought I'd stop by and see if you wanted to go to lunch."

Amazing how a dazzling smile from one good-looking man can do more good than a whole handful of aspirin. "Lunch sounds good," I said. "I have to close up here first."

"No problem. What say we meet at Güero's at twelve-thirty?"

"Great. That'd be great."

I don't remember counting up the money and balancing my cash drawer, but I somehow managed to get all the right numbers in all the right places. Amazing, considering how my mind was otherwise occupied. Was this a date, or just two friends getting together? Was Josh really interested in me? Where was this going to lead? Where did I want it to lead? Did it matter that he was so much younger? Were my stretch marks going to be a turn-off for him?

Whoa! Back up a minute there, Gracie! Who said he was going to even see those stretch marks?

For someone who hadn't had sex in over a decade, I was certainly thinking about it a lot lately.

Maybe I could just turn down the lights....

I got to the restaurant at twenty-five after twelve. I'd hurried so I wouldn't be late, and now I wished I hadn't. Is there anything worse than having to wait to meet someone? The longer I wait, the more I worry they've stood me up. Or that I'm at the wrong restaurant.

I stood by the front door, squinting in the bright sunlight and shifting from one foot to the other. Where was he? Where was he? Next time, I'd be late on purpose. Assuming there was a next time.

"Hi Grace. Hope I didn't keep you waiting long."

I jumped a foot when Josh came up behind me. "Waiting? Oh gosh no. Not at all."

What were a few minutes between friends?

Guero's Taco Bar is an Austin institution, serving up killer margaritas and spicy tacos in renovated warehouse space, complete with lots of hanging plants and skylights and a collection of funky signs and pictures by local artists. Rather than wait for a table in one of the dining rooms, we opted to eat at the bar, which offered the added distraction of being able to watch the cooks in the open kitchen.

Our waitress, who introduced herself as Kiki, had short black hair and a pink halter top that showed off her ample cleavage and the colorful tattoo of an iguana that covered her entire back.

"Cool tattoo," Josh said as she handed up our menus.

She grinned and turned to give us a better view. "Thanks. His name's Louie, after my pet iguana."

I pretended to study my menu, but I was really watching Josh, who was watching Kiki walk away. Was her iguana the only thing that interested him? He looked up and caught my eye. "So you like tattoos?" I asked.

He shrugged. "I think they're an interesting form of artistic expression."

"Do you have one?"

He grinned. "Are you kidding? I was in the Navy. It's practically a requirement." He began unbuttoning his shirt. I stared, mouth open, wondering if this was some strange manifestation of a sexual fantasy. He'd take off his shirt, throw me across the table, and ravage me while everyone around us ate enchiladas and nachos. Then I'd wake up in a cold sweat, wondering if maybe I shouldn't have eaten that pepperoni pizza for supper.

But no, it was broad daylight and I was sitting calmly *in a booth* at Guero's, a silly smile plastered on my face as Josh parted the fabric to reveal an eagle in full flight etched across his chest. I may have panted. I'm sure my blood pressure shot up a few notches. The eagle was magnificent, but frankly, I was more impressed with the chest.

I told you I was pathetic. A man strips for me in a restaurant and I'm reduced to drooling Jell-O. He buttoned the shirt again and laughed. "Now you know all my secrets."

Not as many as I'd like to know. Our eyes met, and I felt a little thrill run through me. There was the potential for something more than mere friendship lurking in those brown depths.

Kiki brought a basket of chips and took our order—margaritas and enchiladas for both of us. In the sudden silence after she left, I looked for a way to keep the conversation going. Small talk has never been my forte.

"You're amazing, you know that?"

This assessment, seemingly out of the blue, startled me. I stared at Josh. "I am?"

He nodded. "Here you are, a single mom with a teenage daughter and you're back in school, going for what you want."

My laughter was a little weak this time. "You're assuming I know what that is. I'm really just feeling my way around."

He cocked one eyebrow and sent a look my way that made me feel warm all over. "Still trying to decide what you want to be when you grow up?"

I nodded. "That's about the size of it."

He crunched a chip. "You'll figure it out."

How did he know that? He hardly knew me. Or was he trying to score points by playing cheerleader? I couldn't decide if the idea made me happy or nervous. "You seem to have your future all figured out." I sliced into my enchiladas. "Why did you decide to major in sociology?"

"I'm interested in society and what makes it tick."

And I'm wondering what makes you tick. I like a man who

can surprise me. A man who isn't afraid to be different. A man with a gorgeous chest.

Who knew it took so little to wake up my sleeping libido? Maybe if I'd gotten out and mingled with the opposite sex more I wouldn't have been so content to sit at home every Saturday night for the last twelve years. And maybe I'd be able to sit here now without continuing to stare at Josh.

I forced myself to look away. "Uh, tell me about this killer senior paper that's going to help you make your mark."

"I haven't decided on a topic yet. I want to do something really groundbreaking. Something that hasn't been done yet that will capture popular interest." He leaned forward, elbows on the table. "What do you think about older women and younger men?"

I stared up at him. "Um, as a topic for your paper, or just in general?"

His grin widened. "Both. I'm thinking it would make a good topic for my paper, and for a little personal study."

I swallowed hard. "Uh….that's nice."

Josh reached across the table and took my hand. "So, would you like to go out next Saturday night?"

I gasped, inhaling a partly chewed chip. Josh had to pound my back while I coughed. That's me, cool, calm and collected. "Is that a yes or a no?" Josh asked.

"I'm sorry. Yes." I chugged margarita and tried to find my voice. "Yes, I'd like to go out with you."

He sat back, smiling. "Good. I know we're going to have a great time."

Sure. A great time. How great? I wondered. I mean, did I need to pack a toothbrush?

I guess you could say after twelve years, I was open to making up for lost time.

CHAPTER 5

I waited until Monday afternoon to tell Trudy about my upcoming date. When she came home from Gil's she was full of talk about the movie she'd seen and the new project Mark was working on. Besides, part of me wondered if my hangover-hampered brain hadn't dreamed up the whole thing. But Monday after class Josh said, "We're still on for Saturday, right?" and I'd been floating ever since.

When I picked Trudy up from school I even smiled and waved at Simon, who gave me a funny look. "Simon thinks you're weird," Trudy said as she climbed into the car.

This was something, coming from a boy with a pierced nose. "Why does he think that?"

"One day you glare at him, today he's your best friend. What's he supposed to think?"

"Tell him I'm on medication."

"Are you?"

"Am I what, dear?"

"On medication. You're acting all funny."

"I'm fine, dear. I have a lot of my mind, that's all." Including a certain young stud.

Apparently convinced this was the best she was going to do, she flipped down the visor and began applying a fresh coat of mascara. "So how's Grandma?"

I turned onto MLK and sped up. *Should I wear the blue gauze blouse or the yellow sundress?* "She's fine, as far as I know. Why?"

"Didn't you have lunch with her today?"

You know the feeling you get just before you throw up, when you think it might be better to just lay down and die? That's how I felt at that exact moment. If someone had come along and offered to shoot me, I would have thanked them.

"Mom, are you okay?" Trudy's voice drifted to me as through a tunnel.

The best I could manage was a low moan. I flipped on my blinker and made a hard right onto Lamar.

"Where are we going?" Trudy asked.

"To your grandmother's. I have some groveling to do."

Wally and the Beaver would have felt right at home at my parents' house on the edge of Austin's Hyde Park neighborhood. The long, low ranch house built of pink brick and cedar shingles in the early '60s sits well back on a manicured lawn, shaded by spreading pecan trees. When my brother and I were teenagers, my parents converted the garage into a rec room, complete with Foosball table and orange shag carpet. It's all still there, as if any minute now the "gang" will stop by for cookies and milk and a game of Twister.

As Trudy and I trudged up the front walk, I could practically feel my mother's eyes on me. I was pretty sure she was watching through the peephole in the door, but of course, she made me ring the bell before she moved to answer.

As soon as the doorbell rang, Mom's dog, a standard poodle with the oh-so-original name of Fifi, started barking. "Quiet, Fifi! Hush!" Mom shouted.

Fifi continued to bark, her toenails scrabbling on the tile entryway. "Shut up!" Mom shouted as she unhooked chains and shot back the bolts of the four locks guarding her front door. Our neighbor, Mrs. Thurston, was robbed four years ago and since then Mom has lived behind barricades. Frankly, I think no burglar in his right mind would want to brave Fifi, but that's just my opinion.

The door swung open and Fifi hurtled past me, practically knocking Trudy over in her enthusiasm. "Fifi, down! You're smearing my makeup!"

Mom's face was all downward lines, like someone in mourning. "Grace Anne. I'm glad to see you're safe. I was telling your father we should file a missing person's report."

When my mother uses my full name, I know I'm in trouble. "Mom, I'm so sorry. I guess I've just got so much going on getting used to school and the new hours at work—I forgot."

She shook her head and turned to walk back into the house. "That's all right, dear. It's a mother's lot to be forgotten. I know you have more important things in your life now. I'm happy for whatever crumbs of attention you throw my way."

"Mom, please, you know that's not true." I hurried to put my arm around her. At times like this, I'm struck by how much smaller she seems than when I was a child. She is shrinking right before my eyes, which holds the frightening possibility that one day, she'll be gone altogether. "I'm sorry I missed lunch. Let me take you and Dad out to dinner to make up for it."

"Nonsense. You and Trudy can eat with us. I made meat loaf." We followed her into the kitchen. Fifi headed for her water bowl and began to drink noisily. Mom tied on an apron, a warrior girding herself for battle. "Trudy, you put ice in the glasses. Grace, set the table.

"Not those dishes. Use the good china," Mom said when I started to take down the beige and white Corelle we always called the everyday dishes. "And use the blue napkins. In the drawer under the telephone."

She whipped potatoes and stirred butter into peas, all the while giving orders. "Trudy, put this butter on the table. Grace, wash your hands before you sit down. And call your father."

I smiled as I headed toward the bathroom. Mom had been saying the exact same things to me since I was five years old. It was always 'Grace, wash your hands' and always would be. When I was a teenager and a young mother, I'd chafed at being treated like a child, but now that I was a little older, I found it very comforting. I'd been looking after myself and Trudy so long it was always nice to have someone fuss over me for a change—as long as the fussing didn't go on too long.

When we were all seated around the table, meat loaf, mashed potatoes and green peas steaming in bowls before us, Mom beamed. "It's so good to have you all here," she said, like a priest giving a benediction. I smiled. All was right with the world again. At least for a little while.

Make that a few minutes. "Trudy, you don't have any meat loaf on your plate. Let me cut you a slice." Mom reached for the platter.

"That's okay, Grandma. I don't want any meat loaf."

"I thought you loved my meat loaf. Last time you were here, you ate two helpings."

Trudy gave me a pleading look across the table. "Trudy's decided to become a vegetarian," I said.

Mom frowned. "A growing girl like her?" She cut a slice of meat loaf and slid it onto Trudy's plate. "Nonsense. You need protein. And iron. You'll get anemic."

"I take vitamins, Grandma." Trudy pushed the offending meat to one side. "Honest, I'm fine."

Mom shook her head and directed her disapproval to me. "You shouldn't allow such nonsense, Grace Anne."

"Leave the girl alone." My father looked up from his plate and made a rare contribution to the conversation. "If she doesn't want the meat loaf, that leaves more for me." He winked at Trudy, who grinned at him.

But of course, my mother couldn't drop the subject. She

frowned at my father, then turned back to me. "I kept my mouth shut when you allowed her to start dressing like a ghoul, but these strange food fads are going too far."

"Vegetarianism is not a strange food fad, Grandma. Buddhist monks have been practicing it for centuries and it's a very healthy way to live."

Mom's eyebrows shot up. "Are you a Buddhist now, too?" She turned to me. "Grace, what are you thinking?"

"Mom, it's all right." I took a sip of iced tea. "Trudy is fine and I'm fine. How are you?"

"I'm fine, too, except that Millie Adamson had the nerve to suggest that I shouldn't be president of the garden club again this year because I've already served two terms." Concerns over Trudy's impending malnutrition gave way to the petty battles of the garden club. I winked at Trudy across the table and nodded toward Mom. Maybe I should study international affairs. I'd make a great diplomat, don't you think?

By the time Mom brought out a chocolate cake and coffee, we were all feeling pretty mellow. Daddy retired to the den with his dessert while the females in the family gathered around the kitchen table. Mom added cream to her cup and smiled at me. "We don't get to visit like this nearly enough. Tell me what all is going on in your lives."

"Well—" I smiled at my daughter "—Trudy has a boyfriend."

Trudy squirmed and mashed cake crumbs with the back of her fork. "He's not really a boyfriend, just a friend."

Mom pursed her lips. "Don't you think she's too young to be dating?"

My heart gave a little lurch, which I did my best to ignore. "She's not dating, Mom."

Trudy shifted in her chair. "People don't date at my school. They just go out with groups of friends."

"How is that different from dating?" Mom asked.

Trudy shrugged. "Nobody's really with anybody else." She looked up at me. "Mom, a bunch of kids are going over to Dave and Buster's Saturday for pizza and to play games. Can I go?"

I think I did a pretty good job of hiding my surprise at this turn of events. Could it be that Cal had actually worked up the nerve to ask her out? And she'd said yes? "Who's going to be there?"

"Just a bunch of kids. Sheila and Mallory and that Cal boy you like."

I smiled. "Will Simon be there?"

She looked away. "Yeah. He might be there." I'd bet money he would be. But what did it matter? I had to start trusting Trudy with boys some time. Now was as good a time as any.

"It's all right with me, if your father doesn't mind picking you up."

It was her turn to look startled. "Why can't you pick me up?"

I flushed and stirred my coffee. "Because I'm going out, too."

"On a date!" My mother and Trudy spoke at the same time.

Mom leaned forward, eyes alight. "Is this someone you met at school?"

Trudy squealed. "I'll bet it's that Josh dude who came by the house the other day."

Mom looked at her. "Who is Josh?"

"He's totally cool, Grandma. He works at a bicycle shop and he is so awesomely hot."

I winced. Trudy made him sound like a teenage sex god. My mother must have thought so, too. She looked at me. "How old is this young man?"

"He's twenty-six." I tried to mumble, but my mother has very good hearing.

"Twenty-six? And he's still in college?"

"He was in the Navy. He's very nice. Very mature for his age." Why was I so defensive? I had no reason to be defensive. Except this was my mother. And I was enough like her to know exactly what she was thinking.

Mom sighed. A sigh that said volumes. It said she'd given up on having a "normal" daughter. "Well, I suppose a younger man is better than no man at all, though I'd feel better if he had a real job."

"Mom, *I* don't even have a real job."

"You've worked at the bank for thirteen years."

"I sit in a cage and count out change for people. I save wheat pennies for Mr. Bob."

Mom brightened and latched on to the change of subject. My strange love life—or lack of it—was obviously too depressing. "Is he still alive? The man must be nearly ninety."

I smiled into my coffee cup. "There's a woman in my class who's eighty and she's decided to get her degree."

"I can't imagine why she'd want to do that. It's not as if anyone is going to hire her at her age."

"Maybe she's doing it for the sake of doing it. For the sake of gaining knowledge and experiencing new things."

"A waste of time and money if you ask me." Mom stood and began stacking our empty plates. "Now, before you run off to your exciting life as a college student, would you do your poor mother a favor?"

I sighed. Payback time. I should have known I wouldn't get away this evening without doing something to make up for the missed lunch. "What do you need me to do?"

"I need you to trim Fifi's nails."

At the sound of her name, Fifi jumped up and barked, pom-pommed tail waving wildly. I made a face at the dog. Trimming Fifi's nails was like trying to brush an alligator's teeth. "Why don't you take her to the groomer?"

"Why should I when I have you to do it for me?" Mom smiled and patted the dog.

I sighed and went to get the nail clippers. I figured it was my penance for forgetting my lunch date with Mom. And it could have been worse. She could have asked me to bathe the dog, too.

* * *

Saturday, 5:00 p.m. Crisis time. Why is it I can never find anything to wear? I'm guessing men don't have this problem. Even Gil, who pays more attention to fashion than the average man, just reaches in his closet and puts something on and it looks great.

I, on the other hand, try on an outfit only to discover it's too tight across the hips. What is it with fabric manufacturers today? I wash in cold water, but you wouldn't believe the things that shrink.

Outfit number two looks okay, but I have no shoes that match.

Outfit number three looks like something my mother would wear. It goes into a garbage bag destined for Goodwill.

Outfit number four looked good in the store, but now makes my skin look like I'm suffering from an unfortunate disease.

I was up to outfit ten when Trudy walked into the room, dressed in pajama bottoms and a pink bra. "Mo-om! I can't find anything to wear."

"I'm sorry, hon. I think it's genetic." I turned this way and that in front of the closet mirror. "Do you think this skirt is too short?"

"Can I have this?" I turned and saw her holding a blue silk blouse I'd placed in a "maybe" pile.

"You want to wear that?"

She clutched it to her chest. "Please?"

"It's not black."

"It'll look good with my black jeans," she called over her shoulder as she ran from the room, blue blouse in hand.

I frowned at the skirt. It was too short. My thighs looked huge. I sank down on the end of the bed and moaned. The problem was, I had no idea what women wore on dates these days. Should I dress up? Dress down? Go all out, or act like I didn't care?

Wouldn't it be easier to stay home in my pajamas and drown my sorrows in a pint of fudge ripple?

"Coward," I said, and went to search the closet again.

In the end, I settled on a red and white sundress that was dressy enough for most restaurants but casual enough for an outdoor barbecue. It also made me look thinner than I was and the full skirt was sort of floaty and feminine.

As I finished my makeup, I wondered where Josh was taking me. I imagined dinner at some cozy restaurant, where we could get to know each other better. Or maybe a fun movie, followed by drinks at some out-of-the-way bar.

I was trying to coax my hair into some semblance of style when the doorbell rang. "I'll get it!" Trudy yelled.

I dropped the brush and scrambled among the mess atop my dresser, searching for a lipstick. My heart raced like the second-place finisher at the Kentucky Derby. He was here! I wasn't ready! Oh God, was my eyeliner straight?

"Stop primping, you look great."

I whirled, lipstick pointed like a gun. "Gil! You almost gave me a heart attack."

"Good to see you, too." He walked over and kissed my cheek, then held me at arm's length. "Very nice. I hope this guy's worth it."

Trudy skipped into the room behind her father. "You look hot, Mom."

"You look good, too." I smiled at her, but inside, I felt a little weepy. My blue blouse was a little big on her, but the color brought out her eyes. The dog collar was gone and in its place was the diamond solitaire I'd given her for her thirteenth birthday. She'd even put little rhinestone clips in her hair. My little girl was growing up.

"You look great, sweetheart." Gil hugged her close. "Maybe I should just lock you in your room until you're thirty."

"Oh, Daddy." She pretended to punch him.

"So tell me about this guy you're going out with," Gil said.

I thought at first he was talking to Trudy, but then I realized the question was addressed to me. I looked at him, surprised. "Why are you so interested? You're not jealous, are you?"

"No. Just concerned." He grinned. "Sometimes it's like having two daughters. Or a daughter and a sister."

I turned back to the dresser, searching for earrings, trying to ignore the funny feeling in the pit of my stomach.

Did Gil really think of me like a sister? I couldn't honestly say I thought of him as a brother. "His name's Josh. I met him in class. He used to be in the Navy and now he's gone back to school, like me."

Gil leaned against the wall beside the dresser. "How's school going?"

"Pretty good. It's harder than I thought it would be, juggling everything."

"It'll get easier, once you've worked out a routine. And you've always been smart. You can do this."

I turned my head and met his gaze. He was smiling, his expression full of fondness, maybe even a little pride. I swallowed a sudden lump in my throat and looked away. "Do you really think I'm smart?"

"I know it. You always got better grades in school than I did."

"That's because you didn't study."

"Because I was too dumb to study." He put his hand on my shoulder. "Don't sell yourself short, Gracie."

This was too much. Why was I so emotional all of a sudden? Must be hormones. I couldn't cry. It would ruin my makeup. I pushed Gil away. "Go on. Trudy's ready to go."

He backed away, a smile on his face that I knew meant trouble. "Oh, I think I'll stick around and meet Josh. See if he passes inspection."

"You wouldn't dare."

"Hide and watch."

Laughing, he left the bedroom. I turned back to the mirror and dabbed powder on my nose. Great. Ex-husband meets new boyfriend. Talk about getting a relationship off to a good start.

When the doorbell rang, we looked like the three stooges, racing to answer it, but I beat Trudy and Gil back with killing looks, then took a deep breath, trying for calm. "Don't keep him standing there all night," Gil said. "Open the door."

I gave him another dark look, then put a smile on my face and turned to greet my date.

No telling what Josh thought when I opened the door. He was so amazingly handsome, dressed in loden green pants and a greenish-brown shirt of some kind of shiny fabric. I stared at him for a full minute, a glazed expression in my eyes, while Trudy and Gil loomed over my shoulders, grinning like a pair of idiots.

"Uh, hello," Josh said, gaze flitting between me and my entourage. "So, uh, are you ready?"

Ready. God, yes, I was ready. Ready to get out of there. I felt like a bug under a microscope. "Yes, I'm ready. Let me grab my purse."

I started to shut the door, but Gil caught it and opened it wider. "Hi, Josh, I'm Gil." He stuck out his hand. "Trudy's father."

Josh went a little green around the mouth, but he recovered well. He shook Gil's hand. "Hello."

"So, Grace tells me you two met at St. Ed's."

"Ye-es."

"What are you studying?"

"Sociology. Uh, Grace, we'd better head out." He tapped his watch.

"I have to get my purse," I said. "I'll be right back."

I grabbed Gil's arm and dragged him along after me. "What do you think you're doing?" I growled. "Why are you interrogating him?"

"You didn't tell me you were dating a *kid*. Is he even old enough to drink?"

"He's not a kid. Besides, Mark's younger than you."

"Three years younger, not a decade."

"It's only nine years." Which I'll admit, sounded like a lot, but so what? I picked up my purse and started to push past him. "I'd better go."

He put his hand on my shoulder and stopped me. "Sorry. I know I'm being a jerk. Who you date is none of my business. I just don't want to see you hurt."

Hurt *again*. The words hung between us, unsaid. Gil had loved me as much as he was able, but the truth between us would always be that in the end, it wasn't enough.

I relaxed and squeezed his arm. "It's okay. I'm a big girl. I can take care of myself."

He nodded and stepped aside. "Have a good time. Call me if you need anything."

To say Josh wasn't his usual friendly self as we drove away from the house was a bit of an understatement. Silence sat between us like an annoying third party. "I think maybe I'd better explain about Gil," I said.

"No need to explain." He reached over and adjusted the radio. "You said you were friends."

"We *are* friends, but that's all. He was just giving me a hard time tonight."

Josh glanced at me. "Maybe so, but I think your ex still has a thing for you."

"He'd be more likely to have a thing for you."

He frowned. "What's that supposed to mean?"

"Josh, Gil is gay. And happily involved with an artist named Mark. There will never be anything else between us."

Josh slumped against the seat back. "Whew." He glanced my way again. "You're serious?"

"Why would I make up something like that?"

"Oh, man."

This is what happens when you try to be honest with a guy. They get all weird on you. I really had planned to keep this particular piece of my past private for a while longer, but Josh sort of forced my hand with the whole jealousy bit. Why couldn't I find a man who would like me just for me, and not care about all the other stuff in my life? I gnawed my lower lip and looked out the window. The green expanse of Zilker Park stretched alongside the road, the bowed limbs of ancient live oaks almost touching the ground, people and dogs gathered on the soccer fields, a trio of swimsuit-clad teens walking to Barton Springs pool. The same scenes that had been a part of all my life in Austin. Yet so much had changed.

"I think that is so cool."

"Huh?" I swivelled my head around and stared at Josh again. "What did you say?"

"I think it's really cool that you and Gil are friends and that he's involved in Trudy's life and all." He looked at me and nodded. "That is such a twenty-first-century kind of social structure, you know?"

"I don't know about that. We're just a family. Maybe not your standard man-woman-child, but still a family."

Josh nodded. "It's just really cool."

Was this a good thing or a bad thing? I wanted to be Josh's girlfriend, not the basis for a future thesis. I crossed my legs and smoothed my skirt over them. It was early days yet. Maybe it was up to me to prove that I could be more than an interesting research subject.

Club Soho specialized in loud. Loud music and loud people in loud clothes. "This place has great energy," Josh shouted as we threaded our way through the crowd toward the bar.

A woman with pink hair shimmied past me. She appeared to be dancing with a five-foot-long stuffed lobster. She looked happy about it, too.

"What do you want to drink?" Josh shouted when we reached the bar.

"Rum and Diet Coke." I hoped they used a lot of rum. I needed a shot of liquid courage. This wasn't quite the intimate restaurant or out-of-the-way bar I'd pictured. Looking around me at the mass of energetic young bodies, I fought the urge to take my tired old self home to bed.

A wall of mirrors behind the bar reflected the action on the dance floor. Thin men and women dressed in skimpy tops and low-slung jeans gyrated around each other in blissful abandon. Many of the dancers had neon-colored hair and most sported tattoos and body piercings.

Don't get me wrong. There was nothing repellant about this bunch. If anything, they were too beautiful. I felt like a wren at a convention of peacocks.

The women had something else I didn't have (besides tattoos and navel rings). They all seemed so self-confident and *comfortable* in their bodies. Even those who weren't model thin didn't seem to have any problem showing off rounded bellies and plump arms. That confidence alone gave them a kind of beauty no expensive cosmetics could have managed.

Me, I worry that ankle-strap sandals make my legs look chunky. I refuse to go without a bra for fear my breasts will end up warming my belly button. Where had these younger women gotten such self-confidence and where could I get some for myself? I'd pick up a side order for Trudy while I was at it.

"So what do you think?" Josh appeared at my side with our drinks.

"Uh…interesting place." I gulped my rum and Coke and came up coughing. Oh yes. Plenty of rum.

"The deejay spins an awesome set." Josh leaned closer,

his breath warm in my ear as he spoke. "He's made this a really happening place."

Personally, I prefer music with lyrics I can understand. But maybe that wasn't the point here. This was music you *felt*. A driving bass rhythm echoed through my chest and the high whine of a saxophone made my teeth hurt. "It certainly has a strong rhythm," I said.

"Let's dance." He drained his drink and set the empty glass down on a table.

I abandoned my own half-finished drink and followed him onto the dance floor. I wasn't too worried about making a wrong move there. From what I could tell, there *were* no wrong moves.

I thought of the ballroom dancing classes I'd taken at Miss Eloise's Dance Academy back in sixth grade. If Mom could see me now, she'd probably demand a refund.

A girl dressed all in black danced past and I thought of Trudy. What was she doing right now? Was she having a good time? Would she tell me about it when she got home, or was she getting too grown-up to confide in her mother? How would I be able to stand it?

Josh was saying something to me. *Pay attention, Gracie.* I gave him a dazed smile. "What was that? I couldn't hear you over the music."

"I said I like that dress," he said. "Very feminine."

"Thanks. I like your outfit, too."

We grinned at each other like a pair of opossums. Maybe in a few minutes, I could talk him into taking me some place quieter. I mean, isn't the whole point of a date to get to know each other better? It was hard to have much of a conversation shouting at each other.

The song ended and Josh grabbed my hand. "Are you hungry? There's a restaurant in the back of this place."

I nodded. Food sounded great. Food and silence.

It wasn't exactly silent, but the restaurant *was* quieter than the dance floor. We ordered turkey wraps and fries and carried them to a booth in the corner. Josh flagged down a passing barmaid and in a few minutes, she returned with more drinks. I sipped mine more cautiously this time. No sense getting drunk and doing something I might regret.

"So tell me what you're feeling now." Josh pointed a French fry at me.

I blinked. Not your standard date question. "Um, well, the turkey wrap is a little dry, but the fries are good."

He laughed. "Not about the food. About us. The whole younger man/older woman thing. What's your take on it?"

I tried not to squirm in my seat. "What do you mean? I'm here, aren't I?"

"Yeah, and I'm glad you're here with me." He looked around. "I don't imagine they had any place like this around here when you were my age."

A girl in a sequined crop top and harem pants shimmied past us. An emerald glinted at her naval. "Uh, no, they didn't."

I laid aside my turkey wrap and looked at him. "So, um, what are your feelings?"

He grinned. "Right now, I'm thinking I'd like to get to know you better."

The look in his eyes made my stomach do a back-flip. It had been a long time since I'd seen that look, but I thought I recognized good old-fashioned lust. Hallelujah! Maybe I wasn't a lost cause after all.

I pushed the rest of the food away. "Maybe we could go someplace quieter," I said.

"Great idea." He finished his drink and pushed up out of the booth. "But first, there's something else I want to do."

I started to get up, but he smiled and slid into the booth next to me. I didn't even have time to think about what was happening when he kissed me.

I felt like Sleeping Beauty, waiting for something within me to be awakened by that kiss. Josh's lips were soft, tasting faintly of whiskey. It wasn't a magic kiss, but it was warm and pleasant, and I could see myself enjoying more of the same.

He drew back a little and looked at me. "Did you like that?"

I nodded. "Yeah."

He kissed me again, deeper this time, and pressed his body against mine. Very nice, but I was conscious of all the movement and noise around us. I pushed him away. "Maybe we should go someplace a little more private."

"In a minute. Besides, nobody cares."

He leaned into me again, his mouth on mine, his hand caressing my breast. I tried to relax, to enjoy the moment, but things were happening so quickly....

"Relax." He smoothed his hand down my arm. "You don't have anything to worry about. I don't mean to brag, but women tell me I'm very good in the sack."

How many women? So maybe that wasn't a fair question, but it was the first thing that popped into my mind. Plus, I didn't think "in the sack" was a very romantic way to put it. "This is just a little sudden for me," I said, trying to put some distance between us, but since I was already pressed against the back wall of the booth, I had nowhere to go. "I thought maybe we'd get to know each other better before things got, um, physical. You know—talk?"

He smiled, still stroking my arm. "I understand. You're just nervous. I'm sure that ex-husband of yours wasn't much of a lover."

Gil? What did Gil have to do with any of this? A knot tightened in my throat. "Is that what this is all about? Here's the poor woman whose husband left her for another man, so you're going to show her a good time?" I shoved him away from me, hard enough to rattle the dishes on the table.

He backed away, straightening his clothes. "Hey, you got it all wrong—"

I wasn't in the mood to listen to any explanations. Nothing about tonight had worked out the way I'd hoped.

I pushed past him and headed toward the one place I was sure he wouldn't follow me.

The ladies' room at Club Soho had everything a girl could want when she's facing an impending meltdown: poor lighting, plenty of toilet paper, an orange vinyl sofa and a working telephone.

I fully intended to call a cab to carry me away from here, but I couldn't make out the phone number through the tears, so my fingers ended up punching out the number I knew by heart.

He answered on the third ring. "Hello?"

"Gil, I'm at Club Soho downtown. Could you come get me, please?"

CHAPTER 6

After I hung up the phone, I slumped down on the sofa and tried to blot my tears with a wad of toilet paper. It wasn't doing a very good job and my mascara dripped down my cheeks in inky streams. I looked like a refugee from a Marilyn Manson concert.

A brunette in four-inch platforms and a Betty Boop T-shirt came into the room and looked at me. "Is your name Grace?"

"Who wants to know?"

"A really good-looking dude out there in the hallway is looking for you."

I sniffed and tried to find a dry space on my wad of tissue. "Tell him I'm not here."

I figured she'd leave then, but no such luck. Instead, she sat down on the couch next to me. It's bad enough crying and looking like a wreck, but the last thing I wanted was an audience. "What did he do to you, hon?"

I blew my nose and shook my head. "Nothing. Not really."

"Did he ogle some other chick?"

"No." Josh had been very attentive. Too attentive.

"Then he probably said something jerky." She sighed. "Some men just don't know when to keep their mouths shut."

I looked at her. With her short dark hair and red-lip-sticked mouth, she resembled the cartoon character on her shirt. "Can I ask you a personal question?" I asked.

She shrugged. "Sure. I don't have to answer if I don't want to."

"How old are you?"

She grinned. "Twenty-two. Was that the question?"

I shook my head and wadded the mess of toilet paper into a tight ball. "So what do you expect from a first date?"

She tilted her head to one side, considering. "I guess I want the guy to show me a good time. Maybe a nice dinner, or a movie that I want to see." She wrinkled her nose. "One time this dude took me to a Jean-Claude Van Damme film festival. Whose idea of a date movie is *that*?"

"Then you don't think it's too much to ask for an evening that's a little romantic?"

"Of course not. If that's what you want, that's what you deserve." She grinned. "I get it! Handsome out there wanted to go straight from hors d'oeuvres to dessert, didn't he?"

"Uh yeah. I think so."

She made a tsking sound. "Some of these guys can't understand why a woman wouldn't just jump at the chance to crawl into bed with them. As if they're doing us some big *favor* or something." She patted my arm. "Don't worry, chickie. There are some good ones out there, it just takes a while to find them sometimes. Meanwhile, I've got one word for you."

"What's that?"

She grinned. "Duracell."

It took me a minute to get her drift. So I'm a little slow. "Uh yeah. I'll remember that."

The bathroom door opened again and a familiar face appeared around the corner. "Gracie, are you ready to go?"

Betty Boop squealed. "You can't come in here!"

Gil came around the corner and took my hand. "It's all right, honey. You don't do a thing for me." He looked at me. "You all right?"

I nodded. "Yeah. Let's go."

I didn't really want to run into Josh, but I couldn't help watching for him out of the corner of my eye. "He was over by the bar when I came in," Gil said, doing his mind reading thing again. "Drowning his sorrows."

Crowds of Saturday night partiers clogged the street outside the club. Groups of laughing people jostled past us, couples arm in arm, eyes alight with excitement. The night brimmed with possibility for them. I felt like a visitor from another planet, someone who had failed to crack the secret code and was being sent home in disgrace.

Gil didn't say anything else until we were in the car. "What happened?" he asked.

I shook my head. "It just wasn't what I expected." I'd wanted a nice dinner and conversation, not bad food, psychoanalysis and groping.

He glanced over his shoulder, back toward the club. "You know I'm not the fighting type, but if it'll make you feel better, I've probably got one good punch in me."

I smiled at the thought of Gil beating up anyone. More likely, muscular Josh would reduce him to a bloody pulp. "It's not worth that."

"Well, you know I'm always ready to defend your honor."

He put the car into gear and pulled out into traffic. I leaned against the window, my face turned away from him. I didn't want him to see the fresh flood of tears his words had brought. Why was it nothing ever changed for me? Gil and I had been divorced twelve years and I was still calling on him to run to my rescue. Why did I still need him that way? When was I going to let him go?

I tried to remember what Josh's kiss had felt like, but all I could manage was the sense that it had been a pleasant experience. A good kiss, but nothing special. Shouldn't there be more? I didn't want pleasant. I wanted passion. Something to make my heart sing. Something to make my ordinary life not so ordinary.

I'd wanted hearts and flowers and I'd gotten loud music and groping in a restaurant booth. Was I being unrealistic? Would I be happier if I learned to settle for less?

Maybe what I needed was to loosen up and just let life happen. Maybe if I'd gone to bed with Josh, I'd find out something about myself I didn't know. Maybe I'd have been happier in the morning.

That's a lot of maybes. And I've never been much of a gambler. What I wanted was a sure thing. Someone I could depend on not to let me down.

I glanced toward Gil. Someone like him. Only straight.

I stifled a sob and looked out the window. Oh God, am I messed up or what?

I thought Gil would drive me home, but instead, we headed out MoPac toward 183. "It's almost time to pick up Trudy," he said.

I nodded and started digging in my purse, hoping for a scrap of tissue. The last thing I wanted was for my daughter to see me looking like this.

I felt a tap on my shoulder and Gil held out a handkerchief. "There's a bottle of water in the backseat if that'll help."

I sniffed. "I must look a wreck."

"Your makeup job is ruined, that's for sure."

I found the water bottle and scrubbed off the rest of my makeup, then combed my hair. Since it was dark, maybe Trudy wouldn't notice anything odd. I'd just tell her I'd decided to come home early. With any luck, she'd dismiss it as "a mom thing" and not ask questions.

Gil found a parking space with a good view of the front door of Dave and Buster's and checked his watch. "Ten o'clock. She ought to be out any minute now."

A crowd of teenagers emerged. I recognized her friends Sheila and Mallory, and some other kids from her class. But where was Trudy?

Just then, the crowd parted to reveal a couple twined around each other. The girl's face was hidden by the boy, who was kissing her. I think my heart stopped when I realized the girl was Trudy.

Gil took hold of my hand. "It's all right, Gracie."

"Let go, Gil. You're hurting me."

He released my hand. "Sorry. You just looked like you were about to bolt out of the car."

I sank back against the seat. "I guess that would be a bad move, huh?"

"Yeah." His voice sounded strained. When I looked at him, he was gripping the steering wheel with both hands, white-knuckled.

I smiled. "It's hard for you, too, isn't it?"

He nodded. "Just the other day she was a baby, giggling on my lap. I'm afraid if I blink, she'll be gone altogether."

I looked toward the restaurant again. Trudy and Simon had stopped kissing and were walking toward us, hand in hand. She was smiling, a bounce in her walk that told me she was happy. Could I ask for anything more? All her life, I'd prayed that Trudy would be healthy and happy. So far, I'd gotten my wish. It was up to me not to screw that up.

I rolled down the window. "Hello Trudy. Hello, Simon."

"Mom! What are you doing here?" Trudy released Simon's hand and hurried to the car.

"I missed you," I said, opening the car door and holding up my arms for a hug.

It was exactly the kind of thing to make her roll her eyes and moan, but I got a hug and a quick kiss on the cheek.

"Hello Mrs. Greenleigh. Mr. Greenleigh." Simon nodded solemnly.

"Hi Simon," Gil said. "Do you need a ride somewhere?"

"No. My brother's picking me up." He nodded toward a red pickup across the lot. "That's him over there." He turned to Trudy. "I'll call you."

"Okay. Good night." She climbed in the backseat without a glance back.

I bit my lip in an effort to keep quiet.

Instead, Trudy began questioning me. "So how did it go with Josh, Mom?"

"We went dancing," I said. "At Club Soho."

"I've heard of that place. Very 'in.'"

"Very loud." I put a hand to my head. "I got a headache and left early." So it was a little white lie. I did have a headache now. Crying does that to me.

"What do you mean, you left early? You don't just leave a date early. Especially not with a guy like Josh."

"You can do anything you like, Trudy." Gil looked at her in the rearview mirror. "Just because a guy takes you out doesn't mean you have to go along with everything he wants to do."

"You're talking about sex, aren't you? I know that, Dad."

"I'm going to keep reminding you anyway."

"What does that have to do with Mom?" Her eyes widened and she stared at me. "Do you mean Josh made a pass at you and you didn't like it?" I imagine she was trying to fit the idea of "mom" and "sex" into the same sentence. The two concepts just don't go together.

I was grateful for the darkness to hide my blush. "I didn't have as good a time as I thought I would," I said. "But what about you? Did you have a good time?"

"I had a blast. There's this game there, where you…"

I smiled as she poured out endless details of the evening's fun. What they did and what they ate, who they saw. Not what they talked about or what they felt. Nothing too revealing, but enough that we felt included, still a part of her life. Our daughter was growing up, but she was still ours for a little while.

The rest of my life might be a mixed-up mess, but I had this one jewel in my crown. I didn't understand men, and I didn't know what I wanted to do five years from now, or even next year, but I had a daughter who loved me. That was worth everything.

I dreaded walking into economics class Monday. I was still angry at Josh, and embarrassed about the way the evening had ended, too. I didn't know what to say to him, and I didn't want to make a scene.

Of course, if I was lucky, he wouldn't even talk to me, and then I wouldn't have to worry.

I held up my chin and faced myself in the mirror. "You have nothing to be embarrassed about," I told myself. "You'll walk into class and if he's there, you'll ignore him. It's the least he deserves after the way he treated you."

I sounded a lot more positive than I felt. Though Josh had been a jerk, I'd enjoyed his company before our disastrous date, and I'd looked forward to getting to know him better. For the first time in a long time, I'd looked forward to being part of a couple. To having a *boyfriend*. I had begun to get excited about the prospect and having it end badly was depressing.

It turned out my pep talk to myself was wasted. Josh was nowhere in sight by the time the bell rang to begin class. I took some comfort in imagining that he was too ashamed of his behavior on our date to show his face.

Professor Hauser handed back the exams we'd taken Friday. I moaned when I saw the large D scrawled at the top of mine. I was doing well in my other classes, but economics was eating my lunch.

"Ms. Greenleigh, will you see me after class?" Dr. Hauser said.

I nodded, glum. He was probably going to suggest I drop the course. I obviously wasn't cut out for this stuff.

I stayed behind when everyone filed out at the end of class. I felt like a kid who'd been called to the principal's office. "You seem to be having some trouble with the class," Dr. Hauser said. "Generally, with my younger students, I find it's because they don't study the material, but I don't think that's the problem in your case, is it?"

I shook my head. "I study the material but, well…" I glanced at him, not sure how he was going to take this. He didn't look particularly upset. I took a deep breath. "I think economics is really boring."

His laughter surprised me. "It can be, yes. Tell me, Ms. Greenleigh, what do you do when you're not in school? Do you have a job?"

"I work in a bank." I made a face. "Sometimes that's boring, too."

More laughter. He had a deep voice and his laughter vibrated through me, like the reverberations of a bass drum. "Maybe you need to think about this class like the boring parts of your job. Something that has to be done."

I nodded. "Maybe I can do that. And maybe it would help if I stayed awake while I read the text."

"So you're working and going to school. That can be a lot to handle at once. Do you have a family also? A husband and children?"

"I have a daughter." I hesitated, then added, "Trudy's fourteen."

"My daughter, Jeanette, is fifteen. Teenagers can be a handful, can't they? We think because they're older, they don't need us as much as they did when they were babies, but sometimes they need us even more."

"Yes!" I turned toward him. "It's one of the biggest surprises I've had as a parent. Do you have other children, Dr. Hauser?"

"I have a son, Daniel. He's twelve. They both live with their mother in Houston."

"Trudy's father lives here in town. It's good for her and it makes it easier on me."

"Perhaps you could arrange for him to take her one extra day during the week so you'd have time to study."

"I hadn't thought of that. I'm sure he wouldn't mind."

He stood. "I think if you concentrate more, you'll get a better grasp of the class material and you'll do better on the next exam. In the meantime, I'm always available between classes and during my off period to answer any questions you might have." He smiled again, an expression that transformed his face to heart-stopping handsomeness. "I want you to know it's a pleasure having you in my class."

"It is?" Did he mean it, or was this just some comment meant to inspire me to do better?

"Yes. I find that when students return to school later in life, they're more interested in learning. Perhaps it's because they're doing this for themselves, and not because it's expected of them."

I flushed. "I guess that's true. I hadn't thought about it much."

He held out his hand. "It was good talking with you. And remember, I'm here if you need me."

His handshake was warm and firm. I left class feeling

better than I had in days. *I'm here if you need me.* Where had I heard that before?

Mondays are always busy at the bank. Weekend deposits have to be processed and lots of people use the drive-through to cash checks and make loan payments. The nice thing about being busy is it makes the time fly, and less opportunity to think about things.

Of course, it also meant I wasn't prepared when my mother pulled into the drive-through.

"Mom! What a nice surprise," I lied. "I didn't know you had an account here."

"I don't." She pressed the button to retrieve the carrier. "I need change for a twenty."

She could have gotten change for a twenty at the grocery store. I had a good idea why she was *really* here. "I was going to call you later," I said. Much later, but I would have eventually gotten around to it.

"I'm here now. So tell me—how was your big date?"

I didn't consider it a good sign that my night out with Josh had been elevated from "a" date to a "big" date. "It was okay, Mom. Nothing special."

"Are you going to see him again?"

I counted out three fives and five ones and shook my head. "No." Who was I kidding? It would be a cold day in July before I went out with Josh again.

"What happened?" Mom asked. "Trudy said he was young and good-looking. What did you do?"

Of course, this was all *my* fault. I must be the one who's defective. "He behaved like a jerk," I said.

"Oh? What did he do?"

"I don't want to talk about it." I put the bills in an envelope and dropped it in the carrier.

"There's no need to take that tone with me. I was only trying to help."

I sighed and hit the button to return the carrier. "I know. And I appreciate it."

"Maybe you should see a sex therapist."

I blinked. "A *sex* therapist? Why in the world would you think that?"

"Well after all, dear, Gil seemed perfectly fine until he married you."

I didn't know whether to dissolve into tears or hysterical laughter. With a line of customers waiting, neither was an option, so I did the next best thing. I smiled sweetly and attempted to shock my mother into leaving me alone. "I'm thinking of getting my navel pierced. And maybe my tongue."

Mom recoiled as if I'd held up a live snake. "Far be it from me to try and tell you what to do. But don't come crying to me when you get a nasty infection." She dropped her sunglasses down on her nose and stepped on the gas. I was still laughing when she pulled away.

CHAPTER 7

When I was in first grade, my teacher gave each student a packet of bachelor's button seeds. We each had a section of dirt on the playground to tend and by the time school let out for the summer, the playground was edged with bright blue bachelor's buttons.

And I was hooked on gardening. No matter where I've lived since then, I've grown flowers. When Trudy and I moved into this house, I began digging up the backyard before I'd even unpacked all the boxes.

Tuesday evening I decided to weed the back flowerbeds. I do my best thinking when my hands are in the dirt and I had a paper to write for my Government and Politics class. Maybe somewhere between the asters and the zinnias I'd come up with the words to fill up the pages that were due Thursday.

"You're a hard woman to pin down, do you know that?"

I looked up from my work to find Joyce leaning over the fence that separated our backyards. "I've been trying to catch you since Saturday."

"I've been in and out a lot." I sat back on my heels and brushed my hair out of my face. "So what's up with you?"

She grinned, dimples forming at either side of her mouth. "I had my first date this weekend."

"You did? That's great." I was impressed. Talk about a fast worker. "Who? How did you meet him?"

"His name is Brad and we met waiting in line for the ATM over on South First."

When I wait in line at the ATM all I ever meet are bums begging spare change and couples squabbling over why the account is overdrawn. Maybe I need to change banks. "What did you do on your date?"

"We had dinner then went to a concert on the UT campus."

Much better than being groped in a loud, "hip" hangout. "And?" I prompted.

She laughed. "And nothing. That was it. He brought me home."

"That doesn't sound like a bad first date."

"A bad *only* date you mean. I haven't heard a word from him since."

"It's only Tuesday." I plucked a handful of dead leaves from around the daylilies.

"Grace, he said he'd call. And he hasn't." She shrugged. "I don't care. I didn't really click with him anyway."

"Click? What do you mean, click?"

"You know, I didn't feel any connection." She waved her hand. "There was no chemistry."

I sat back again and stared at her. "You know that after only one date?"

"Sure. Don't you?"

I hated to admit it, but I was clueless. After all, I thought things were going pretty good with Josh and me until he'd started groping me. I reached out and jerked a stubborn weed from around the base of a dwarf wisteria.

Joyce rested her arms along the top of the fence and watched me work. "Where were you Saturday night?" she asked. "I tried to call you when I got in and you didn't answer."

"Oh, uh, I had a date too."

"Really? Tell me!" When I looked up she was all smiles. "Who was he? What did you do? Did you have a good time?"

"He was this guy I met at school. He took me to this place downtown, Club Soho."

"I've heard of that. Very trendy."

"That's me. I'm such a trendy gal."

She laughed. "So what was it like? Did you have a good time?"

I shook my head. "No. In fact, I ended up calling Gil to come get me and take me home."

"Grace, no!"

I nodded. "I know. It was pathetic."

"What did this guy do that was so awful?"

I pulled a spent blossom off my Peace rosebush. "He started groping me in the booth in the restaurant."

"*Groping* you?"

I nodded. "It's embarrassing, really. One minute we were having a decent conversation and the next, he's all over me. It was…awkward."

"At least he was interested. Brad didn't even try to kiss me good-night."

"Josh was moving way too fast for me," I said. "It just felt…wrong. You know?"

"Yeah." She sighed. "I know. This dating business is harder now than it was when we were younger. I mean, back then, there were rules."

I nodded. "You didn't sleep with a guy on the first date. He always paid for dinner. And in college and high school, we were surrounded by single guys our age, so it wasn't that difficult to find a date."

"Now you have to wonder if he's married or a psycho, or if he's carrying some disease." She sighed. "I want dating to be fun, but now it seems like so much *work*."

Show me anything worth doing that isn't. Raising children, staying married, growing roses. The good stuff is always a lot of work.

Still, that didn't mean I cared to repeat my experience with Josh—or anyone else—any time soon.

"Mo-om! Do we have any more printer paper?" Trudy shouted out the back door.

"Look in the hall closet." I turned toward her. "What are you doing?"

"Making a book of my poems."

I nodded. Even though I have my doubts about Trudy's poetry, she takes her work very seriously. And what do I know? She might be the next big hit songwriter.

"What kind of poetry is she writing?" Joyce asked.

"The depressing kind."

"What do teenagers have to be depressed about? If you ask me, they have it made."

"Growing up is hard." I snipped off a handful of coreopsis and zinnias and took them to the fence. "Don't you remember?"

She shook her head. "I try not to."

I handed her the flowers. "Here you go. Something to cheer you up."

"Thank you. That's so sweet." She held the flowers out, admiring them. "I'm doing better though. At least that's what my therapist says." She gave me a smile that didn't reach all the way to her eyes. "Thanks for the flowers, Grace. Maybe next time we'll both have better luck with our dates."

"Maybe so." I waved and went back to my weeding. I suppose Joyce had the right idea, with her "get back on the horse that threw you" theory. But it would be a lot easier to do if we had some guarantee that eventually things would work out all right.

Would I earn my degree? Get a better job? Find happiness? Would I end up moving in with Trudy and driving us both crazy?

"Mo-om! Where's the stapler?"

"In the desk drawer!" I shouted back.

She appeared in the doorway again. "It's not there. I looked."

I shoved up onto my feet and went into the house to search for the stapler. Why was I worried about Trudy and I driving each other crazy in the future? There were days when I was positive we were already there.

"Gil, have you thought of getting one of those software programs to help you balance your checkbook?" You guessed it—I was sitting at Gil's kitchen table again, going through my monthly routine. Somehow, in the rush of adjusting to my new schedule another month had already flown by.

He looked up from the spaghetti sauce he was making for our dinner. "Why would I want to do that when I can have you come over and do it for free?"

"That's just it. I've got to stop doing this." *I've got to stop depending on you, and letting you depend on me.* I thought this, but I couldn't say it. Gil had been a part of my life for too long. And it's not that I wanted that to change, but I needed to make room for other people.

"You say that every month. And every month you're back over here." He replaced the lid on the stockpot and turned down the heat under it. "Besides, if I'm going to watch Trudy one extra night a week, you can balance my checkbook."

"Ha! Like it's any big hardship for you to have Trudy over here an extra night. You know you love it."

He turned a kitchen chair around and straddled it. "If you really don't have time for my checkbook, I can probably manage to figure it out myself. Or maybe I can pawn it off on Mark."

"Where is Mark anyway?"

"He and Trudy went over to the salvage yard to see if he can find some car parts for a new collage."

"Car parts? Sounds like a big project."

"Something to do with the wastefulness of modern transportation."

"Ought to be a big hit." I ticked off the last check and wrote the final figure in the proper space, then handed the book to him. "I guess it doesn't take that much time. And I do appreciate your watching Trudy."

"Is it helping any? Are you getting any studying done, or are you spending all your time in the backyard with your flowers?"

I grinned. "You know me too well. Maybe I spend a little of that time in my garden, but I'm studying, too. And I think it's helping. I made a C on my last Economics test. And I'm getting better about asking questions when I don't understand something."

"Good girl."

"Dr. Hauser is really a good teacher."

"He'd have to be to make economics interesting." He

got up and started pulling the makings of a salad from the refrigerator.

"I didn't say he made it interesting, just that he helps me understand it better." I joined him at the counter and began shredding lettuce while he chopped peppers.

"Just remember that I won't be able to watch her next week. I'm going out of town."

"I remember. To that sales convention, right?"

"Yes, where Corporate tries to inspire us by hiring washed-up celebrities to entertain and self-styled gurus to pump us up." He tossed a handful of chopped peppers into a salad bowl. "I'd rather stay home, but they're giving me some kind of award, so I have to be there."

"An award! Gil, congratulations."

"Yeah, well I doubt if selling the most widgets in the past year will help the cause of world peace or global reconciliation, but it does get you a nice plaque and a trip to Hawaii. Mark's excited about that."

"And you're not?"

He grinned. "Maybe a little bit." He added mushrooms to the bowl. "There's something I've been meaning to tell you."

His manner was serious all of a sudden. Too serious. I swallowed hard and tried to keep my voice light. "What's that?"

"Mark and I are thinking about having a commitment ceremony while we're in Hawaii."

"You mean…like a marriage?" The last word came out

as a squeak. I cleared my throat and laid both hands flat on the counter, steadying myself.

He nodded. "Sort of. As close as we can get." He lifted his head and met my gaze. "We've been talking about it for a while. This seemed like a good time."

I nodded, and focused on the salad to keep him from seeing the panic and yes, hurt, I was sure was in my eyes. "When?" I managed to ask.

"About seven weeks from now. Just before Thanksgiving. We'll probably have some kind of party when we get home to announce it to everyone, but we wanted you and Trudy to know first."

I nodded, still trying to take it in. "Congratulations." I forced a smile. "I mean it. You and Mark are good together."

It was all true. I was glad Gil had found someone to spend his life with. Someone who made him happy. But I also suddenly felt that much more alone.

We didn't say anything for a while. I tore lettuce and shredded carrots and tried to absorb this new wrinkle in my life. Later, I'd probably cry over the unfairness of life in general, but I refused to do so in front of Gil.

"So has Josh said anything to you about the other night?"

Gil's question startled me. "Uh, no." I sometimes caught Josh staring at me in class. Not with romantic longing or old-fashioned lust or even loathing. No, when Josh looked at me these days it was more…calculating. "I think Josh was too young for me."

"What about someone else? One of your professors maybe."

Why did Dr. Hauser's face immediately come to mind? Sure, he was a good-looking guy, but he'd never shown any *particular* interest in me. "Look, just because you found someone doesn't mean I'm not perfectly happy by myself."

Maybe not *perfectly* happy, but most of the time I did all right.

"I just think you're an attractive woman. The kind of woman lots of guys would go for."

I frowned. "What would you know about it?"

"I'm queer, not blind."

I dumped the salad makings in a bowl and looked him in the eye. "Thanks for being concerned, but butt out."

He laughed. "You say that, but you don't really mean it."

It annoyed me to know that he was right. Again.

"Ta-dah! We're home!" Trudy marched into the kitchen holding a steering wheel out in front of her. Mark followed with two side mirrors and a chrome bumper.

"Looks like you found a few things you could use," I said.

"We got some awesome shit…uh, stuff." He flushed and glanced at Trudy.

She grinned and held out her hand. "You owe me a dollar."

"What for?" Gil asked.

"I bet him a dollar he couldn't go half an hour without swearing."

Gil laughed. "And he was dumb enough to take it? Pay the woman, Mark."

Mark dug in the pockets of his cut-offs and came up with a handful of change. "I've only got eighty-two cents."

Trudy swept up the change. "You can owe me the rest."

Gil came over and put his arm around Mark. "Trudy, Mark and I have some news to tell you."

Gil smiled, but I thought Mark looked nervous. Trudy looked at them expectantly.

"In November, Mark and I are going to Hawaii."

"Awesome! Can I come?"

Gil laughed. "No you can't. But while we're there, Mark and I are going to have a commitment ceremony." He glanced at Mark, who smiled shyly and nodded. "It's sort of like a wedding."

Trudy grinned. "That's cool. Will you have flowers and cake and everything like a wedding?"

"Probably. We haven't settled on all the details yet. Maybe you can help us with that part."

"All right! You could both wear white tuxes. Wouldn't that be cool?"

Mark relaxed a little and grinned. "I think that would be very cool."

Debating the merits of tails versus a standard tuxedo, they headed for the garage, carrying their car parts. I met Gil's gaze. "She's a good kid," he said.

"I think we both can take credit for that." I began to set the table.

Gil put his hands on my shoulder. "Even though I know you're okay on your own, I really hope you do find someone, Gracie. Someone who's as good for you as Mark is for me."

I nodded, blinking back tears. *But where am I going to find someone who could read my mind the way you can?*

"Mom, can I have a tattoo?"

Trudy attempts to catch me off guard with these things, coming at me in the early morning, before I've had my coffee. But even under such adverse conditions, Mom is not as dim as she might think. "No, you may not."

"But Mo-om!" She threw herself across the end of my bed. "Just a little one."

I searched through my bag of tricks, otherwise known as my makeup case, for eyeshadow that wouldn't make me look like an aging punk rocker. "I don't care if it's microscopic. You can't have a tattoo."

"But lots of girls have them these days."

And if lots of girls jumped off a cliff, would you expect me to let you jump off the cliff, too? But I didn't say this. This is something my mother would say, and despite what the mirror tells me to the contrary some days, I am not my mother. "No."

"But I'd get something really cool. On my ankle. You'd hardly even notice."

I sighed. When I was her age, I begged to get my ears pierced. That seemed so innocent now. I plucked a pale brown shadow from the box and began brushing it on. "I'm still not going to let you do it, but just to satisfy my curiosity, what would you get? A flower or something?"

"No!" The idea clearly horrified her. "That's too girly. I was thinking about a wolf. Wouldn't that be cool?"

"No, I don't think so." I leaned closer to the mirror and applied a second coat of mascara. Why is it I own fifteen pounds of makeup and end up using the same two or three items every day? Did I really buy all this other junk, or is it a plot by the beauty industry to make me feel even less beautiful than I already do?

Trudy hopped off the bed and came to stand beside me. "Then I'll just ask Dad."

I laughed. "Not if you're smart, you won't. He'll have a fit."

She selected a lipstick from the box and examined the color. "So what do you think about Dad and Mark getting married?"

The needle on my Mom Alert pegged to the right. Something told me this wasn't necessarily a casual question. "What do *you* think?" Mom as psychiatrist.

She outlined her lips with the brick-red lipstick and leaned back to admire the effect. "I think it's kind of cool."

"Yes." I kept my voice deliberately neutral, watching her in the mirror. "Your father and Mark have been together a long time. This is a way for them to affirm their commitment."

"Yeah. I like Mark. And it's kind of like having two

dads. Or a dad and an uncle." She pawed through the makeup again. "And I think Mark's artwork rocks."

I suppressed a laugh. Yes, when it came to artistic endeavors, I suppose you could say Mark and Trudy were kindred spirits.

She picked up a hairbrush and began rearranging her hair. She hadn't dyed it in a few weeks and a thin strip of brown showed above the dead black. "It's kind of weird, though."

"Mark's artwork?"

She wrinkled her nose. "No. I mean, dad marrying another guy." She glanced at me. "I mean, I know he's gay, but it's still weird, you know?"

I slipped my arm around her shoulders and hugged her close. Weird is another way of saying "different" and what's worse to a teenager than being labeled as different? "It's not something most of your friends have to deal with, is it?"

"No." She laid down the brush. "I mean, it's always been a part of my life, but some people wouldn't understand."

I smoothed her hair back from her forehead. "Do some of the kids give you a hard time about your dad?"

Her face had that closed-up expression I dread, the one that meant I wasn't going to get the whole truth. "A couple of them have said some things, but they're losers anyway."

"What does Simon think?"

She pulled away and retreated to the door. "He thinks it's weird, but he doesn't care." She picked up my backpack. "Can I have five dollars for lunch?"

End of discussion. I wanted to tell her I understood, that I knew it was hard when people you cared about couldn't accept the things about you that were out of the ordinary. That a more conventional life looked easier but that didn't mean it was necessarily so. Instead, all I could manage was "My wallet's in the inside pocket."

I watched her take out the money and leave the room. I had a feeling I'd failed her somehow. She'd come to me wanting advice on how to deal with the strange curves life threw her and I hadn't had the answer she needed.

But I couldn't answer Trudy's questions because they were the same ones I was asking myself. The kind of questions that maybe didn't have answers at all.

CHAPTER 8

The trouble with trying to pay attention to a lecture on microeconomic theory is that there are so many other things that are at least twenty times more interesting. For instance, the grounds crew was mowing outside the classroom this morning, which reminded me my own grass needed cutting. If I let the St. Augustine runners get longer than three inches, General Edison has a fit. (And who was St. Augustine, anyway? The patron saint of lawn care? I think about these things when my mind is trying to avoid any real work.)

Myrtle was wearing a tunic of purple Kinte cloth that caught my eye. This reminded me my own wardrobe could use an update. After class, I'd have to ask her where she got it. But was purple really my color?

Then there was the fact that Josh was sitting beside me. He was staring at me again, though I tried to ignore him. What exactly was going on with him and me? We certainly weren't friends anymore, but I didn't think of him as an enemy. We'd had a bad date and that was the end of it. So why did he keep studying me as if I was one of his sociology research subjects?

So anyway, my mind was on anything but economics that morning. I guess I wasn't the only one because about midway through class, a ripple of laughter worked its way around the room.

Dr. Hauser stopped in the middle of a comparison of consumer demand and production theories and peered at us over the top of his reading glasses. "Apparently, I'm missing the joke."

"There's a strange young man outside in the hall." Myrtle nodded toward the door. "He keeps looking in the window and gesturing. Perhaps we should report him."

It wasn't much, but I welcomed any diversion. I turned toward the door and about that time a face loomed in the glass panel above the knob. My mouth fell open as first a familiar cheek, then an ear, then a nose squashed against the glass. Surely it couldn't be… A hand came up to wave frantically in my direction.

Dr. Hauser strode to the door and opened it. Mark stumbled inside. "Grace, you have to come with me right now."

Dr. Hauser turned to me. "Ms. Greenleigh, do you know this man?"

I stood and started toward him, numb. "Mark, what are you doing here? What's wrong?" Images of plane crashes and car wrecks flashed through my mind. Fear squeezed my chest. "Is Gil all right?"

He nodded his head, mouth twisted in agony, tears brimming in his eyes. "No, it's Trudy. Grace, it was awful. They wouldn't let me see her."

The world went gray and I had to sit down. I groped for an empty chair. A strong arm slipped around my shoulder and guided me to a seat. "What's happened?" Dr. Hauser asked. His voice was firm. Reassuring. "Has her daughter been hurt?"

"There was an accident at school," Mark said. "But I don't know what's wrong. They wouldn't tell me anything."

I sucked in a deep breath. I felt like bursting into tears, but I had to be strong for Trudy. "Tell me everything you know, Mark. Where is Trudy now?" I know the words came from me, but it was like listening to someone else. Some calm, rational person far removed from the panic that threatened to overwhelm me.

Mark swallowed. "Breckinridge Hospital."

"When did they take her there?" Dr. Hauser asked. I realized then that he was the one who'd guided me to the chair. His hand still rested on my shoulder, anchoring me.

"The school called about nine." Mark twisted his hands together. "Of course, they wanted Gil. I told them he was out of town and they wouldn't even talk to me. I thought it was about some parent-teacher conference or something. No big deal." He wiped at his eyes and sniffed. "But then they called back and said it was an emergency and did I know where to find you? I know you don't have a cell phone, so I couldn't call you. I went to the school, but they'd already taken her to the hospital. They wouldn't tell me anything, just said I should get you."

I stood, wobbly, but determined. "We'd better get to the hospital and find out what's going on."

"I'll take you." Dr. Hauser pulled his keys from his pocket.

"No, really. I can manage." I started toward the door. I was vaguely aware of everyone staring at me, like rubber-neckers at an accident scene, their expressions ranging from shocked to mildly curious.

"You're in no shape to drive." Dr. Hauser took his jacket from the back of his chair and slipped it on. "Class dismissed."

He took my arm and guided me toward the door. As we passed Mark, Dr. Hauser put his hand on his shoulder. "You come, too."

Nothing much about the drive to the hospital registered. I had the vague impression of a nice car smelling of leather. As we threaded through traffic, I was aware of Mark swearing under his breath in the back seat. But these things were minor sensations in the background. They were crowded out by the visions of my daughter, hurt and alone, crying for her mother. Trudy, who wore grown-up mascara and polka-dotted cotton underpants. The little girl who pretended to like coffee, because she thought it was more mature, but who would drink all the chocolate milk when I wasn't looking.

What had happened to her? How was she hurt? Why hadn't I been there when she needed me?

Guilt isn't logical or reasonable or related to any standard reality. It's a two-year-old who throws a temper tantrum in your head, refusing to be placated. And it was having a full-blown conniption in my brain right now.

By the time we reached the emergency room entrance at Breckinridge Hospital, I was ready to scream and wail and demand to see my daughter. Only Dr. Hauser's hand on my elbow pulled me back from the edge of hysteria.

"I'm here to see Trudy Greenleigh," I told the woman at the front desk.

"And you are?" She didn't even look up from her computer as she asked this. Apparently whatever was on that monitor was a lot more interesting than a mere human being.

I gripped the edge of the counter. "I'm her mother. Grace Greenleigh. Please tell me, what's wrong with her?"

"Please have a seat, Mrs. Greenleigh. Someone will be with you in a moment."

I automatically turned and started toward a grouping of upholstered chairs, then some part of my brain woke up and I did an about-face. "No, I will not have a seat. I want to see my daughter now."

This pulled the biddy's attention away from her computer screen. "That kind of behavior is uncalled for," she said frostily.

"My *daughter* is here and I am going to see her *now*."

Dr. Hauser stepped forward. "I'm sure you can understand a mother's concern for her child."

Whether it was the words he said or the smile that accompanied them, the woman's expression softened. "Just a moment. I'll see what I can do."

When she was gone, I looked at the professor. "It annoys the hell out of me that she listened to you and not me, but thanks all the same."

He shrugged. "Must be my natural charm." But the glimmer in his eyes told me he didn't take the words, or himself, too seriously.

Dragon Lady returned. "Come through here, please."

The three of us started past her, through the double doors leading into the emergency room, but she put out a hand to stop Mark. "Who are you?" she demanded.

"He's with us." I stepped back and took Mark's arm.

The Ice Queen looked like she'd just eaten a lemon. "Only family members are allowed in the treatment rooms."

I stared at her. If she only knew how close she was to having her hair torn out by the roots…. "He *is* family." I pulled Mark along with me.

Mark muttered something under his breath that sounded like "trucking witch" but I promise you, those weren't his exact words. "If I was somebody's skanky second wife, they'd have let me in without blinking," he said. "I've helped take care of Trudy since she was five years old, but that doesn't mean shit to people like her."

I patted his shoulder. "I know. It's not right. But you're here now and Trudy will be glad to see you."

We found her in a curtained alcove, seated on a gurney, her left arm propped on a stack of pillows. Her face was pale and streaked with tears, but she'd never looked more beautiful to me. "Mama!" she cried when she saw me.

I hugged her close, careful of her arm, my tears flowing freely. "What happened, hon? How did you hurt your arm?"

"I fell in gym class." Her face crumpled. "They think my arm's broken."

I cradled her head on my shoulder. "It'll be all right, baby."

Mark moved in on the other side of her. "I went to the school, but they wouldn't let me see you."

She gave him a weak smile. "That's okay. You got my mom to me and that's good."

"Mrs. Greenleigh! When did you get here?" A frazzled-looking blonde in gym shorts and sweatshirt rushed around the corner. "I'm Connie Rogers." She stuck out her hand. "The school sent me with Trudy when we couldn't find her family."

"You located *me*," Mark said, but that was old news now and no one paid him any attention.

"Ms. Rogers, what happened?" I asked. "How did Trudy get hurt?"

"Well…there was something about a dare to race up the

bleachers. Trudy slipped and fell." She frowned at Trudy. "I believe there may have been a boy involved."

"Trudy?" I looked at her and waited.

Her face flushed pink. "Simon bet me I couldn't do it, so I had to show him."

Ms. Rogers collected her purse from beneath the gurney. "Well, now that you and Mr. Greenleigh are here…" She glanced at Mark. "And your friend—I'll just be going."

"Mr. Greenleigh?" I looked around the room. "Is Gil here somewhere?" Surely he couldn't have flown in from California so quickly….

Ms. Rogers turned to Dr. Hauser. "Aren't you Trudy's father?"

He only half-hid his smile. "No. I'm another, uh, friend."

She was still standing there with her mouth open when the curtain parted and Myrtle and Josh burst in. "Grace, is everything all right?" Myrtle gasped.

I smiled. "Everything's going to be fine. Thanks. We think Trudy broke her arm." I introduced everyone to Mark and Trudy.

"How did you get past the bitch at the front desk?" Mark asked.

"We didn't even stop to talk to her," Josh said. "We just blew right past."

Myrtle grinned. "My theory is, if you act like you know what you're doing, people assume you do. For all they knew, we were a couple of doctors."

I looked at Myrtle in her purple Kinte cloth, and Josh in his *Butthole Surfers* T-shirt. "I'm not sure the medical community has stooped that low."

Dr. Hauser chuckled, so I think he was the only one to hear me. Everyone else was busy getting acquainted.

"Who *are* you people?" Ms. Rogers demanded.

I'd forgotten she was still here. Everyone turned to stare at her. "Friends," we all chorused.

She sniffed and compressed her lips into a thin line. Her expression told us she suspected we were all crazy. And certainly not respectable.

Fortunately, she didn't hang around. If she had, there might not have been room in the alcove for the doctor when she arrived. Dr. Sahir was an efficient woman who didn't seem fazed by the crowd that greeted her. "Well, young lady," she said to Trudy. "Looks like you have quite a fan club." She snapped a sheet of X-ray film onto the light box against the wall. "You have a greenstick fracture. Right there."

We all leaned closer to squint at the tiny fissure in the bone. "How long will it take to heal?" Trudy asked.

"Six weeks in a cast, you'll be better than new," the doctor said. She opened a cabinet to reveal boxes of plaster wrap and gauze. "Now, what color cast would you like?"

I waited for Trudy to say "black" but a fourteen-year-old is full of surprises. She leaned forward and studied the rainbow of colored wrappings. "I think I'd like the purple."

* * *

An hour later, Trudy had a bright purple cast that already boasted half a dozen signatures, from Dr. Sahir and the rest of us "friends." I finished the paperwork required to spring her and turned to go, running smack into Josh's broad chest.

"I'll take you home," he said.

"My car is still at St. Ed's."

"Can you have someone take you to pick it up later, after Trudy's settled?"

"I suppose I could have my neighbor take me." I looked back at Trudy, who was admiring her cast. "I guess it would be better to take Trudy straight home."

"I'll take you," Josh said again.

"That won't be necessary." Dr. Hauser stepped up and took my arm.

I looked from one to the other. They were both doing that macho guy thing, where they straighten their shoulders, expand their chests and jut out their chins. I would have laughed if I hadn't known they'd be terribly insulted. Big macho men have easily bruised feelings.

As it was, I merely stepped back and watched, enjoying the show.

"You brought her here," Josh said. "The least I can do is take her home."

"Since she came here with me, I should finish the job and take her home. Besides, you've got Myrtle with you."

"You've got Mark with you."

I considered Josh. Young. Studly. Brash. A man who had made a pass at me on our first date and hadn't acted the least bit interested since.

There was Dr. Hauser. Older. More serious. My teacher, so something of an authority figure. I didn't know him all that well, but I liked the way he'd taken charge of things this morning. He'd kept me calm.

"Thanks, Josh, but I'd better go with Dr. Hauser," I said.

He didn't hide his annoyance. "I'd have brought you here in the first place."

"I know."

I turned to Myrtle, who gathered me close in a hug. "You have a beautiful daughter," she said. "She's going to be just fine."

Oh damn! Now I was getting all choked up again. "Thanks for everything." I backed away. "Guess we'd better be going."

Dr. Hauser already had Trudy situated in the back seat when I walked out to the car. Mark slid in beside her. "How you doin' kid?" he asked.

She smiled wanly. "I'm feeling kind of floaty. I guess it's the medicine they gave me."

"You can go right to sleep when we get home," I said as I climbed into the passenger seat. Later, we'd have a talk about the dangers of trying to impress men, but for now, she deserved a little rest. Besides, when the pain medication and adrenaline wore off, I had a feeling she'd come to her own conclusions about Simon's dare and its consequences.

"My daughter broke her arm last year," Dr. Hauser offered as he guided the car onto I-35.

"You have a daughter?" Trudy asked. "How old is she?"

"She's fifteen. She broke her arm in gymnastics class."

"Is she okay now?"

"Oh, yes." He glanced at her in the rearview mirror. "They say when a broken bone heals, it's stronger than ever."

She frowned. "I still wish I hadn't broken it."

"Allison was an instant celebrity when she returned to class. Boys vied to carry her books."

Trudy's expression brightened. "That would be cool."

"Most bad things have a good side, too." He glanced at me. "Sometimes, they provide an opportunity to get to know people better."

"The only person I got to know better today was Ms. Rogers. Ugh." I didn't have to see Trudy's face to picture her expression. Yep, that was about my opinion of Connie Rogers, too.

Meanwhile, I was trying to process what Dr. Hauser had said. What exactly had he meant?

When we got to the house, Mark helped Trudy up to her room while I said goodbye to Dr. Hauser. "I'll stay and help if you need me," he said. "But I really ought to get back to class."

"I've kept you too long already. Thank you so much."

He took my hand. "Though the circumstances were unfortunate, I'm glad I could be of some help to you."

His grasp was warm and firm. I was reluctant to let go, but I finally did. "Thanks," I said. "For everything."

I'm not sure how long we stood there looking at each other before I managed to break out of my trance. "I'd better go in and see about Trudy."

"Yes. I'll see you at school."

"Yeah, see you." I turned and sort of floated back up to the house. Economics class was definitely going to be much more interesting from now on.

Gil came in on a late flight, looking worse for wear when he showed up on my doorstep at 2:00 a.m. "How's Trudy?" he blurted as soon as I opened the door.

"She's fine." I ushered him inside. "It was a clean break and she should be good as new in six weeks."

He headed past me down the dark hallway, to Trudy's room. A thin sliver of light from her night-light stretched across the floor as he eased open her door and slipped inside.

When I came in after him a few seconds later, he was standing beside her bed, looking down on her, relief smoothing the lines of his face.

Trudy lay on her back, her left arm in its purple cast cradled across her chest, her right arm wrapped around a pink stuffed bear Joyce had sent over as a get-well present. When Gil bent and kissed her, she sighed and rolled onto her side.

I smiled and left them alone. Whatever confusion or pain our unconventional family life had caused Trudy, she couldn't have had two parents who loved her more. I think she knew that. I hoped she did.

Gil met me in the kitchen a few minutes later. I found two clean glasses while he went to the cabinet where I keep my liquor and took out a dusty bottle of Chivas. "I think we both could use a drink," he said, holding up the bottle.

I nodded and slid the glasses toward him. Now that Gil was here, I felt like I could finally stop fighting the fear and anxiety I'd been beating back all day.

"I got back from my seminar this afternoon and there was a frantic message on my voice mail from Mark," he said. "Something about not being able to get in to see Trudy and not being able to find you."

"I know. I was in class and the school wouldn't let Mark see Trudy because, technically, he's not related to her."

"Fuck technically." He filled both glasses halfway, then added ice to both and a splash of soda to mine. "That's what's wrong with this picture. If it's not mom, pop and the youngsters, it doesn't count, anything else's not family. But there's so much more. Family is caring and commitment and…"

I nodded. I'd heard this all before. And despite the longing I had sometimes for a more conventional family life, I believed he was right. But Gil didn't need me to agree with him. All he needed was for me to listen while he blew off steam.

After a few minutes, he wound down and sagged back in his chair. I leaned forward and refilled his glass. "It must have been terrible for you, flying home and not knowing what was happening. I died a dozen times between St. Ed's and the hospital."

"I managed to get hold of Mark from the airport and he had calmed down enough to let me know Trudy was okay. But part of me didn't believe it until just now, when I was here, seeing her with my own eyes."

"I know. It was a terrible mix-up from the beginning. Tomorrow, I'm going to make sure the school has a copy of my schedule and St. Ed's number. *And* I'm going to insist they have Mark listed as one of the people to be contacted in case of emergency."

"You ought to have a cell phone," Mark had said. "Then they could contact you directly."

I realize every third person you see these days has a cell phone stuck to their ear, but so far, I'd resisted the urge. My budget is tighter than last year's jeans and cell phones are not cheap. I sighed. "I don't like cell phones. And I don't think I can afford one."

"You don't have to afford it. I'll get one for you."

"Gil, no!"

"I'm not doing it for you. I'm doing it for Trudy."

What could I say? As much as I hated to keep depending on Gil, I didn't want a repeat of what had happened today. "All right. But I'm only going to use it for emergencies."

I finished my drink and poured another one, letting the fuzzy, warm feeling seep through me. My gaze drifted to Gil. He looked tired, his shirt rumpled, his tie loosened, his hair falling boyishly across his forehead. But he looked good, too. Handsome, in a very GQ way. So different from the awkward boy he'd been in school, and yet the boy was there, too. I could see him, in Gil's shy smile, and in the way his lips quirked up at the corners when he saw the irony in an otherwise serious situation.

He had nice lips. Full, but not too full. I'd kissed those lips once, but I couldn't remember what it felt like. What would happen if I kissed him now? Just leaned across the table and planted my mouth on his? Would either of us feel anything at all?

"Why are you looking at me that way?"

I started. "What way?"

Deep frown lines creased his brow. "You were looking at me…I don't know. Funny."

I flushed and stared into my half-empty drink glass. How many of these had I had? Too many if I was having these kinds of thoughts. One kiss wasn't going to turn Gil straight.

"I think it's time I went to bed." I stood and carried my glass to the sink. "You'd better spend the night here. You're in no shape to drive."

"I'll call Mark and have him come pick me up. He'll be anxious to see me, anyway."

"That's a good idea." Suddenly, I wasn't comfortable with the idea of him here in the house any longer. Or, more truthfully, I wasn't comfortable with myself with him here. Gil was my friend and the father of my child, but it was past time I stopped fantasizing he could ever be anything more.

CHAPTER 9

When I showed up for coffee with Myrtle after class the next day, I was surprised to see Josh there. He'd made himself scarce since our date. Maybe he figured our encounter at the hospital yesterday had broken the ice.

Whatever. I could certainly be civil to him. He was Myrtle's friend and I wouldn't ask him to leave.

"Hey, Grace," he said, then went back to staring into his coffee.

I nodded to him, then turned to Myrtle. "Good morning."

"Good morning. How is your little girl?"

"A little sore, but much better, thank you." When I'd dropped Trudy off at school that morning, she'd been swallowed up by a crowd of well-wishers, eager to admire and sign her cast.

"I'm sorry I said your friend Mark was strange," Myrtle said. "I realize now he was only upset."

I laughed. "That's okay. Mark *is* a little strange. He's an artist."

"My third husband was an artist. A sculptor." She smiled. "That's how we met. He hired me as a model."

Was there anything she hadn't tried? "Mark makes collages. Unusual collages."

"Well, he seemed like a nice young man."

"So he's your ex-husband's—what do they call it—partner?" Josh bit off a hunk of bagel and spoke around it.

"Yeah." I fiddled with the lid on my coffee cup. "Mark and Gil have been together almost nine years."

"That's really interesting." He chewed bagel and chased it with a swig of coffee. "I've been thinking it would make a really good subject for a paper for my sociology class."

"What would make a good subject?" I set aside my cup, already getting the feeling I wasn't going to like his answer.

"The gay family in America. I could interview you."

I shook my head. "No. I don't think so."

"But why not? I'd do a good job."

"I'm not interested in being a research subject."

His expression grew sullen. "I'd think you'd welcome the chance to tell your side of the story."

"Tell it to whom?" I couldn't keep the tension from my voice. "I don't feel the need to defend myself to anybody."

"Maybe there are other people in your situation who would be helped by what you have to say."

I knotted my hands into fists. It was either that, or deck him. "This isn't the freaking *Oprah* show. It's a research paper. And I resent your trying to use our friendship that way."

"Is that what you call it—friendship?" He stood and glared down at me. "Because I don't know what to call it. Especially after you left me yesterday to ride off into the sunset with Hauser."

"The man was doing me a *favor*. It would have been rude to refuse him when he'd gone to so much trouble."

"I think he was hoping you'd do *him* a favor."

I flushed. "And what difference would that make to you? You're the one who can't decide whether to maul me or shake my hand."

"You're the one who doesn't know what you want—"

"My, this is certainly an interesting conversation, but are you sure you want everyone to hear it?"

Myrtle's gentle voice cut through the haze of my anger. I glanced at her, then around the crowded student union. Dozens of curious eyes looked our way. "I think I've said enough," I mumbled, and sank onto the sofa once more.

Josh sent me a hurt look, then grabbed up his backpack and left. I sagged back against the sofa cushions. "What a mess."

"Emotions are messy things." Myrtle began gathering up our discarded cups and napkins. "And a man's pride may be the messiest."

"Do you think that's what this is about? Josh's pride?"

"He's very young, dear, but he's not dumb. I'm sure he picked up on the way Dr. Hauser was looking at you yesterday."

I stared at her. "He wasn't looking at me any special way."

Myrtle clucked her tongue. "Yes, he was. Trust me, I've seen that look before. Experienced it myself a few times, too." She patted my shoulder. "Don't worry, dear. Josh will get over it."

I sat up straighter. "I really don't care if Josh 'gets over it' or not." His suggestion that my family situation would be a good topic for a paper had really ticked me off. I was also a little annoyed at Myrtle for suggesting that Dr. Hauser had been making eyes at me. The man was my professor—for my least favorite course, as it happens. Why would he be ogling me when I was so worried about my daughter?

Still, those few seconds when he'd held my hand I'd felt…something.

Probably just the after-effects of finding out Trudy was all right. Stress does crazy things to people.

How else to explain why two of the most popular brands in America are Xanax and M&M's?

On Friday, Gil delivered a brand-new cell phone to me and the following Wednesday afternoon it rang for the first time, while I was once again counting out wheat pennies for Mr. Bob. (What can I say? I'm a sucker for lonely old men.)

I was so startled I dropped a whole handful of penny rolls and lunged for my backpack.

"What is that ringing?" Mr. Bob asked. "You got one of them cell phones or something?"

My heart galloped in my chest and I felt like throwing up. Not Trudy again! Oh God, what was it this time? A chemistry lab explosion? Cafeteria food poisoning? Or the results of another attempt to impress Simon?

"I'm sorry. I'm sorry," I muttered as I scrambled frantically to silence the ringing phone. I groped in my pack, past a bottle of water, a makeup bag, two tampons, assorted notebooks and half a peanut butter sandwich before my fingers curled around the phone.

Almost sobbing with relief, I found the phone and flipped open the cover. "Hello! Is this Trudy? Is this the school?"

"No. This is your mother. I haven't heard from you in days and thought I'd better make sure you were still alive."

All the breath I'd been holding escaped in a rush. I sagged against the counter. "What?" I squeaked. I stared at the back of Mr. Bob's balding head as he stooped down and gathered up the scattered rolls of pennies. "Mom, I gave you this number for emergencies," I said. "I'm working right now."

Mr. Bob dropped the rolls of pennies in the open cash drawer and leaned down to study the drawer's contents more closely. "Any more pennies we can look through in here?"

"Mr. Bob, only employees are allowed behind the counter." I gently steered him to the other side of the counter.

"Grace! Are you there?"

"I'm still here." More's the pity.

"How is my granddaughter doing? Of course, if you would think to call me once in a while, I wouldn't have to go to all this trouble."

I kept my voice even. "Mom, I did call you on Monday."

"And now it's Wednesday. She could have developed complications. Blood poisoning. Gangrene."

"She's fine. Believe me, if anything was wrong, I'd let you know."

"I'm sure you would. Eventually."

Mr. Bob helped himself to a handful of mints we keep on hand to pass out to customers. He admired one of the pens stamped with the bank name, then slipped it into his pocket as well. "Uh, I'm kind of busy right now, Mom. Was there something else you needed?"

"Fifi needs clipping. She's starting to look like a sheep."

I stifled a groan. "Why don't you take her to a groomer?"

"Why should I, when you do such a good job?"

Mr. Bob read the bank brochure, his lips moving silently. "Mom, I'm really busy with school and work and looking after Trudy. I don't have time to clip Fifi."

"I warned you going back to school was going to be too much for you. Though I'm sure you'd do better if you were more organized. Come by tonight. I'll make pot roast."

My mother makes the world's best pot roast. But the side order of guilt she serves up with it is sometimes hard to swallow. "I can't come tonight," I told her. "I have to help Gil and Mark hang Mark's new exhibit at Sud Your Duds."

Mom sniffed. "So you have time for them, but not time for me."

"I don't have time for anybody, but I promised them weeks ago that I'd do this. And you know you always taught me to keep my promises." See? This was all her fault.

"Dear, do you really think you should spend so much time with Gil and his friend?"

Mom is never sure how she should feel about Mark. Is he the rival who stole Gil's affections? A friend who should be accepted as one of the family? Or should she give up trying to figure out where he fits in and pretend he doesn't even exist? At various times, she's tried all these approaches, though she doesn't seem comfortable with any of them.

"I don't spend that much time with them," I said. I mean, I don't. Not really.

"You're over there all the time. Or one of them is over at your house."

"Gil and I are still friends. And we have Trudy."

"But you're not married to him anymore." The gentleness in her voice caught me off guard. "You ought to have other men in your life."

"I do have other men in my life." Some days, I'm surrounded by men. Mr. Addleson. Mr. Bob. Josh and Dr. Hauser. But I knew that wasn't what Mom meant.

"Mom, I really don't want to get into this right now." I

watched Mr. Bob pick up a blown glass paperweight, examine it, then return it to the counter.

"Then I'll let you go. But tomorrow night I'll expect you for dinner." She hung up without saying goodbye.

I replaced the phone in my backpack and turned to Mr. Bob. "No more pennies today," I said. "I won't keep you any longer." I tried to look cheerful, though my smile felt a little strained.

He smiled back. "I don't have anything else to do this afternoon. Thought I'd keep you company." He held up a half-filled Crown Royal bag. "I'm getting quite a collection here. Want to see 'em?"

I suppose to some people all wheat pennies do not look alike, but I'm not one of them. "Uh, not right now, Mr. Bob," I said. "I really do have work to do."

His smile never faltered. "That's okay. I'll head on over to Albertson's. They put the donut holes on sale for half price at four. I like to get there while the selection is good."

After he left, I felt a little guilty for running him off like that. He was such a sweet old man, and even wheat pennies had to be more interesting than the economics chapter I had to read before class tomorrow.

Whatever possessed me to think I could handle a job, a teenager and college? And I was supposed to fit a social life in there somewhere, too? Sure, and while I was at it, I'd handcraft all my Christmas presents and find a cure for cancer.

Or maybe I'd cry "uncle" and hide under my bed.

I am woman, hear me whimper.

* * *

Sud Your Duds was what you might call a high-class coin laundry. All the machines worked and instead of orange plastic chairs there were actual sofas to sit on.

And now they had artwork. Or at least, Mark's collages. I studied the work in my hand. Assorted bottle caps were arranged to spell the word *POP*. "It's pop art," Mark explained, coming up behind me. "Clever, huh?"

"Uh, yes." But would anyone actually pay for it?

"Mark, do you think this should hang over the washers or next to the pay phone?"

Mark left to help Gil and I unpacked the next piece. Titled *Iguana*, it featured a lizardlike figure fashioned out of discarded candy wrappers.

"Cool!" Trudy stood on tiptoe and peered over my shoulder. "If that one doesn't sell, do you think Mark would let me have it for my room?"

"You'll have to ask Mark. But not now. He's got a lot on his mind, getting ready for this show."

"Yeah. He does seem a little tense."

I followed her gaze over to the washers, where Gil and Mark were squabbling over where to hang the auto parts collage. Like an old married couple.

"I've decided I'm glad they're getting married, or committed, or whatever." Trudy started unwrapping the next collage in the packing box. "I mean, it's good for Dad to have somebody. It's good that he's not alone."

Alone. Why did that word conjure up images of microwaved dinners in front of the TV, of long Saturday afternoons crying in darkened movie theaters? Why was I afraid of that word—alone? As if I'm not good company for myself.

"Lots of people live alone," I said. "Lots of people are perfectly happy by themselves."

She shrugged. "Yeah. But not most people. I don't think Dad would be." She worried her lower lip between her teeth and glanced at me. "Mom, maybe you should join a dating service or something."

I swallowed a lump in my throat. "You don't have to worry about me, honey. I'm fine."

"Parents always say that. But it can't be true all the time."

When did my baby get to be so smart? I resisted the urge to throw my arms around her, knowing that would be a signal to switch on the waterworks. As it was, I turned away and dabbed at my wet eyes.

"What's going on over here?" Gil joined us. He peered at me. "Are you crying?"

"Just hormones." I sniffed and held up the iguana picture. "Where do you want this?"

"Ask Mark. I'm just the slave labor."

"I'll ask him." Trudy snatched the collage from my hand and skipped across the room.

"You sure you're okay?" Gil asked when she was gone.

I nodded. "I'm sure. Trudy just said something really sweet and it hit me how quickly she's growing up."

"Too fast." He leaned against a dryer, arms folded across his chest. "But there's nothing we can do to stop it." His face was glum. I realized my expression probably matched his.

"Could we talk about something a little cheerier?" I cut open another packing box. "How are the plans for your commitment ceremony coming?"

"Good. We have our reservations, and we've found a minister to officiate." He glanced toward Trudy and Mark, who were pretending to wrestle over the iguana collage. "I'm wondering if I should try to get you and Trudy out there."

Call me a coward, but the last thing I wanted was to watch my ex-husband exchange vows with someone else. I accepted the idea and I was happy for him. But I didn't have to join in. I shook my head. "No. This should be just for you and Mark. We can all celebrate together when you get back."

He looked relieved. "As long as you're okay with that."

"I am. And Trudy is, too."

"Good. Do you think you could watch the house while we're gone? Water the plants and bring in the mail?"

"Sure, I can do that." I gave him my best Polly Perfect smile. Watch your house, balance your checkbook, clip your dog—that's me. I can do anything—I just wasn't sure how long I could keep it all up.

CHAPTER 10

The last person I expected to slide in next to me at break the following Monday was Josh. Since he'd stormed out of the student union the other day, he'd been keeping his distance, pretending not to see me in class. Fine by me.

When he sat down at my table in the student union, I almost choked on my danish.

"Hi, Grace."

"Uh, hello." I regarded him warily. "What's up?"

"Nothing much. I just wanted to see how things are going with you."

"Things are fine." Though maybe not so fine now that he was here. Was he trying to be friends, or did he have another "study" planned? "Is there anything in particular you wanted from me?"

He scratched at an invisible spot on the table. "I guess I wanted to apologize for the way I've been acting. I don't see any reason why we shouldn't still be friends."

I could think of a few. "I don't know if that's such a good idea."

He shifted in his seat. "Give me a break. So maybe the

dating thing didn't work out, but that doesn't mean we have to be enemies, does it?"

Guilt nudged some of my irritation aside. As long as I wasn't going to date Josh, what could it hurt to be friendly with him? I mean, when he wasn't being a jerk, he was a pretty interesting guy. And he *had* rushed to the hospital when Trudy was hurt. Maybe I'd misjudged him. "I guess we don't have to be enemies."

"All right." He nodded and sat up straighter. "How's Trudy?"

That was a safe enough topic. "Doing great. Except for the cast, you'd never know she was hurt."

"And Mark and Gil? They okay?"

"Yes, they're fine."

"Job going well?"

"Ye…es." What was going on here? Why was Josh acting so…well, *nervous?*

"So what's been going on in your life?" I asked. "Anything new?"

He put his hands behind his head and looked up at the ceiling. "I finally got approval for my senior paper. My advisor's real excited about it."

"Oh?" The hair on the back of my neck rose in warning. "And what did you decide to write about?"

"I'm going to write about the gay family in America. Remember? I told you."

How was it that a man could be so devious and look so innocent? "Yes, you told me. And I told you I didn't want any part of it." I moved my chair back, physically distancing myself from him.

He threw up his hands. "No, no! It's all right. You don't have to be a part of it. I'm going to do it without you."

He looked like a regular choirboy. A studly choirboy, but still… "There'll be nothing about me or my family in there?"

"Only my observations as a researcher." He must have seen the thunder in my eyes, because he immediately added, "But I don't have to use your real names. I can make up a name. I can call you Ms. Smith. How does that sound?"

I gave him a withering look. "Why do we have to be in your paper at all?"

"This could be a groundbreaking piece of work. Something that could point to fundamental changes in the structure of the American family in the twenty-first century."

"Something that will get you noticed." I remembered his words from an earlier conversation. Josh was ambitious. He wanted a plum fellowship and fame.

His expression turned pleading. "You don't know how hard good graduate fellowships are to come by."

I stood and slung my backpack over my shoulder. "I can't stop you from writing anything you like," I said. "Just don't expect me to be happy about it."

"I'll do a good job, Grace. You'll see."

But I didn't want to see. I didn't want to be a research

subject or a groundbreaking statistic or anything other than an ordinary woman. A goal that seemed more elusive all the time.

Dr. Hauser obviously didn't let any attraction I'd imagined he felt for me effect my grade in his class, as witnessed by the lowly C inscribed across the top of my most recent test paper. I frowned at the disappointing grade and decided a business degree might not be in my future.

Of course, Myrtle would probably tell me I could do anything I wanted to do if I put my mind to it. This was the philosophy she lived by. On Friday, she'd announced her intention of wallpapering her dining room that weekend. "I'm ready for a change," she'd said.

Personally, I'd had my fill of change in my life. I was ready for a nice, predictable routine to set in. I glanced over my shoulder at Myrtle's empty desk. It wasn't like her to miss class. I hoped she was all right.

"Ms. Greenleigh, will you speak with me after class, please?" Dr. Hauser didn't even look at me when he spoke. Clearly, I'd imagined the feelings I thought had passed between us the afternoon Trudy was hurt.

I remained at my desk while everyone filed out. Josh gave me a questioning look as he walked by. I shrugged. I had no idea what the professor wanted.

Dr. Hauser took a seat at the desk next to mine. "How is Trudy?"

I folded my hands on my notebook, trying not to look

as nervous as I felt. "She's fine. Her cast comes off in four weeks."

"That's good." He spread his hands out flat on the desk top. His fingers were long and thick, the nails neatly trimmed. A scholar's hands, stained with ink.

I shifted in my seat. What was it with me and these awkward moments with men lately? Was I really that difficult to talk to? I searched for something to jump-start the conversation. "I wanted to thank you again for all your help the day Trudy was hurt," I said. "That was so thoughtful of you to drop everything to take me to the hospital and stay with me."

"Oh, yes, I'm a thoughtful fellow all right." He looked as if he was trying not to smile. Then his eyes met mine and I felt as if he'd grabbed hold of my heart and squeezed. Oh wow. "You do realize I didn't merely take you to the hospital that day out of the goodness of my heart, don't you?"

"You didn't?" I stared at him, determined to keep my crazy emotions hidden. To play it cool. That's me. Ms. Cool.

"No. I saw the opportunity to get to know you better and I took it." He leaned closer. "And if circumstances had been different, I would have asked you out."

"You would?" Why was I suddenly incoherent?

He smiled now. A really sexy smile. He had great teeth. And really nice lips…I blinked. "I'm sorry, what did you say just now?"

"I said, looking back, I can see my timing wasn't the best, considering what you'd just been through. So I want to try again."

I stared at his hand resting on the desk between us. He had long fingers. A scar on the knuckle of his index finger. A ring with a black stone in it. "Try what?" Apparently, I was no longer capable of communicating with more than two syllables at a time.

"I'd like to take you out. On a date."

"You can do that?" I swallowed and tried again. "I mean, can a professor date a student? There aren't rules against that?"

He straightened. "This isn't high school, Grace. We're both adults."

"Right."

"So, will you go out with me?"

I wanted to say yes. I really did. But when I opened my mouth, what came out was. "I don't think that would be a good idea."

It was his turn to look stunned. "What do you mean? I happen to think it would be a very good idea."

I shook my head. "It's just…my life is a little…complicated right now." There was my insane schedule to deal with, and Mark's crazy art show, and Gil and Mark's commitment ceremony and Josh's paper with Gracie Greenleigh, aka "Ms. Smith" and company as exhibit number one. Dr. Hauser would take one look at the circus that passed for my life and run in the opposite direction. I'd lose any hope of a relationship with him and probably flunk economics to boot.

"I'm not afraid of complications."

He sounded so calm when he said it. I wanted to believe him. "Maybe next semester. When I'm not in your class." By then maybe things would have settled down more on the personal front. One could hope…. "I really have to be going." I gathered up my books and stood.

Dr. Hauser rose also. "Have dinner with me, Grace. Try it and we'll see how it goes."

I shook my head and blindly shoved my books in my pack. "No. I don't think that would be a good idea at all."

"Grace, please reconsider."

But I was already out the door and headed down the hall, a little voice in my head berating myself for blowing this chance at a simple evening out with a nice guy. When had I turned into such a gutless wonder?

I ran into Josh on the front steps of the building. "I was on my way to get you," he said. "I just found out some bad news."

"What? Somebody beat you out of a plum fellowship? *Sociology Today* rejected your article proposal?" I was in a nasty mood and Josh was unfortunate enough to be directly in my line of fire. Not to mention I was still pissed at him for using me and my family as his ticket to fame and fortune.

He frowned. "No. It's about Myrtle. I was worried about her, so I called her house. Her daughter was there."

I felt like someone had dumped a bucket of sand on my burning anger. I stared at Josh. "Is Myrtle all right?"

He shook his head. "She fell off a ladder yesterday and broke her hip. They did surgery last night at St. David's."

I started down the steps, Josh on my heels. "Where are you going?" he asked.

"To see Myrtle." She was eighty years old. She should have known better than to be up on a ladder at her age. Why hadn't I volunteered to do the wallpapering for her? What if she ended up in a wheelchair for the rest of her life? Oh, God, what if she didn't make it?

Josh grabbed my arm and pulled me back. "You'll have to wait. She can't have visitors yet."

"Damn." I stopped and squinched up my eyes, fighting tears.

"Her daughter said she came out of the surgery fine, and the doctors predict she'll do well. But at her age, you can never tell."

I nodded. I'd be all right in a minute. I just needed to compose myself. The last thing I wanted was to burst into tears on the steps of the School of Business.

"What did Hauser want?"

The change of subject almost gave me whiplash. I shook my head, trying to clear my thoughts. "Oh, he just wanted to discuss my grades. And I thanked him again for helping me with Trudy."

"That all?"

No. But the rest was none of Josh's business. If I told

him that, though, he'd know the conversation had been personal. "I had a question about the last test. I want to bring my grade up, but I'm having trouble."

Josh snorted. "Maybe if the subject matter was more interesting. Why do you think I dropped the class the first time?" He glanced at his watch. "We've got time for a quick cup of coffee if you want."

I shook my head. "I need to get on over to the horticulture department and work on my class project." I needed to be alone with my thoughts and my hands in the dirt. Nothing like a bit of gardening to soothe my jangled nerves and help me organize my thoughts. If only people were as easy for me to manage as my flowers.

Trudy and I went to visit Myrtle in the hospital on Friday evening. We stopped off first at my favorite nursery, Travis Gardens, to buy a plant to take with us. "Hey, Grace. We've got some great new perennials in." The clerk, Kimmie, greeted me as I came in the door. "You should take a look."

"Thanks, Kimmie, but I don't have time right now. I need a plant for a friend who's in the hospital."

"Mom, these are cool." Trudy stopped beside a display of New Guinea impatiens.

I eyed the brightly colored flowers. "Myrtle would probably like those, but I was hoping for something fancier."

"I can put one of those in a nice planter for you," Kimmie said. "Throw in some ribbon, it'll look real nice."

"Thanks." I selected a plant and handed it over.

"Be just a minute."

I followed her to the potting section. "Where's Graham?" I asked. The nursery manager was usually busy up front.

"You didn't hear? He quit." She picked up a clay planter shaped like a hedgehog. "Is this okay? Or do you want sometime more sophisticated?"

I laughed. "I think a hedgehog would be perfect. Why did Graham quit?"

"I think he decided to move back east." She scooped potting soil from a bin into the planter. "Anyway, until they hire a new manager we're shorthanded."

"Why don't you take the job?"

She shook her head. "No way. With three kids at home still, I don't want any more than my twenty hours a week."

I could understand that. I'd cut my hours at the bank to thirty and would love to trim them more, but there were pesky things like rent and grocery bills that forced me to work almost full-time even while I was in school. Still, as my mother constantly reminded me as I was growing up, things could be worse. I could be Joyce, with two children and an ex-husband who complained about every cent the court required him to pay for their support.

I paid for the plant and Trudy and I headed for the hospital. "I don't see why I had to come with you," Trudy said as I steered the car up the ramp at the hospital parking garage. "I only met this woman once."

"And she asks about you all the time. I think it would really cheer her up to see you." I glanced at her. "And it will help me, having you here." I wasn't sure I was ready to see my friend, whom I'd come to think of as indestructible, reduced to a little old lady in a hospital bed.

As it was, when we walked into that semiprivate room and I saw her lying still in that bed, I almost turned around and walked out. She looked so much smaller than she had before, and her coffee-colored skin had a gray tinge to it. "Is she okay?" Trudy whispered.

I knew what Trudy meant. Myrtle was so still, she could have been dead. I tiptoed up to the bed and set the New Guinea impatiens on the bedside table. Myrtle stirred and looked up at me. "Grace? Is that you?"

I took her hand and squeezed it. "It's me. How are you doing?"

She squinted at me. "Hand me my glasses, would you? On the table."

When she had the glasses on, she smiled. "That's better. And what a lovely flower. Did you grow it?"

"No, I bought it. It's a New Guinea impatiens. They're very hardy and it should bloom all year with the right conditions." I was yammering away about nothing. I've always admired people who know just what to say in these situations. They're the ones who always do the right thing at funerals and bring the perfect gifts to hospitals. Me, I'm always afraid of sticking my foot in my mouth, so I tend to avoid any mention of illness or bereavement, even though I know this is probably not the best way to handle things. My gaze drifted toward her hip, which was of course, covered up with blankets. Myrtle's daughter had said they'd done surgery, but what did Myrtle think of the results?

"If you're going to tell me I'm a foolish old woman who had no business up on that ladder, save your breath," Myrtle said. "My daughter and my doctor have already given me their opinion more times than I care to listen."

I could imagine Myrtle tuning them out, or maybe arguing with them. I smiled. "How are you feeling?"

"Like my whole head is wrapped in cotton wool. That's from the drugs they give me." She lifted her right arm, from which protruded an IV. "Then when the physical terrorists get after me, everything hurts but my little toe. That will probably start acting up tomorrow." She raised her head a little and looked past me. "Who's that with you? Is that Trudy?"

Trudy stepped forward, smiling nervously. "Hi, Mrs. Busby."

"How's your arm doing?"

Trudy held up the purple cast. "It's better. I'll be out of this thing soon."

"Raise the bed for me, dear. The button is on the table there, by those lovely flowers your mother brought."

Trudy found the bed control and adjusted it until Myrtle was sitting. She smoothed the covers across her chest and looked at Trudy. "Thank you. I hear you're a poet."

Trudy's whole face lit up when she smiled. "Yes. I love poetry."

Myrtle nodded. "When I lived in Colombia, the village poet was one of the most revered persons in the community."

"Mom told me you were in South America with the Peace Corps."

"That's right. I was older than your Mom when I went over there. Don't make such a face, dear. That's not as old as you think." She turned and winked at me. "What are you looking so down in the mouth about?"

I hadn't realized my expression had betrayed my feelings. "I guess I'm just upset that you're hurt," I admitted.

"It's not as if I'm going to die here in this bed. Not unless the doctors have told you something they haven't revealed to me."

I shook my head. "Oh, no. It's just…well, a broken hip is rather serious, isn't it?"

"For some people maybe. As for me, I intend to be on my feet again in a few weeks. The physical terrorists tell me there's no reason I shouldn't be, as long as I put up with their torture every day." She gave me a stern look. "Let this be a lesson to you. Take your calcium and get plenty of exercise." She looked at Trudy. "You too, young lady. It's never too early to start taking care of yourself."

"Yes ma'am."

I backed away. "We'd better be going. I don't want to tire you out."

"Nonsense! I'm not tired. I'm bored." She looked at Trudy. "I know she's not going to want to tell me, so I'll ask you. Has Grace been out with that professor, Dr. Hauser, yet?"

Trudy glanced at me, a question in her eyes. "I don't know what she's talking about," I said.

"She hasn't been out with him." Trudy turned back to Myrtle. "Do you think he's asked her?"

"If he hasn't, then I've seriously misjudged him. But the way your mother is blushing right now, I'd say he has."

Trudy leaned against the bed and crossed her arms. "So why haven't you gone out with him, Mom? He's kind of cute, for an old guy."

"I doubt if he's more than forty. Not that old."

"He's forty-one," Myrtle said. "He's been divorced three years and has two children who live with their mother and see him every other weekend and holidays. His hobbies are kayaking and rock climbing, which accounts for the very nice body under those suits of his, in case you haven't noticed."

My mouth dropped open. "How do you know all that?"

Her smile would have made the Mona Lisa proud. "Most people enjoy talking about themselves, especially to someone like me, who knows how to listen."

"I'm impressed." And a little afraid. Myrtle was a one-woman intelligence agency.

"So why haven't you gone out with him?"

I glanced at Trudy. "It's complicated."

Trudy rolled her eyes. "You're not still using me as an excuse, are you?" She turned to Myrtle. "When I was a baby, she wouldn't go out because she didn't want to leave me with a sitter. When I got older, she had to stay home and help me with my homework. Now she has this idea that men don't want to date someone with a teenager. Duh! This professor guy has *two* teenagers."

Nothing like finding out your kid can see right through you to make you feel about two feet tall. Not that I'd realized at the time that I was hiding from the big bad dating world behind Trudy, but now it seemed so clear. "It's a lot more complicated than that," I said, not sure I believed it myself. "There's Gil and Mark, and the fact that Dr. Hauser is my teacher and—"

"It's not easy when you've been hurt before to put your heart on the line again, but don't you think it's time you tried?" Myrtle's voice was so gentle I felt like crawling into bed beside her and burying my face against her shoulder, the way I'd done with my mom when I was a little girl afraid of thunderstorms.

That was the whole problem, wasn't it? "I guess I am a little afraid of screwing things up," I said. After all, I hadn't read the signals right during my date with Josh. If I had, maybe I wouldn't have freaked out when he came on strong. Come to think of it, I hadn't read Gil's signals right, either. When it came to men, I obviously had poor reception.

"I was afraid when my first husband left me with two

little children to support. I was afraid when I got on that plane to fly to Colombia. I was afraid when my daughter was sick with cancer. If you're never afraid, then your life is too safe. Too dull." She reached out and grabbed my hand. "You're allowed to make mistakes, and you have to allow other people to make them, too."

I nodded. I knew she was right, but knowing and *believing* are sometimes two different things.

"Are you going to go out with the professor, Mom?" Trudy asked.

"I don't know." I squeezed Myrtle's hand. "But I promise I'm going to think about it."

"Don't think too long. A fire goes out if you don't tend it." She released my hand and lay back on the pillows. "All right, you can go now. I guess I am a little tired."

We said our goodbyes and left her. I was almost out the door when she called after me. "Grace!"

"Yes?"

"If it doesn't work out with Dr. Hauser, I know a nice young orthopedic surgeon I could introduce you to."

CHAPTER 11

Gil and I had agreed that Trudy would go to his place after school on Wednesdays so that I could use the time to study. Though I still struggled to juggle everything, those extra hours to myself helped.

Except when I didn't have them to myself. I was scarcely in the door that Wednesday when Joyce appeared on my front steps. "I need you to go shopping with me," she said.

I stared at her. Since I'd seen her that morning, she'd cut off her long brown hair. She now had a short, short cut with blond highlights. "Joyce! Your hair!" I was too stunned to say anything else.

Her face crumpled. "You don't like it? It's too extreme, isn't it? I knew I shouldn't have listened to a stylist named Nemo."

"No, I love it! It's gorgeous." It was true. While I would look ridiculous in a style like that, the shorter cut drew attention to Joyce's delicate features and gorgeous eyes. "You're a new woman."

She smiled with relief. "That's sort of the idea. A new

look for my life. Now I need to go shopping for clothes to go with the hair and, I hope, my new attitude."

"I can't tonight," I said. "I've got all this reading to do and questions to answer and…"

"Please! I promise it won't take long. You'll have time to do the reading later. I already hired a sitter for the boys and everything."

"What's your hurry? Why don't we go this weekend? Maybe Saturday afternoon, or Sunday?"

She shook her head. "No, I have to go now. Before I chicken out."

I glanced at the clock. It was just after five. If I only took a couple of hours and stayed up a little later… "Okay. But I'll drive." That way I could make sure we got back to the house at a decent hour.

"Thank you!" Joyce gave me a big hug. "I need you to tell me if I'm making a complete fool of myself."

"You're not making a fool of yourself." Not yet, anyway. Sure, this transformation seemed a little sudden, but considering her whole life had been turned inside out a few months ago, who could blame Joyce for wanting to rearrange things, including her appearance?

We climbed into my car and headed for Barton Creek Mall. Two blocks away, I decided on a slight detour. "What are we doing here?" Joyce asked as I pulled into the Travis Nursery lot.

"I have to pick up some rose food," I said. "I promise, it'll only take a minute." And getting the food now would save me a trip later.

"The economy must be picking up. I see Help Wanted signs everywhere these days," Joyce said as we made our way up the walk to the nursery office. She nodded to the sign on the door. "Looks like this place needs a manager."

"I think the old one moved." I pulled open the door and led the way toward the fertilizer section at the back.

"You ought to apply for the job." She stopped to admire a display of miniature wind chimes. "You know more about plants than anyone I know."

"I don't know anything compared to a professional horticulturalist." I studied the shelves. They were out of my usual brand of rose food, which meant I'd either have to come back later, or choose another brand.

"Still, you are more educated than the average person off the street. And I'll bet you'd enjoy working here a heck of a lot more than your job at the bank." She grinned at a row of plaster gnomes.

"The job at the bank has good insurance and flexible hours. I'm not likely to find that at many other places—not that will pay enough to support me and Trudy."

"You'll never know if you don't look, will you?" She stopped behind me and studied the shelves. "How do you decide what to use? All these boxes look alike to me."

"Some of them are alike. Then it comes down to cost." I plucked a box from the shelves. "It's like jobs. They're mostly the same. You have to pick which pays the best or has other features you need. Which means I'm stuck at the bank for a while."

"You could at least ask about this job." She followed me to the register.

"Hey, Grace." Kimmie took my box of rose food and ran it over the scanner. "How are you?"

"I'm good. How are you?"

"Still overworked."

"No new manager yet?"

She shook her head. "Nope. We've had some applicants, but I guess none of them were right."

Joyce elbowed me in the ribs, but I ignored the hint. Working in a nursery would be terrific, but I'd looked into this kind of job before. The pay and the hours were both bad. If I was alone, I might consider it, but I had to think of Trudy. For her sake, I had to stick with the bank a while longer.

"Where to first?" I asked as we sped toward the mall once more.

"Someplace that has hip, stylish clothes that aren't too expensive."

"There are places like that?" I laughed at her crestfallen expression. "I'm just kidding. But why the sudden urge for hip and stylish?"

"Kyle told me last week that I dressed too much like a schoolteacher."

"But you are a schoolteacher."

"Yes, but I don't want everyone to know it the minute they look at me."

It was true that Joyce's wardrobe consisted mainly of

denim jumpers and appliquéd sweater sets and dark slacks, but I'd thought of them as more of a practical uniform for an elementary schoolteacher than any serious fashion statement. "So what kind of look are you going for?" I asked.

"I don't know. Something that says sexy and fun." She grinned at me. "That's the kind of life I want. Maybe if I dress the part it will help me get it."

By that token, I should be dressing in the most staid, unexciting clothes I could find, to go with the calm, uneventful life I sometimes fantasized about.

We headed for the junior section of Macy's, reasoning that that was as "hip" as two thirty-somethings could get. Joyce collected a handful of outfits from the racks and retired to the dressing room, only to return fifteen minutes later, crestfallen.

"What's the matter, didn't they fit?" I asked, looking up from the stack of sweaters I'd been refolding. (They were a mess, okay? And I had to do *something* while I waited.)

"The size fourteens fit." She shoved the clothes back onto a nearby rack. "I've never worn a size fourteen in my life."

"They're fourteen *juniors*. It's not the same."

"I don't care. I refuse to let a size fourteen in my closet. Let's go down to that new boutique by the food court."

A row of mannequins slouched in the front windows of the boutique, bored expressions on their porcelain faces. "Apparently being hip requires bad posture and a worse attitude," I said as I studied one mannequin's outfit of gathered army-green fatigues and a T-shirt that was two sizes too small.

"Maybe the idea is if you look pissed off, no one messes with you." She rifled through a rack and pulled out a sleeveless top in muted purple stripes that melted into each other. "This is cute."

"It is. Try it on."

An hour later, we emerged with two pairs of pants, a skirt, a dress and two shirts that met Joyce's definition of "sexy and fun." All the clothes looked cute on her and I had to admit she'd looked happy trying them on.

"Thanks for coming with me, Grace," she said as we headed toward the parking lot.

"No problem. It was fun." I'd pay for it with lost sleep, but what are friends for?

"I feel great," she said, hefting her stuffed shopping bags into the trunk of my car. "I should have done this months ago."

"I wish I'd thought of it," I said. I'd been so busy with the big change of going to college that I hadn't thought of this little one. I'd handled things pretty well so far, but there were so many more things I wanted to do. If I overhauled my wardrobe, along with my attitude, no telling what I could accomplish.

"Mom, instead of going to Mark's show tonight, can I just go home from school with Sheila? Her mom can bring me home later."

Friday morning, I looked up from the stack of towels I was folding. Trudy was hunched over the kitchen table, inhaling a bowl of Frosted Flakes. "Don't you want to go to Mark's show? I'm sure he'll be disappointed you're not there."

"No he won't. He'll be too nervous to even know whether I'm there or not. And there'll be tons of people there that I don't know. Besides, Sheila and I have this project we need to work on for Language Arts."

"I still think you ought to be there, just for a little while. This is a big deal for Mark."

"I know. But it's just a bunch of people standing around looking at his artwork. It sounds like it'll be really boring."

I couldn't argue with her there. I expected to be pretty bored myself. "Is it all right with Sheila's mom if you study over at her house?"

"Mo-om!" She shoved back from the table and stood. "What is this? The inquisition? All I want to do is study with a friend. Is that a crime?"

I sighed. Are all the things you say as a teenager destined to come back at you out of your own children's mouths? Nothing is trivial at that age. Everyone is out to get you. Every obstacle to getting your way is a sinister plot. Your parents are evil demons determined to trap you with them forever and thwart your every plan.

The temptation, of course, is to try to argue with your child. To force them to take off those dark-tinted glasses and view the world as it really is. Or at least as you see it.

My advice is not to waste your breath. I was willing to put my foot down for important stuff. No tattoos. No drugs or alcohol or going places with people I don't know. But the little everyday battles weren't worth the effort to fight.

"You can go to Sheila's, but be home by ten," I called toward Trudy's retreating back. "And next time don't spring this kind of thing on me at the last minute."

She didn't answer, but a few moments later, she returned to the kitchen wearing her backpack. "Can I borrow these earrings?" She tucked her hair behind her ears, revealing big silver loops from my jewelry box.

I shrugged. "I guess so."

She smoothed the front of her sweater. "Does this look okay, or do you think the one with the purple stripes is better?"

"You look fine." I picked up my keys. "We'd better go."

On the way out to the car my second cup of coffee kicked in, and I started wondering why Trudy was suddenly so interested in her appearance. "How are things with Simon?" I asked as she settled into the front seat next to me.

"Okay." She looked out the side window, practically turning her back on me. Translation: I can't believe you're asking me such a personal question.

Fine. She was obviously in one of her "moods" this morning. I sympathize. Sometimes we're all at the mercy of our hormones and teenagers have it worse than most. The best I could do was take comfort in the knowledge that this too would pass.

I dropped her off in front of the school. "Call me when you get to Sheila's," I said.

She made a face. "We're gonna be really busy."

"Humor me. One day you'll be a mother, too, and you'll understand."

I was trying for a joke, but it didn't get a smile out of her. As I watched her walk across the courtyard, I had a sudden vision of a grown-up Trudy—taller, more filled out, more sure of herself than I'd ever been. The image took my breath away. Then it was gone and there was present-day Trudy, caught between childhood and adulthood, feeling her way through life as blindly as I ever had. I wanted to run after her and pull her close in a hug, but being her mother, all I could do was let her go and say a silent prayer that she'd have a happy life ahead of her, even when I wasn't around to smooth the path.

It's amazing what a few tablecloths, some candles and an abundance of fancy finger food can do for a humble coin laundry. I might not have recognized Sud Your Duds, if it hadn't been for the neon sign flashing in the front window. Someone (I'm betting Gil) had made up a banner that announced the title Mark had come up with for the show: Life Collages by Mark Leland.

I found Mark at the portable bar in the back, his white-knuckled hands wrapped around a scotch and soda. "Everything looks great," I said. "And you have a good crowd."

"All my friends came. They felt sorry for me. Figured no one else would show."

"Isn't that a reporter for the *Statesman?*" I indicated a tall blonde with red cat-eye glasses. "She's not a friend of yours, is she?"

"Shit! The press!" He took a swig of scotch. "Oh God, I think I'm going to be sick."

Gil came over and clapped Mark on the back. "Save your nervous breakdown for another night. There's a couple over here who might actually want to buy one of your pieces."

"Buyers?" Mark set aside his drink and smoothed back his hair. "Lead me to these paragons of good taste."

They headed off toward a couple who were contemplating the auto parts collage, and I checked out the buffet table. I had just stuffed a fried shrimp into my mouth when a familiar figure hailed me from across the room. "Grace!"

I almost choked as Josh came toward me. He was wearing black jeans and a black leather jacket and more than a few heads—both male and female—turned when he entered the room. I had a good idea why he was really here, so I kept my expression cool. "I didn't know you were into art."

He looked around at the various collages displayed above the washers and dryers. "Interesting stuff. I really came more to soak up the atmosphere."

"The atmosphere?"

"You know. For my paper."

Oh, yes. The infamous paper. "Josh, you're not going to ruin Mark's big night by asking a bunch of nosy questions, are you?"

He looked pained. "Now Grace, I have better manners than that. I'm here to observe." He reached past me and helped himself to a shrimp.

"Have some free food while you're at it," I said, and began refilling my own plate.

Determined to mingle, I wandered over to where a woman about my age was contemplating the *Pop Art* piece. "What do you think of it?" I asked.

"Very perceptive," she said. "A real statement about the disposable nature of art. Or perhaps the way trivialities overwhelm our lives."

I looked at the piece again. "Hmm." I was just wondering how he got the caps to stick up there like that, but I didn't say anything. So I'm not into modern art. Sue me.

The woman moved carefully away and I turned to survey the crowd. If you ask me, people are more interesting than pictures any day. As mentioned, a lot of Mark and Gil's friends were here, some single people and couples, both gay and straight. A lot of good-looking men in the crowd; the trouble was determining which ones of them were available.

It felt strange, being here with Gil and Mark, but without Trudy. We were family, weren't we? Not the more traditional family I'd always pictured having, but one that, until now, did things together.

I sighed. When I was fourteen, I didn't want to be seen with my family, much less spend a Friday night with them. I ought to be thankful Trudy wasn't making me drop her a block from the school so no one would know she even had a mother.

During the teenage years, you count your blessings where you can find them.

Josh seemed to be having a good time. He stood in front of the iguana piece (which already had a big red Sold tag on it, I was glad to see) talking with another young man. Whatever they were talking about, they both seemed to be really into it, with lots of serious looks and expansive gestures. I just hoped Josh wasn't going to do too much research tonight. I didn't trust him not to ask embarrassing questions. I wished I could read lips.

About that time, the other man slipped his arm around Josh's shoulder. He kept talking, a pleasant expression on his face, but Josh's eyes got big and his face turned the color of printer paper. Without warning, he lurched across the room toward me.

"Grace, you've got to help me," he whispered.

"Josh, what is it? Are you ill?" He certainly looked ill. I moved out of the way, just in case he was about to be sick. Not that I wasn't sympathetic, but I had on a practically new pair of shoes.

"That guy just made a pass at me." The words came out in a hoarse whisper.

I glanced over his shoulder at the man, who was staring at us, a puzzled expression on his face. "Are you sure?"

He nodded. "We were just standing there, talking, and he put his arm around me and said I should come over to his place later."

I frowned. "What were you talking about?"

"I was telling him about my paper. I mean, he seemed really interested in the subject, and had a lot of good things to say…." A horrified look came into his eyes. "You don't think he thought I was gay, do you?"

I tried hard not to laugh. "It may have crossed his mind. But I'm sure it was an honest mistake. He probably thought you were one of Gil and Mark's friends. You can explain it to him now—he's coming this way."

"Oh, my God, no!" Josh glanced over his shoulder. The other man was smiling, headed our way.

Josh turned around and before I could say anything, pulled me into his arms and covered my lips with his.

Maybe it was because he caught me off guard, or because the one drink I'd had had gone to my head. Whatever the reason, I enjoyed the kiss a lot more than I expected to. Either Josh's technique had improved, or desperation made him let go of his inhibitions. He didn't seem in any hurry to end it either, so I relaxed and tried to go with the flow, so to speak. I was just starting to enjoy myself when he released me, almost dropping me in the process. I stumbled back, red-faced and disoriented. "What the hell was that all about?" I asked.

"I was going to ask the same question."

Do you ever have one of those moments when you are sure you are going to die of embarrassment? When you wish it were possible? At least if you were dead, you wouldn't have to try to come up with a plausible explanation for an awkward situation.

That's how I felt when I turned and found myself face-to-face with Dr. David Hauser. "Hello Grace," he said, his face expressionless, eyes cold. He looked at Josh. "I see you're busy, so I won't keep you."

He turned and left, and all the warmth in the room left with him. I sagged back against the buffet table and stared after him. I didn't know whether to scream or cry, but frankly, I don't think I had the energy to do either.

"Gracie, are you all right?" I hadn't noticed Gil standing there, but now he looked from me to Josh, a grim expression on his face. "Would someone mind telling me what's going on here?"

CHAPTER 12

If I were the dramatic type, I would have slapped Josh. He certainly deserved it, and my palm did itch to connect with the side of his face. But I was reluctant to draw any more attention to myself than I already had. So I settled for glaring at him. While not as physically gratifying as striking him would have been, the glare did make him squirm.

"Josh was just leaving," I said.

"I was?" He looked startled, but when Gil took a step toward him, he moved back and angled toward the door. "I guess it is late. Nice to see you all. Goodbye."

He scuttled sideways toward the exit, bumping into the tall man he'd been so engaged with earlier, then abandoned all semblance of cool and bolted toward the door. I turned away and headed for the bar.

I was halfway through a stiff gin and tonic when I felt a familiar hand on my shoulder. "Okay, spill," Gil said. "What's going on? I thought you and Josh had called it quits."

"We had. We have." I turned to face him, cradling the

drink in both hands, letting the cold seep through the numbness creeping over me.

Gil raised one eyebrow. "You looked pretty cozy just now."

"He was just using me." So what else was new? The fact that I'd actually enjoyed the kiss—to a point—made me that much more disgusted with myself.

Gil waited, the obvious question unasked.

I sighed. "He thought one of the other men here tonight had made a pass at him."

"He should feel flattered. There are a lot of hot guys here tonight."

Right. I could think of one guy I thought was pretty hot who'd left in a hurry when he caught me in a lip-lock with Josh. I sighed and set aside my half-finished drink.

Gil put his hand on my shoulder. "Don't stress about it, okay? He's not worth it."

I started to tell him Josh wasn't the man I was stressing about, but decided some things were better kept to myself.

Mark joined us, bouncing up and down on the balls of his feet like a hyperactive chihuahua. "Dudes, I'm so stoked! Is this a trip or what?"

"It's great." I manufactured a smile for his sake. "I saw a lot of Sold signs on your work."

"The reporter from the *Statesman* interviewed me and they got a great shot of me and Gil in front of the *Pop Art* piece."

"You're a celebrity." At least someone's life was going

the way it should. I yawned. "I'd better head home. I've got an early day tomorrow."

"Do you want me to drive you?" Gil asked.

"No, you stay with Mark. Go celebrate. I'll be fine."

"If you're sure."

"I'm sure."

Trudy was waiting at home, looking curiously grown-up in a pair of pajamas that used to belong to me, her makeup still in place. When I walked in the door she looked up from the bowl of Lucky Charms she was eating. "How was the show?"

"Great." I assumed my best false cheerfulness, something motherhood had helped me to perfect. I might be in a black mood myself, but no sense inflicting it on Trudy. "There were tons of people there. Mark sold almost all his pieces."

"Cool!"

I put my arm around her. "How's the project coming?"

"The project?" Her spoon rattled against the bottom of her bowl.

"The Language Arts project? Isn't that what you went over to Sheila's house to work on?"

"Yeah. It's going okay." She raised her bowl to her mouth and drank the last of the milk. "We're almost finished."

My mom alarm started to ping. Trudy was avoiding looking at me, a sure sign something was up. I moved around to face her. "What's this project about?"

"Oh, you know. Language Arts stuff."

"Language Arts stuff?" I narrowed my eyes. "Trudy, are you up to something you're not telling me?"

She looked at me then, completely open and honest. "Awww Mom, you're so suspicious. Our project is on communication and technology."

"How do you do a project on that?"

She flushed. "I was gonna surprise you, but we're making a film."

"A film?"

"Yeah, we're using Sheila's parents' videocamera and we're filming people talking on cell phones and using computers and stuff and setting it to music. And I even wrote some poetry."

Poetry about communication technology. Okaaay. "That's great, honey."

"Yeah, it's hard work. I'm wiped." She stood and kissed my cheek. "I think I'll go to bed now. You look pretty tired too."

"Yeah, I am." Emotional gymnastics like I'd experienced tonight would wear out anyone. I stumbled into the bedroom expecting to toss and turn half the night, rehashing the evening's events. But the minute my head hit the pillow, I passed out. Some nights even reruns are too much to take.

Over the weekend, I'd almost convinced myself that David Hauser seeing Josh kissing me was no big deal. Almost. But when I woke Monday morning my first thought was that I had economics class today. I buried my face in the pillow and moaned. After Friday night I couldn't face Dr. Hauser. What must he think—that I'm the kind of woman who engages in flagrant PDA over the canapes?

Trudy appeared in the doorway. "Mom, are you okay?"

I was tempted to tell her no, but instead uncovered my head. "I'm fine. Just a little tired."

"Should I call Sheila and ask her to give me a ride to school?"

"No, I'm getting up."

Sheer willpower and long practice got me out of bed and into my clothes. I went through the motions of making coffee and getting ready for class—class I had no intention of showing up for. Not until I'd decided what to do.

Should I confront Josh about what happened? Should I go to Dr. Hauser and try to explain? Should I tell him I'd decided to accept his offer of a dinner date?

Or should I pretend nothing had happened and ignore both men?

I mean, why do things have to be so difficult? Couldn't I just once have good things fall in my lap all nice and neat without having to work so damn hard for them?

I thought about all this as I drove Trudy to school. Instead of dropping her off in the front, I pulled into the Visitors' parking lot. "What are you doing?" she asked.

"I thought as long as I was here, I'd check with the office and make sure they added Mark's name to the list of emergency contacts, like I asked."

"You called Mrs. Lazarus about that already, didn't you?"

I shut off the engine. "I talked to her on the phone, but I want to make sure she really did it. I've learned it pays to follow up on these things." Besides, this would give me a legitimate excuse for missing economics class.

I followed Trudy into the building, not protesting when she made a point of walking five steps ahead of me. As we passed the trophy cases outside the gymnasium I heard giggling and turned to see a trio of girls on the stairs watching us. When they saw me they laughed harder, their mouths twisted in nasty smirks.

The hair on the back of my neck stood at attention and I was immediately plunged back in time to my own high school days. The girls on the stairs were the "popular" girls who said nasty things behind my back when Robert Cavanaugh bragged about having "done it" with me in his car out by the lake. I had that same sick feeling in my stomach now that I had had then.

I glanced ahead to Trudy, and saw her stiffen and raise her head a little higher. So I hadn't imagined the vicious undertone in that laughter. What the hell was going on?

I caught up with Trudy at her locker. "What was that all about?" I asked.

She jerked open the locker door. "What was what all about?"

"Those girls were laughing about something."

"I'm sure it's nothing." She pulled books from her backpack and shoved them into her locker. "I thought you were going to talk to Mrs. Lazarus."

"First I want to talk to you." I touched her shoulder. "Look Trudy, I know what it's like to be singled out by a clique of girls. They can be cruel."

She shrugged off my hand. "It's no big deal, Mom. I can handle it."

That wasn't a good enough answer, but it was all the answer I was going to get. Cal showed up just then and the grateful smile Trudy bestowed on him made his eyes light up. Apparently even boring Cal was an improvement over actual conversation in the school hallway with your mother.

"Hello Mrs. Greenleigh," Cal said. "How's it going?"

"It's going okay, Cal. How are you?"

Trudy slammed her locker and glared at me. "Mom was just leaving," she said.

I got the message. I nodded goodbye to them both and made my way to the office.

As I'd suspected, Mark's name was *not* on the emergency contact list. Mrs. Lazarus apologized and said our conversation had "slipped her mind."

"Of course, emergency contacts are usually only parents and immediate family," she said with a hint of disapproval.

"Mark *is* family," I said as I picked up a pen and wrote in his name on the form. I returned the paper and pen to her. "I don't want any more mix-ups like we experienced the day Trudy broke her arm."

."How is she doing?" Mrs. Lazarus asked, wisely changing the subject.

"Trudy is fine." I hesitated, then decided I had to ask. "You don't know anything about any other students who might be picking on her, do you?"

"Picking on her?" She frowned. "Has Trudy said something to you?"

"No, but I heard some girls laughing in the hall and wondered…"

Her expression relaxed. "If I worried every time girls laughed in the halls here I'd be a nervous wreck." She shook her head. "I'm sure it was nothing." The way she said it let me know she had me pegged as an overprotective mom.

I would have pressed the issue, but I didn't see any point. Trudy had said she was handling it—whatever *it* was—so I'd have to trust her. But I'd keep a close eye on her, and she and I would talk again about this.

First bell hadn't rung yet, so I stopped by the cafeteria on my way out to say goodbye to Trudy. At first I didn't see her in the crowded room where all the students gathered to wait for classes to begin. Then I spotted her off to my left, surrounded by the trio of girls who had smirked at us as we'd passed. Cal was with her, looking troubled, though Trudy's face was a mask of nonexpression.

I knew better than to charge into the middle of things, but I wanted to know what was going on. I moved closer, ducking behind a vending machine, knowing Trudy would be mortified if she caught me spying on her.

"Saw your dad's picture in the paper with his *boyfriend*," one of the girls said.

"What's it like having a faggot for a dad?" said another.

"Is that why you hang out with a faggot like Cal?" the third asked.

My fingers curled into fists at the ugly words. So that's what this was all about. For all the supposedly liberal ways of modern youth, I'd forgotten how judgmental they could be of anyone different.

"You'd better shut up," Cal said. "You can't talk about Trudy's family that way."

"What are you gonna do about it?" the third girl asked. "Faggot!"

Trudy's gaze flickered to him, then back to the girls. "Mark's a talented artist and a really cool guy," she said. "And my dad's really cool, too."

"He's still a faggot," the first girl said.

The withering look Trudy gave them made me want to cheer. "Like I care what you think." She shook her head. "You're all so lame."

She turned away. "Come on, Cal. I've got better things to do than waste my time with these losers."

"Who're you calling a loser, you bitch!" The third girl lunged toward Trudy but Cal stepped in front of her. He wasn't very bulky, but he had a couple of inches and at least twenty pounds on the girl, and the determined look in his eye apparently made her think twice about starting anything with him. He stared at her a long moment, then turned and caught up with Trudy.

I sagged against the vending machine, shaking, but also inflated with a rush of pride. Trudy was so strong. So beautiful. She absolutely radiated strength. I could believe she really didn't care what those girls thought, and that she really did see them as losers.

Could I take a little credit for instilling that kind of strength and self-assurance in my daughter? Gil deserved his share of praise, too. And Mark.

But the lion's share probably went to Trudy herself. She was one amazing girl.

The kind of girl I'd always wished I was. Truth be told, the kind of woman I was still trying to be.

Seeing Trudy stand up to those girls galvanized something in me. By the time I pulled into the student parking lot at St. Edward's, I knew what I had to do.

I sought out David in his office. When I appeared in his open doorway and cleared my throat, he looked up from his desk, clearly startled. "Grace. What are you doing here?"

"We need to talk."

He shuffled paper, not looking at me. "Is it something in the course work? I can refer you to a tutor."

I stepped inside and shut the door. "We need to talk about last night."

"I understand from this morning's paper that it was quite a successful show. I must admit Mark's artwork is quite…interesting."

I sat in the hard plastic chair across from his desk. "I don't understand half of it, but people who do say he's very good."

"Yes, I've never been a student of modern art myself."

I leaned toward him. "I don't want to talk about Mark. I want to talk about why you left in such a hurry."

"I never intended to stay long. I had other things to do." His eyes met mine. "And you were obviously otherwise occupied."

I felt my cheeks warm. "What you saw…it wasn't what you thought."

He sat back and studied me a moment. I held still, refusing to look away, remembering Trudy's courage.

"You were kissing Josh Campbell," he said. "Quite enthusiastically, I might add."

I made a face. "*He* was kissing *me*." Not entirely the truth, but if I had it to do over, I definitely wouldn't have kissed him back. "He thought one of the men at the party had made a pass at him and apparently decided kissing me was the best way to send the message that he wasn't available."

"And you just happened to be the closest female."

"Something like that." I picked invisible lint from my slacks. "Look, Josh and I did date—once. It didn't work out." I looked at David again. "I just wanted you to know there's nothing going on between us. You didn't need to run out like that last night."

He nodded. "I'm glad to hear it. And I apologize for leaving. Is there anything else?"

His attitude wasn't exactly warm, but I could appreciate his reserve in this situation. I took a deep breath. "Yeah. If you're still interested in going out sometime, I'm game."

His smile was sudden and devastating, hitting me in the gut and sending warmth through my torso. Oh, wow.

"I'm definitely interested," he said.

"Yeah?" I smiled too, giddy.

"How about Saturday night? What would you like to do?"

Oh, no. He asked me out. I wasn't going to be stuck in the role of social planner. I stood on shaky legs and smiled down at him. "Surprise me."

Saturday night I agreed to let Trudy spend the night with Sheila. Sheila's dad picked her up at five, which left me an hour to fuss over my outfit for my date with David. I changed clothes four times, finally settling on black slacks and a blue knit shirt with bell-shaped sleeves and a daring (for me) plunge neckline that revealed a hint of cleavage.

I studied my image in the mirror. "Grace Greenleigh, you look *hot*," I declared. No way was David going to see me as a struggling economics student tonight.

When the doorbell rang, my heart started beating double-time. By the time I made it into the living room I was out of breath. Unfortunately, all my excitement was wasted on Joyce, who stood on my doorstep. "Can I borrow your rhinestone hair clip?" she asked, her hands clasped in a pleading gesture.

"Sure. Come on in." I held the door open wider and she rushed past me into the living room. "Do you have a date?" I asked.

"No, but Peter is coming to pick up the boys and I want him to think I do." She followed me into the bedroom and watched while I dug through my jewelry box.

"Why do you want him to think that?" I handed her the hair clip.

"I don't want him knowing the truth—that I'm sitting home alone crying over sappy movies and eating frozen cheesccake right out of the box." She adjusted the clip in her hair. "How do you think this looks?"

"You look gorgeous. Definitely not like a woman sitting home eating cheesecake."

"Good." She turned back to the mirror and smoothed her hair. "I want him to take one look at me and be sorry he ever left."

I didn't like the direction this conversation was taking. "You don't want him back, do you?"

She glanced over her shoulder at me. "God no! But I want him to realize how badly he screwed up."

I studied her while she continued primping in the mirror. She was wearing a black satin shift that clung to every curve, killer high heels, a rhinestone bracelet and my hair clip. But underneath all that glam lay a genuinely good person. The kind of woman who promised to "love, honor and cherish," and meant the words with all her heart. She was a good mother and she'd been a good wife. No matter what Peter had now, how could it be better than what he'd given up?

"What brought this on?" I asked.

She turned away from the mirror, all the bravado gone from her eyes, replaced by desperation. "I saw the soon-to-be second Mrs. Peter Dilly today."

I made a face. "What did she look like?"

"Grace, it was awful!" She wrung her hands. "I mean, I felt so bad."

"That gorgeous, huh?" Men always went for the eye candy.

"No! She's not beautiful at all. She's—plain." Joyce sounded as stunned as I felt. "And she's older than I am. What does he see in her?"

So much for easy generalizations. Who knew? Was it possible Peter had found true love with an older, plainer woman? Then what had he and Joyce had all those years? "The question is, what does *she* see in *him?*" I said.

"I don't know. What did *I* ever see in him?" She turned to the mirror again and squared her shoulders. "The important thing is, I want him to see what he cheated himself out of. I know that's probably immature and vindictive, that I shouldn't care what he thinks, but I can't help it. I have fantasies about him groveling at my feet."

I grinned. "What do you do in these fantasies when he grovels?"

"I walk all over him in three hundred dollar high heels, right into the arms of some gorgeous man who treats me like a princess." She extended one foot and admired the black stiletto pump she wore. "So far I only have forty-six dollar shoes and I'm still looking for the man, but it's a start."

I patted her shoulder. "It's a good start. You show him. And while you're all dressed up, why don't you go out somewhere nice? You might even meet someone."

"Why don't you go with me?" She looked me up and down, and gave a low whistle. "Wait a minute. Do you have a date?"

I nodded, fighting to keep the smugness out of my smile. "Yes, I have a date."

"So tell me all about him. Where did you meet?"

"At school. He's one of my professors."

"Now there's an idea. Maybe I should take some classes."

The doorbell rang and we both jumped. "That's probably him now," I said. It had better be. My heart couldn't take many more false alarms.

When I opened my front door David smiled at me, another one of those looks that made me feel feverish. "You look wonderful," he said.

"You look very nice yourself." He was wearing khakis

and a short-sleeved tropical print shirt in shades of blue and green that brought out his eyes. I relaxed a little, relieved I'd made the right choice in going for a casual look.

"Hello." Joyce stuck her head around the door. "I'm Joyce, Grace's friend and next-door neighbor." She edged around the door, out onto the steps. "I'd better go now. Y'all have a great time tonight." As soon as she was on the walkway behind David, she turned and gave me a big thumbs up. *He's gorgeous!* she mouthed.

I nodded in agreement, my smile bigger than ever.

"Do I pass inspection?" David asked.

I laughed. "Yes, I'd say you do."

We walked to the car and he opened the door for me, a gentlemanly gesture I found touching. I managed to keep quiet for all of five minutes, but finally I couldn't stand it anymore. "Where are we going?" I asked.

He laughed. "You strike me as someone who might be up for something a little different."

Memories of Josh and our disastrous evening at Club Soho flitted through my mind and I swallowed hard. "Such as?"

"There's a carnival in town. I thought we might go."

A carnival. I smiled. "I haven't been to one of those in years."

"Then how do you feel about going with me?"

It would be an unconventional first date, but then, I

didn't seem to pull off conventional all that well. Maybe this was a better way to start. I gave him my best smile. "I think that's a great idea."

CHAPTER 13

An hour into my evening with David, I'd decided he was some kind of dating genius. I'd just spent the past week obsessing over my lack of experience with the opposite sex, my years of self-imposed celibacy and my cluelessness as to what adults really did on dates these days, and David took me to a place where I didn't have to worry about any of these things.

I mean, who isn't a kid again at a carnival? Put a seventeen-year-old or a thirty-year-old on a Tilt-A-Whirl and they both act the same, screaming and giggling and holding on to their fellow passenger for dear life.

David certainly didn't seem to mind the holding on part, which may have been his intent in the first place. In any case, after the first spin in the teacups and crash in the bumper cars I was more relaxed than I'd been in, well, years.

"Do you come to carnivals often?" I asked him as we walked down the midway, enjoying our dinner of mustard-smeared corn dogs and beer-battered onion rings. (Carnival cuisine holds that everything is better battered and fried. So far I'd spotted battered and fried potatoes, pickles, Oreo cookies, corn and ice cream. And don't forget funnel cakes—fried batter. I could practically feel my face breaking out.)

"I haven't been to one of these in probably twenty years." He glanced at me. "I saw the Ferris wheel this afternoon and thought maybe it would be a fun way for us to relax and get to know one another better."

"Economics apparently isn't the only thing you know a lot about."

"Hmm. That's debatable. But tell me—what do you know a lot about?"

I puzzled over this one a minute. I could say I knew about being a single mom, but then again, Gil had always been there to help me, so how single was that? I knew about banking, but I wasn't interested enough in it to become an expert. I knew how to handle despondent neighbors and friends and could probably name ten ways I'd screwed up my life in the past. But what did I really know about?

"Flowers," I said after a minute. "I know about flowers. And shrubs and trees. Plants." I glanced at him. "I like gardening."

"Who loves a garden, finds within his soul, Life's whole." His eyes found mine. "Louise Seymore Jones. My mother had it painted on her garden gate."

An economics professor who quoted poetry. I was beginning to feel a little out of my league. "Um, not that it's any of my business, but do you date your students very often?"

He looked amused. "Actually, you're the first."

"I am?" The idea shocked me. I mean, he was surrounded every day by attractive coeds, and I knew from overhearing conversations around campus that he was considered very sexy "for an older dude" as one of the twenty-somethings had phrased it.

"After my divorce I wasn't interested in dating again for a while. When I was ready, I knew I wanted someone with a bit more...maturity."

Funny word, maturity. When you're a teenager it's something you strive for. When you're my age it makes you feel a little long in the tooth. I added more mustard to my corn dog. "I thought every man's dream was a nubile young thing who wouldn't make too many demands."

"That doesn't quite describe my dreams." He gave me a devilish look that could have melted ice cream, if I'd had any. I polished off the last of my corn dog and tried not to think of the phallic implications of my meal choice. Why hadn't I opted for a hamburger?

If he noticed how much I was blushing, he had the grace not to mention it. Instead, he stepped up to a baseball pitch and proceeded to win me a stuffed Minnie Mouse. "I'm impressed," I said as I accepted the gift. "You have quite an arm." I'd noticed those nice biceps right off.

"I played on my college baseball team."

A professor who quoted poetry and was a jock. My

black-and-white picture of him was taking on color. It was a little scary. Time to head for familiar territory. "Tell me about your children."

"David Junior is on the track team this spring and spends every weekend at meets, which makes it tough for his old man to get any time with him, but we do our best. Allison just landed a part in the school musical, which has made her happy and makes me proud and nervous at the same time. I anticipate watching an actual performance will be excruciating."

I winced. "I know exactly what you mean. You want so much for them to do well that you feel every little blow to their pride personally."

"My father used to say being a parent required both a soft and a hard heart. I think I'm only just now learning what that means."

He put his arm around my shoulder and it was all I could do not to melt into a puddle right there in front of the House of Mirrors. It felt so *good* leaning on someone this way. At the same time, I had never felt more vulnerable. I said a silent prayer that I wouldn't screw this up.

We were standing in line for the Ferris wheel when I heard familiar laughter. The hairs rose up on the back of my neck and I told myself I had to be imagining things. But when the laughter came a second time I did a slow turn and scanned the crowd.

I spotted them over by the bumper cars—four teens dressed in black. Trudy was back to full Goth mode, complete with dog collar and heavily mascaraed eyes. She was standing next to Simon, laughing, though to me the mirth sounded forced.

As I stared at her several emotions fought a battle within me. Anger welled up, quickly followed by sadness and a deep disappointment. This was the Language Arts project she'd said she was working on? Had the glib story she'd told me been all lies, a cover for sneaking out with Simon?

And why did she feel the need to sneak around behind my back? Except that she knew I wouldn't have approved of her continuing to see the boy who had indirectly led to her broken arm. Still, why hadn't she at least tried to talk to me about it? Was this what having a teenager meant— these lies and secrecy?

"Grace, what is it? Is something wrong?" David nudged my arm.

"I'm afraid our wonderful evening is about to come to a not-so-wonderful end." I gave him an apologetic look, then turned back to my daughter.

"Is that Trudy?" He frowned. "Did you know she was going to be here tonight?"

"I did not." I sighed and started toward the group by the bumper cars, David following.

I was about ten feet from Trudy when she looked up and saw me approaching. Her mouth dropped open and her face bleached white as paper. She squeaked something I thought might have been "Oh shit," then averted her eyes. As if pretending not to see me was going to make this encounter not happen.

I stopped in front of her. Her friends moved away, out of the danger zone, I presumed. I didn't say anything, just stared and waited for her to acknowledge me.

"Mom, what are you doing here?" she finally mumbled, not looking at me.

"No, I think that's my line," I said. "What happened to working with Sheila on your Language Arts project?"

"We finished early?" She dared a glance at me, seeing if I bought it.

I shook my head. "Come on. We'll talk about this at home."

"But Mo-om! We just got here. We've hardly ridden any of the rides."

"Too bad. We're going home."

"At least let me say goodbye to my friends."

I glanced around. Simon and the others were nowhere in sight. Apparently they'd abandoned Trudy to me. So much for friends. "Looks like they already left," I said flatly.

"I guess so." She ducked her head, but not before I saw her bottom lip tremble. My heart twisted and it was all I could do not to hold out my arms and pull her close. But I wasn't sure she'd welcome my embrace just now. And I wasn't ready to forgive all without talking about things first.

Sometimes being a parent is damned hard. And the older your child gets, the harder raising them turns out to be. David's comment about needing a soft and a hard heart came back to me. So true. And so tough to find the right balance.

Trudy huddled in one corner of the backseat of David's car, enveloped in a chilly silence. I couldn't think of anything to say to ease the tension and David was smart enough to keep silent. So much for my big romantic evening. Maybe I wasn't meant to enjoy a normal date— whatever that was.

As soon as David pulled into my driveway, Trudy bolted out of the backseat and into the house. I stared after her, reluctant to move. "I suppose I should go into the house and talk to her," I said.

He nodded. "You're a good mom. You'll do the right thing."

In spite of everything, I had to smile at that. "Even if you're just saying that to score points, you have."

He slid across the seat toward me. "You couldn't have come this far with her if you weren't a good mother."

"I had some help from her father."

He nodded, eyes locked to mine, as if searching for something. I was suddenly aware of how close we were. I could feel the warmth of his body against mine, and see gold flecks in the brown of his eyes. It made me a little breathless, but I was determined not to run away from my feelings, no matter how mixed up and scary they were.

"I…I'm sorry our evening was ruined," I stammered.

"It wasn't ruined." He caressed my shoulder. "I had a

good time even if I didn't get to take you into the tunnel of love."

There went my mind, creating sexual euphemisms where maybe none existed. "We didn't even get to ride the Ferris wheel." I tried to make it a joke, but my voice shook too much.

He shrugged. "Things happen. Maybe some other time?"

I nodded. "Yeah. I'd like that."

My lips were tingling, waiting for him to move in closer for a kiss. I debated grabbing him and laying a big one on him, but wasn't sure I could pull it off.

He rescued me from my indecision by leaning forward and touching his lips to mine. He didn't linger long, didn't put his arms around me or open his mouth or anything. But all the same it was a kiss that warmed me to my toes.

I think I mumbled a "good night," though I have no memory of actually opening the door and getting out of the car. I might have floated all the way to my front door and into the house, I felt that giddy.

Of course, once inside my feet landed firmly on the ground again. Trudy was slumped on the sofa, wrapped in an afghan and glaring at me. "Thanks for ruining my evening," she said.

"Quit stealing my lines." I sat down at the other end of the sofa and hugged a pillow to my stomach.

She looked away. I fought back a flood of words and waited, hoping the right ones would sort themselves out of the jumble in my head. As it was, she spoke first. "So, I guess I'm in a lot of trouble for going out with Simon, huh?"

"No, you're in trouble for lying to me."

She ducked her head and plucked at the fringe of the afghan.

"Was there even a Language Arts project?" I asked.

She whipped her head around to face me. "That part was true. Sheila and I are making a film."

"So how did you end up at the carnival with Simon?"

She dropped her gaze again. "Simon asked me to go with him. I told him you wouldn't let me, because of my arm."

"I never said you couldn't go out with Simon."

"Yeah, but I knew you didn't really like him." She bit her lower lip, hesitating. When she spoke again, the words came out in a rush. "I couldn't tell him I'd changed my mind about dating him. I mean, part of me still really likes him, you know? But the other part of me thinks maybe that's not such a good thing."

I stared at her, swallowing tears, amazed once again at how self-aware she was. At her age I'd been completely at the mercy of hormones and peer pressure. I reached over and put my hand on her shoulder. "You should trust that part of you that said it's not a good thing. You have good instincts."

She leaned her head against my hand, a tender gesture that sent tears spilling down my cheeks. I'll admit it, I'm a sentimental watering pot when it comes to my baby. "Yeah, but Simon and his friends are really popular and it feels good sometimes to think that people might see me as popular, too."

I remembered the girls who had teased her in the cafeteria. How many times had she faced similar derision before? How tempting it must have been to be one of the "in" crowd, supposedly immune to that kind of ugliness. But then I remembered that I was still her mom, and I had to be tough.

"Understanding why you lied doesn't make the lie any better," I said.

She sighed, a heavy expulsion of air that deflated her further, so that she sank down into the cushions. "I know. And it was dumb. But when he called Sheila's tonight and asked us to meet him, I thought, just this once...." She glanced at me, a little girl peeking about from behind the heavy makeup. "I was actually glad you saw me. Embarrassed, but glad. I wasn't having a good time."

My mom antennae stood at attention. "Why weren't you having a good time? Did Simon do something to hurt you?" If he had, so help me he would regret it. And then he'd regret it all over again when Gil and Mark got through with him.

She shrugged. "He didn't *do* anything to me. They were just drinking and stuff. Doing stupid stunts on the rides."

"Trudy! You know better than that. You should have called me."

"I know, but you were on your date. I didn't want to spoil that." Her lip trembled and her eyes filled with tears. "But I guess I did anyway. I'm sorry."

I slid closer and cradled her head on her chest, smoothing her hair. "You can call me anytime you need me. It doesn't matter what I'm doing. And you can call your father, too, if you can't reach me."

She sniffed. "Were you having a good time, before you saw me?"

"Yes, I was." I smiled, remembering the feel of David's hand on my shoulder, and the pressure of his lips on mine. Small things really, but things I'd missed so much.

"I'm sorry," she mumbled into my shirt.

"It's okay. David has kids. He understands these things."

"Do you think you'll go out with him again?"

"Maybe. Probably." I hoped so. I needed to take things slow, though. Right now I couldn't trust my feelings. How much of these sensations was my wanting to be with *someone* and how much was my reaction to David himself? Until I could figure that out, I was being cautious.

I patted Trudy's shoulder. "So what do you think we should do about what happened tonight with you and Simon?"

She whimpered and burrowed tighter against me.

"Trudy?" I put my hand under her chin and forced her to raise her head and look at me. "You know I'm going to have to punish you?"

She nodded. "I guess you could ground me."

"You're grounded for two weeks. And that includes when you're at your father's."

She made a face. "Do we have to tell him?"

"Yes we do. And I imagine he'll have a few things to say to you, too."

She rolled her eyes. "It's not fair. I bet kids whose parents aren't divorced don't have to endure *two* lectures."

"Consider yourself lucky to have two parents who care about you so much. Now look at me."

Her eyes met mine again.

"No more of these games with Simon," I said. "I know some of the kids at school can be mean sometimes, but hanging out with people who do 'dumb' things isn't a good way to be popular." I smiled. "You've always been your own unique person. Don't give that up now. Concentrate on hanging with the people who can appreciate you for you."

She collapsed back against the sofa in a dramatic gesture. "That was a great speech. Very momlike."

"I meant every word of it. Now get up off the couch and go upstairs and take off all that makeup. You look like a ghoul."

"I look like a rock star." But she grinned and jumped to her feet. "So did the professor kiss you good-night?"

"That's none of your business." But my blush gave me away, I know. She was still laughing as she ran toward her bedroom. I leaned back against the sofa, smiling. Considering how our conversation had started, I was happy with the way things had ended up. Trudy and I were still on good terms and David hadn't been scared off by tonight's turn of events. I'd survived another parenting crisis with only a few more gray hairs to show for it.

Thank God for hair color and expensive face cream. A little sleight of hand and I could pass for one of those serene women you always see in television commercials, the ones for whom life is all roses and champagne.

But I knew their secret. Even those perfect women have their share of thorns and hangovers. I figured I was getting all that out of the way first. To my way of thinking, I was owed a lot of smooth sailing ahead.

CHAPTER 14

Of course I should have known all those warm fuzzy feelings wouldn't last. By Monday morning Trudy had decided that being grounded for two weeks was "so unfair," and I wasn't even trying to understand her. Nobody understood her. In fact, she was the most miserable girl in the world and it was all my fault.

There's something to be said for being hit with all this at seven in the morning. For one thing, I hadn't had my coffee yet, so I wasn't awake enough to try to argue with her. For another, I had to drop her off at school, which limited the amount of time I had to listen to her whine.

If I thought I was home free once Trudy was out of my hair I was only dreaming. I scarcely had the car parked at St. Ed's when Josh hailed me from across the parking lot. "Hey Grace! Wait up."

For two seconds I thought about pretending I hadn't heard him, or maybe taking off running in the opposite direction. But Josh could outrun me any day of the week and all my mother's admonitions not to be rude were carved deep in my character. Not only can you not fight Mother

Nature, you can't win a battle against Mother Nurture either.

So I slowed and waited for him to catch up. I hadn't talked to him since the night of Mark's show. I thought he'd been wisely avoiding me, but no such luck. "Sorry I haven't been around," he panted as he skidded to a halt beside me after his sprint across the parking lot. "I've had a bad cold."

I made a face. And he'd kissed me. "Thanks for nothing," I said.

He gave me a puzzled look. Then he laughed. "Are you still upset about that kiss the other night? I didn't mean anything by it, you know."

"I know." That was the problem, wasn't it? I wasn't interested in Josh as a potential boyfriend, but it still hurt to be used that way.

"You've got a break now, don't you? Let me buy you a cup of coffee."

"Why?" I knew by now that Josh always had an ulterior motive.

"It's just a cup of coffee. To make up for the other night."

"I have to get to class."

"We still have twenty minutes. That's plenty of time for coffee."

I didn't particularly want to spend the next twenty minutes with Josh, but I didn't want to show up for class early and have David think I was waiting for *him* either.

(Another of my mother's teachings—*don't look too eager.*) "All right. I could use some caffeine anyway."

We made our way to the student union. I thought fondly of Myrtle and the talks we'd had here. "I miss Myrtle," I said.

"Yeah, me too." He paid for our coffees and led the way to an unoccupied table. "I talked to her a couple of days ago and she said she was moving into a rehab facility."

I made a mental note to take Trudy to see her again soon. Both of us could benefit from Myrtle's wisdom.

"So how did Mark's show turn out?" Josh asked. "It looked to me like he was selling a lot of pieces."

You couldn't accuse Josh of shying away from an uncomfortable subject. Me, I'd just as soon forget that night, and that kiss, ever happened. "I think it went very well," I said. "He's already talking about a larger show later in the year, and he's had inquiries from a couple of galleries." Who would have guessed there was such a market for junk art?

"Great. I'm glad for him. He and Gil seem like really nice guys."

"They are." I watched Josh, wary.

He wrapped both hands around his coffee cup. "So, uh, what did you think of Mark when you first met him?" he asked.

I frowned. "What did I think?"

"It must have been awkward. I mean, like meeting the other woman. Only in this case, it was a man, of course."

229

"I knew Gil was gay. I wasn't surprised he'd date another man."

He leaned toward me, his expression avid, like a girl-friend getting ready for a good gossip session. "Yeah, but you and he had been married. And it's obvious you still have feelings for him."

I stiffened. "What's obvious?"

"Well, you know. There's got to be a reason you haven't remarried after twelve years. I figured it was because you were still carrying the torch for Gil."

I gripped my coffee cup so hard my fingernails dug grooves in the cardboard sides. Of all the arrogant, asinine presumptions. Josh had the nerve to psychoanalyze my life and smile at me while doing it. "You don't know what you're talking about," I snapped.

He raised both hands, the picture of innocence. "Hey, don't get upset. If you don't want to talk about it, I understand."

"There's nothing to talk about." I stood and picked up my backpack. "I have to go now."

"No, stay." He laid his hand on my arm. "I have some more questions I need to ask you."

I shook him off. "I knew it. You didn't want to buy me a cup of coffee to make up for the other night. You wanted to pick my brain for your damn paper."

I didn't give him a chance to answer, just turned and fled, stumbling through the crowded student union back onto the mall. So he thought I still had feelings for Gil.

Of course I had feelings for him. He was the father of my daughter. One of my best friends. My first love. I couldn't forget those things just because he hadn't been able to love me the way I wanted to be loved.

In the business building I ducked into the women's restroom and into a stall, where I sank down on the closed toilet lid and rested my head against the metal stall divider. Oh God, what was happening to me? Not forty-eight hours ago I'd been half in love with a man I'd dated *once* and today I was being asked to analyze my feelings for Gil. Couldn't I just get on with my life without having to *think* about it so much?

Someone knocked on the door of stall. "You okay in there?"

I opened my eyes and raised my head. "Yeah. I'm fine." I checked my watch. I had five minutes to get to class. Oh joy—now I'd have to deal with Josh and David in the same room.

I stood and flushed, just in case the knocker was still listening, and emerged from the stall. Ignoring the stare of the blonde who'd been waiting, I went to the sink and washed my hands. I fluffed my hair and studied my reflection in the mirror. For a woman whose life was so chaotic, I looked pretty together. Enough to fool most people.

I took a deep breath and shouldered my backpack. I could do this. I could deal with these two men. I wasn't going to let them see me sweat.

Being new to the adult dating game, I had no idea how

David would act when he saw me. Part of me wanted him to pull me into his office, kiss me passionately and declare he'd been miserable these past forty-eight hours without me. The saner, more practical portion of my brain hoped for some small acknowledgment that he was serious about seeing me again.

What I got was a small smile and a "Good morning, Grace."

I smiled back. "Good morning Da—Dr. Hauser."

When Josh walked past, I pretended to be engrossed in the next chapter of my economics text, and he had the good sense not to try to talk to me.

If anyone wondered why I was smiling throughout the deadly dull lesson on economic indicators they didn't say anything. David at least noticed. At one point he stopped and asked if I understood his explanation of the various indicators. "Of course," I lied. I'd been so busy admiring everything about him from the way he held the chalk to the way his butt looked in his gray suit trousers that I hadn't heard one-fifth of what he'd actually said.

When class ended, David stopped by my desk. "Would you stay after class a moment, please?" he asked.

I nodded, avoiding his eyes, too afraid I'd give my feelings away to everyone around us.

Someone cleared his throat. I looked up and saw Josh lingering in the aisle. I figured he planned on continuing our earlier conversation and scowled at him to let him know that wasn't going to happen.

"Did you need something, Mr. Campbell?" David asked.

"Oh, no." He glanced at me. "I guess not."

"Then I'll see you Wednesday." David ushered Josh to the door and shut it behind him.

He turned to me, looking severe. "Can you tell me the chief economic indicators used by the federal government?" he asked.

I grinned. "No. But I promise to go home and read all about them."

"Having trouble concentrating in class?" He stood very close to me, but didn't touch me. At least not with his hands. His eyes were doing a thorough job of caressing me, making my heart tap dance and my face feel flushed.

"M-maybe a little," I stammered.

He smiled. "Me too. Are you worried this relationship could be bad for your grades?"

I shook my head. Bad for my poor starved libido maybe. "It's not as if I was an A student before."

"True." He stroked his hand along my cheek. "I'd say something about offering you private tutoring, but I'm afraid it would come across as a bad line in a movie."

A nervous giggle escaped. "It probably would." His finger moved back and forth along my jaw, evocative and sensual.

"I'd like nothing more than to kiss you again," he said softly, his eyes locked to mine. "But if someone walked in and saw us it would be awkward."

"You're right." Just knowing he *wanted* to kiss me was enough.

"I'd like to take you out again."

"I'd like that." Soon. And then what? If one brief kiss could get me this heated up, what was going to happen to me when we progressed? I could self-combust. But it was a chance I was willing to take.

"Would you have dinner with me Friday evening?"

"Yes."

"Perhaps your ex-husband would agree to look after Trudy so you wouldn't have to worry about her."

I grinned. "Good idea."

"How did it go with her after I dropped you off Saturday?"

"It went okay. We had a good talk. I grounded her for two weeks. Of course now she thinks I'm the meanest mother in the whole world."

He laughed. "The lines never change, do they? Allison said the same thing to her mother only a few weeks ago."

"I said the same thing to *my* mother."

We stopped talking then, and just looked, staring into each other's eyes. I smelled the herbal scent of his shampoo and the starch in his shirt and studied the feathery edges of his neatly clipped moustache. I wished I'd taken more care with my makeup. Was my mascara crooked? Had I eaten off all my lipstick?

I'm not sure how much time passed before he sighed and took a step back. "I have another class," he said.

"So do I." I gathered up my backpack and he walked me to the door. Then I was out in the hallway, sailing past Josh, deaf to his entreaties.

I floated to horticulture lab and didn't even realize I was smiling until the teacher asked me what I found so amusing about the discussion of the treatment of plant diseases.

At work that afternoon, Monday hit with full force. Mr. Bob was waiting for me when I took over the drive-through. "Found any more pennies for me?" he asked, falling into step with me as I crossed the parking lot.

"I haven't had time to look for pennies, Mr. Bob," I said. I slid my ID through the card reader on the door and shoved it open.

Mr. Bob slipped in behind me. "That's okay. I can look myself."

"Customers aren't allowed in here," I said, shooting a *why me?* look to the morning drive-through employee, Sharon.

"Oh, Mr. Bob isn't going to hurt anything, are you?" Sharon patted the old man on the back, then waved good-bye to me and made her exit.

I stashed my purse under the counter and pressed the button to open the cash drawer. Did I mention before that I'm a sucker for annoying old men? I fished out four rolls of pennies and handed them to Mr. Bob. "Let me know if you find anything good."

"Hope this lot is better than last week," he said. "I only found two wheat pennies in the whole batch."

"Life's like that sometimes," I mused. "Good stuff doesn't come along all that often."

He looked at me over the top of his glasses. "You're awful young to be so cynical," he said.

I laughed. "I'm not cynical. I'm realistic. Besides, I didn't say good things *never* happened. After all, nobody would collect wheat pennies if they weren't a little unusual."

"Hmph." He went back to sorting pennies. "If I'd known they were going to be so hard to find, I'd have started collecting something else."

The phone rang, saving me from having to continue the conversation. "Grace, I need you to come in early tomorrow." Mr. Addleson didn't waste time with pleasantries. "Margo is having surgery or something." His tone said he couldn't believe one of his tellers would be so inconsiderate.

"I have class tomorrow morning." *As you very well know.*

"Can't you skip it? I skipped plenty of classes in my college days and it didn't do me any harm."

That was debatable. "I have an exam tomorrow that I can't miss." An exam I ought to be studying for, but that was beside the point.

"Hey, what do you know? I found two of 'em in the same roll!" Mr. Bob waved his two finds under my nose.

"That's great, Mr. Bob." I smiled and nodded, my mind

working overtime to think of a way to get Mr. Addleson off my back.

"What? Who are you talking to?"

"Mr. Bob. You know, he's—"

"What is that crazy old man doing there? You tell him to get out right now."

"I'll do that. 'Bye."

I hung up before he could protest, and turned to Mr. Bob. "My boss says you have to leave now."

"Okay. There's nothing else good in this lot." He shoved a pile of pennies across the counter toward me. "Want me to reroll 'em for you?"

"That's okay. I'll run them through the machine in a minute."

He glanced at the clock on the wall, then cinched up the old Crown Royal bag where he kept his pennies. "I'd better go, then. It's almost time for the French bread to come out of the oven over at Albertson's. If you don't get there right away, all the free samples are gone."

When he left, I sagged into the chair at the teller window. Blissful silence. At least until the next customer came along.

Everything was routine for a Monday. I took a few deposits from businesses, counted garage sale proceeds for one woman, made change and cashed checks. I was even beginning to think I might be able to sneak in a little studying for tomorrow's Government and Politics exam when a motor home lurched into the drive-through, almost taking out the corner post that held up the awning.

I'm not talking some little travel trailer here—I mean one of those behemoths that ought to come with its own zip code. I watched, one hand on the phone ready to call nine-one-one as the driver, who was barely visible over the dash, inched under the drive-through awning, breathing a sigh of relief when the top of the trailer cleared with a scant three inches to spare.

The thing was so huge the driver couldn't lean out and reach the speaker button for his lane, so the passenger door opened and a platinum-haired woman trotted around to do the honors.

"Mom, what are you doing in that thing!" I stared at my mother, who looked like a midget next to the massive trailer. The window eased down and my father waved at me from the driver's seat.

"Isn't it fantastic?" Mom leaned over and almost shouted into the speaker. She'd never quite gotten the concept that she could speak normally and I'd still hear her ten feet away. "We bought it this morning."

"What are you going to do with it?" I shuddered to think of the damage my father—not the best driver in the world—could do with something this large.

"We're going to explore the open road! Find adventure! See the world." She beamed at me.

"You're going to see the world in that thing?"

"Only North America, but you know what I mean."

I nodded weakly. On one hand, having them out of my hair for a while might be nice, but I knew I'd worry the whole time they were gone. They might be overbearing and interfering at times—especially my mom—but they were my parents and I loved them, and they were getting older.

And why was I suddenly so maudlin?

"We're leaving after the first of the year and we plan to be gone three months," my mother said. "So we'll need you to look after Fifi while we're gone."

Look after Fifi for three months? I shook my head so violently I made myself dizzy. "No. I can't possibly do that. Why don't you take her with you?"

"We can't do that, dear," Mom said. "You know she gets carsick."

"That thing isn't a car. It's an ocean liner on wheels. I'm sure she wouldn't be sick in that."

"We can't take the chance. Not when you're here to look after her."

"Mom, I can't—"

"Of course you can." Someone in the line of cars that had formed behind them honked a horn. She glared at them, then turned back to me. "We have to go. Come for dinner Friday and we'll discuss the details."

"I can't come Friday," I said.

"Why not?"

"I…I have a date." As soon as the words were out of my mouth I wanted them back. I wasn't ready to share my budding relationship with David with anyone else.

"What? With that young man you went out with before? I thought you'd broken up with him."

"No, this is someone different."

"Oh. Well, try not to scare this one away."

"Mother, it's time for you to leave now." I nodded at the line of cars behind her that stretched to the street.

"You don't have to get huffy with me. I'm only trying to give you good advice."

"Goodbye, Mom." I switched off the microphone, leaving her no choice but to frown at me, then hustle back around to the passenger side.

Grinding gears, my father steered the motor home out of the drive-through, narrowly avoiding the Dumpster as he made the turn toward the street.

Seven irate customers later I had a break in the traffic. I pulled out my Government textbook and tried to study, but there's nothing like a ten-page chapter on the importance of political debate to focus your mind on more pressing matters. For instance, was Trudy going to forgive me and resume normal conversation, or was her current unpleasant mood the beginning of the "terrible teens" and four more years of arguments and tears?

What was I going to do with that damn poodle for three months? General Edison would have a fit if he thought I was keeping a dog at my place.

My cell phone rang and I lunged for my backpack. I was getting better at finding the thing before it stopped ringing. Gil's number flashed on the screen, so I answered. "Hello?"

"Hey Gracie. How's it going?"

"Fine, Gil. I'm at work. How are you?"

"Okay. A little nervous, to tell the truth."

Nervous? Mr. Suave was nervous? "What's wrong?"

"Nothing's wrong. It's just that the ceremony is less than a week away and I've never done anything like this before."

"You married me and survived the ceremony. Remember?"

"Well, yeah. But that wasn't the same."

Ugh. What did it say about me that those words hurt? Of course, I knew what he meant. This commitment ceremony with Mark was something Gil wanted to do, something he'd been led to do by the feelings in his heart. Marrying me had been a matter of guilt and obligation. Not to mention that, although my father did not actually own a shotgun, Gil didn't know that at the time, and threats had been made.

"Everything will be fine," I said. I didn't know that, of course, but it's what people want to hear. Sometimes those words alone are enough to pull them through. "When are you leaving?"

"The plane leaves Saturday morning, but we're going to spend Friday night at the airport hotel so we won't have to rush around to get there at the crack of dawn."

Friday! Damn. That meant he couldn't watch Trudy for me. Maybe Joyce could do it. Or my mom. Though after my less-than-enthusiastic reaction to news of her vacation plans I'd have to apologize and maybe even grovel a little.

"Listen, do you have a big suitcase? One with wheels?"

His question pulled me away from my fretting. "Yeah. I have a new one I won in an employee appreciation contest a couple years ago." At the time I hadn't missed the irony that someone who never went anywhere had ended up with a set of luggage.

"Could you drop it by tomorrow night? One wheel fell off Mark's case and we really don't have time to shop for another."

"Sure. I can bring it by."

"Thanks. You're a lifesaver. Now if I can just remember where I put my gold cuff links."

"They're in a box in the pocket of your tuxedo jacket." Even in college, Gil had owned his own tux. Which, now that I think about it, might have been a clue as to his true nature, but I wasn't into deciphering such things back then.

"They are? I think you're right. Thanks."

"It will be great, Gil," I said. "The ceremony will be beautiful. And even if something goes wrong, it doesn't matter. What matters is the commitment you and Mark have already made to each other."

"You're right." I heard him take a deep breath. "You're absolutely right. Thanks."

"You're welcome." I watched a car turn into the drive-through. "I have to go now. I have a customer."

"Okay. But Gracie—"

The tenderness in the way he said my name formed a knot in my throat. "Yes?"

"I just…I hope you find someone like Mark. I mean, someone who'll love you as much as you deserve to be loved."

"Thanks." The word came out in a croak, and I switched off the phone before the waterworks started.

As it was, my eyes fogged with tears. I groped for a tissue, and blotted my eyes, sniffing mightily. My customer pressed the speaker button. "Are you okay?" he asked.

"Allergies." I sniffed again and blinked rapidly. It wasn't a complete lie. Obviously I was allergic to sentiment, especially the heartfelt kind.

Criticism, sarcasm, irritation and even real anger I could handle. I prided myself on being able to deal with the hard stuff in life. But the softer stuff confused me. Maybe it was because I could usually see the difficult stuff coming, whereas love sneaked up on me every time.

CHAPTER 15

Tuesday evening, after slogging through my English exam and enduring another fun-filled afternoon at the bank, I came home and dragged my never-used suitcase out of the hall closet. Trudy wandered out from the kitchen, a bowl of microwave macaroni and cheese in her hand. "What are you doing with that?" she asked.

"Your dad wants to borrow it for his trip." I unzipped the case and made sure there was nothing inside, then zipped it up again. "Want to come with me when I take it over there?"

"Nah, I got homework."

I straightened and stared at her. Since when did homework take precedence over seeing Gil? "Honey, is everything okay?"

She shrugged and poked at her macaroni with a fork. "I'm fine."

"School's going okay?"

That shrug again. "Yeah."

My mom alarm was still pinging. I tried again. "So

you're okay with your dad and Mark having this commitment ceremony and the trip to Hawaii and all that?"

She poked at the macaroni again, but didn't eat it. "Yeah. Whatever." She turned and shuffled toward her room. It took everything in me not to follow. But memories of my own annoyance at my mother's oversolicitous attitude, which I dismissed at the time as sheer nosiness, held me back.

I slumped against the wall and watched her go. Right. This was it, then. Everyone had warned me this was coming. My generally happy, talkative daughter had morphed into a sullen, uncommunicative teen right before my eyes. I hadn't believed it would happen, and I hadn't realized how much it would hurt when it did.

Leaving Trudy to mope in her room, I drove to Gil's and handed over the suitcase. Mark was attending a Tae Kwon Do class downtown while Gil had what looked like the entire contents of his closet spread across the bed. "Do you think I need more than three dress shirts?" he asked.

"You're only going to be there a week. And I'm pretty sure they have dry cleaners in Hawaii."

"Right. Maybe just two, then." He glanced over his shoulder at me. "As many business trips as I pack for, you'd think I'd have this down cold."

"This kind of trip is different." I couldn't quite bring myself to call it a honeymoon, though I guess that's what it was. Anyway, what *I* called it was irrelevant. "Have you talked to Trudy lately?" I asked.

"Not since Sunday. Why?"

"When she was here Sunday, did she seem okay?"

He looked up from folding socks. "I guess so. Is something wrong?"

I chewed my thumbnail. "I'm not sure. She's acting... different."

"She's probably still ticked at you for grounding her." He tossed a roll of socks onto the pile on the bed and picked up another pair.

"You'd have grounded her, too, if you'd been in my place."

"Yes, but you're the one who did it, so that makes you the bad guy."

Oh, the joys of single motherhood!

"Don't worry," he said. "Trudy will be all right. She's a good kid."

"I know." Knowing doesn't stop me from worrying though. The day you become pregnant the part of your brain responsible for worrying immediately enlarges to twice its previous size. For the rest of your life, the slightest hint of trouble on the part of your offspring sets it to throbbing. Which might explain why I'd had so many headaches lately.

"Do you have everything you need for your trip?" I picked up a bottle of cologne from the dresser and set it down again.

"I think so. We have reservations at the Oahu Hilton and the ceremony is all set."

"Did you find your cufflinks?"

"Yes, they were in the pocket of the tux, just like you said."

I hugged my arms across my stomach and watched him fold a handkerchief into a neat square. "Do you have a camera? Don't forget to take pictures."

"I won't." He moved away from the bed and steered me out the door to the living room. "I'm a big boy. Everything's under control."

I flushed. "Sorry. Since Trudy won't let me mother her these days I think I'm overcompensating."

He looked me in the eye. "Everything will be okay."

"I know it will." Say it out loud often enough and I might even believe it.

He continued to study me. "And you'll be okay?"

I nodded. "Yes, I will." I stepped back from Gil and looked at the suitcase waiting by the front door, the tickets on the hall table and all the other preparations for a trip. Gil's life was moving in a new direction, farther away from me.

I examined the idea, prodding at it like a bad tooth. It didn't hurt nearly as much as I'd expected. In fact, I was really okay with the idea. "I'll be fine," I said, a little breathless with a combination of relief and excitement. My world was shifting, little tremors that rearranged feelings and attitudes. Today I was letting go of Gil.

Who knew what I'd accomplish tomorrow.

* * *

When I stopped by the rehab facility the next afternoon to see Myrtle, she was riding an exercise bike, her attention focused on the latest episode of *Oprah* playing on the television mounted in the corner. "I remember her when she was a lowly news reporter. She's done pretty well for herself."

"Pretty well, yes." I crossed the room and stood beside her. "Hello there."

She had one of those smiles that makes anyone within range feel better. "How are you dear?"

"I'm fine. How are you?"

"Making progress. The physical terrorists have me up to five miles on this thing. They say that's good."

"I don't know if I could ride five miles on an exercise bike." In fact, I was pretty sure I couldn't. Though I know it's blasphemy in this day and age, I'm a slacker when it comes to physical fitness.

"Of course you could if you had to," Myrtle said. "Be grateful you don't have to." She climbed off the bike and settled between the bars of a walker. "Let's sit and chat a bit." She led me to a pair of armchairs beneath a window. "How is that darling girl of yours?" she asked.

"Not so darling these days." I filled her in on Trudy's latest escapades, including our confrontation at the carnival and her subsequent moodiness.

"Sounds like something is eating at her." She nodded.

"She'll either work through it alone or confide in you sooner or later."

"I wish I believed that were true. I hate to see her hurting and I want to help her."

"Of course you do." She patted my hand. "But part of growing up is learning to heal your own hurts."

Could we really do that—heal our own hurts? "I just…I was so young when I had her. I'm worried I've done things to screw her up." I laughed without mirth. "Isn't every mother's nightmare to have her child grow up to write a tell-all bestseller blaming mom for everything that ever went wrong in her life?"

"I've seen plenty of screwed up children in my day. Trudy is not one of them." She shifted in her chair to face me. "Look at it this way. You've learned things raising her that will come in handy with the next child."

"The next child?" I choked on the words. "Myrtle, what makes you think there's going to be a next child?"

She offered me another beatific smile. "Why not? You're still young. I had my youngest when I was thirty-eight."

"Well, yes, I know it's possible, but…" When I'd first married, I had anticipated having at least two, maybe even three children. But of course, things hadn't worked out that way. It had been so long since Trudy was born, so long since there was even a possibility of another child, that I'd taken for granted that she was my only chance.

"You don't think it would be, well, *unfair* to Trudy for me to have a baby after all this time?" I asked.

"Unfair to give her a brother or sister? Unfair to teach her about caring for someone younger, someone who will look up to and even depend on her? Unfair to allow her to share her love with a child? What's unfair about any of that?"

"When you put it that way, nothing. Still, she's been an only child for so long."

"And she's old enough to realize you have enough love for more than one child in your life. Besides, we worry too much about being fair to children these days. Life is unfair and while I would never condone unnecessary hardship or cruelty, there's nothing wrong with them having to deal with unfairness now and then."

"Why are we even having this conversation?" I laughed.

"We were talking about the challenges of being a parent. How is David?"

The mention of David Hauser in such close proximity to our discussion of children made me a little nervous. It was way too soon to be thinking along those lines, I was sure. "He's fine," I said. The less said on the subject, the better.

"Did you enjoy your date at the carnival—at least until you saw Trudy?"

"Yes." I smoothed my hands down my thighs, unable to keep the good news to myself after all. "We're going out again this Friday."

"Excellent. She grabbed hold of the walker and hoisted herself to her feet. "I have to go for my whirlpool now."

I stood also and kissed her cheek. "It was good to see you."

"Good to see you, too. Come back next week and tell me all about your evening with David." Her eyes sparked with mischief. "And don't leave out any details. It's been a long time since I was in a relationship with a man, but I still enjoy remembering what it was like."

I hadn't seen Mom since she and Dad showed up at the bank in their new RV, but I couldn't avoid her forever. After all, she was my mom. Plus, I needed her to look after Trudy Friday night. Since she'd managed to survive my own stormy adolescence, maybe she knew a way to banish my daughter's sulkiness that I hadn't hit upon yet.

Of course, Trudy objected to the idea of having to stay at her grandmother's. "Why can't I go to Dad's house?" she asked.

"Because he and Mark are staying at the airport hotel Friday night since their plane leaves early Saturday morning to go to Hawaii. Besides, your grandmother loves to see you."

"She can see me anytime."

"She and Granddad are planning a big trip. They'll be gone for three months, so you won't see them for a while."

She folded her arms across her chest and looked stubborn. "Why can't I stay here by myself?"

"Because you're fourteen and if anything happened the child welfare people would haul me to jail and put my name in the paper and it would be very embarrassing."

She studied me, apparently weighing whether or not I was serious. "Where are you and this professor dude going on your date?"

"I don't know. Probably to dinner." How wonderful to have a meal with pleasant conversation and no pouting children at the table!

"Can Grandma come here instead of me having to go over there? I have a lot of homework and it's a big hassle to tote all my stuff over there." She indicated the various books, papers and notebooks scattered around the room.

"Since when are you so interested in homework on a Friday night?"

She scowled at me. "Mo-om!"

"All right. I'll ask Grandma to come over here." Though it would mean more groveling. I hate to grovel, especially to my mother.

Fortunately, Mom was in a good mood when I called. "I'm so excited about this trip," she said. "It will be like a second honeymoon for your father and me."

"So you're going to the beach?"

"The beach? I hate the beach. I can't stand sand in my shoes and the salt water makes my hair look like straw."

"But I thought you and Dad spent a weekend on Padre Island for your honeymoon."

"We did, and it's a wonder we stayed married after that.

I got food poisoning from eating bad shellfish and spent the entire weekend lying on the bathroom floor with a wet washrag on my head."

"So where *are* you going for this 'second honeymoon'?"

"Everywhere. Except the beach."

"Could you come over to my house first and look after Trudy Friday night?"

"That's right. You told me you have a date."

I winced. Did Mom have to sound quite so gleeful about this? "Yes, I have a date. With one of my professors."

"Wonderful. Of course I'll look after my granddaughter. But why don't you bring her here?"

"She says she has a lot of homework. But it's probably because we have cable and you don't."

"All right then. I'll stop by early and we can talk about Fifi's schedule."

"Fifi's schedule? Why does a dog need a schedule?"

"It's important for animals, like children, to have a routine. She likes to eat at specific times of the day, plus you'll need to walk her and take her to the vet. She's due for her shots while we're away."

Had Mom not heard me when I told her I couldn't take care of her dog for three months? "Don't come too early, Mom. I have to get ready for my date. We'll talk later."

I was afraid if I refused Mom now, she'd get mad and I'd be out a sitter for Friday. I could just see me telling David I was bringing a fourteen-year-old chaperone on our date.

CHAPTER 16

Joyce called while I was dressing for my evening with David. "What are you planning to wear?" she asked.

I looked at the contents of my closet scattered across the bed. Times like this I wished we all wore uniforms, like on *Star Trek*. Lieutenant Uhura never had to obsess over what she wore on a date. "I'm not sure. I'm thinking a floral skirt and a shirt."

"Sleeves or no sleeves?"

"Um, sleeves, I guess. What if we go someplace where the air-conditioning is turned down to frostbite level?"

"Cleavage or no cleavage?"

"What?" I glanced at the modest valley between my breasts.

"Is the neck of the top low enough to show a little cleavage or not?"

"Um, not, I guess." I held up the blue knit blouse that was my top choice so far.

"I recommend you go for low-cut and sleeveless. You've got a nice body, why not show it off a little?"

"Joyce! I don't want to come across like I'm advertising myself as tonight's special."

She laughed and I heard the ice in her glass rattle as she took a sip of her drink. Gin and tonic, I guessed. She was probably getting ready for her own date. "What are you wearing tonight?" I asked.

"A red chiffon sleeveless, backless dress that would make Marilyn Monroe proud. My plan is to dazzle Trevor into worshiping me from the very beginning."

"Trevor? Who's Trevor?"

"I met him when I took Kevin in to have his ears checked and he seemed so nice. I thought, why not give him a try?"

"You picked up a patient in the doctor's office?"

"No, silly, I picked up the *doctor*." She laughed. "He's not really the doctor, though. He's a physician's assistant. And I didn't pick him up. We flirted a little and he asked me out."

How did she do it? Joyce hadn't been officially divorced even three months and men flocked to her. "Have a good time. The dress sounds gorgeous."

"Go for a slinky tank top," she said. "David won't get the wrong idea. If you're lucky, he'll get the right idea and ask you back to his place."

"I don't want to go back to his place." Not yet, anyway. Call me old-fashioned, but this was only our second real date. I need to know someone longer than that before I let them see me naked. "Besides, what if I get cold?"

"It's been twelve years since you slept with a man. I don't think anyone would say you're rushing it. And if you get cold, you ask him to keep you warm. It all works together, see?"

"I'll keep that in mind. Have a great time tonight."

"*You* have a great time. Talk to you tomorrow."

She hung up and I reached for the blue top. At this point in my life, comfort won out over my desire to appear sexy. Besides, I hadn't noticed David disliking anything he'd seen so far.

I was brushing a second coat of mascara on my lashes when Trudy came into my room. "You look really pretty," she said, standing behind me and watching me in the mirror.

I smiled at her reflection. "Thanks."

She hesitated, then leaned forward and slipped her arms around my neck, hugging me tightly. The suddenness of the movement, and the tenderness of it, made my throat tighten. I reached up and awkwardly patted her arm. "Everything okay?"

She nodded. "I'm sorry I've been such a butt lately."

"It's okay, honey. We're all butts sometimes." And a few, unfortunately, are butts on a permanent basis but thankfully my daughter was not one of those.

"I don't mean to be a pain, but I have a lot of stuff going on, stuff to think about. It makes me feel all weird sometimes."

Adolescence in a nutshell. "You're a good kid," I said. "And smart. You'll figure it out. And you know I'm here for you if you ever need to talk about anything."

"I know." She withdrew her arms and stepped back. "What time do you think you'll be home?"

"I don't know," I said. "Not too late."

"Grace! Trudy! Anybody home?" My mother's shout carried through the house.

"Be right there, Mom!" I answered.

Trudy and I met Mom in the kitchen. She was fussing with a casserole she'd set on the counter. "I made spinach lasagna," she said when we walked in.

"My favorite." Trudy gave Mom a hug. "Hi, Grandma. How are you?"

"Pretty good." Mom slid the casserole dish into the oven and turned the dial to three-fifty. "I've been busy planning this trip. I've been trying to decide if it would be better to get maps from Triple A or Rand McNally."

"Triple A has them for free so I'd go for those," Trudy said.

Mom patted her cheek. "That's my girl." She turned to me. "I've been thinking, Grace. Why don't you and Trudy move into our house while we're away? That would be less stressful for Fifi and you could save the money you'd spend on rent during that time."

"I have a lease, Mom. I can't break it. Plus, I don't want to lose the house."

"So rent it out."

"General Edison would have a conniption." Not to mention I didn't relish the idea of strangers living in my house. "Maybe you should hire a house sitter," I said. "There are whole lists in the paper."

"Fifi would hate living with a stranger."

And I would hate living with Fifi, but I was only her daughter. Apparently the dog outranked me these days. I was saved from making any comment by the phone. Trudy and I raced to answer it, but I won.

"Grace? I need a big favor." Joyce sounded panicky.

"What is it? Is something wrong?"

"My sitter cancelled. Could your mom watch Trudy and my boys?"

I covered the phone with my hand and addressed my mom. "Joyce's sitter cancelled. Could her two boys come over here and stay with you?"

"I suppose I could manage that. Trudy can help."

Trudy's expression soured. "I guess I could help with the evil twins."

"They're not evil," I said. "They're not even twins."

"They're ten- and eleven-year-old *boys*," she said. "They can't help being evil."

I shook my head at her and uncovered the phone. "Send them on over."

"Thanks. And thank your mom for me, too."

I suspected Joyce had had her kids poised on the doorstep when they showed up within two minutes of my hanging up the phone. But I sympathized with her desperation. If my night out with David had been threatened I'd have been tempted to go door-to-door searching for a neighbor to keep an eye on Trudy.

"Thanks, Mom." I kissed her cheek on impulse. I think the gesture startled us both.

"What was that for?" she asked.

"Just because. I really appreciate you helping me out tonight."

"Trudy is my granddaughter, for goodness' sake. Why wouldn't I want to spend time with her?"

If only all relationships were so simple. I didn't have time to contemplate this further, as the doorbell rang. "David's here," Trudy said, and raced for the door, Kevin and Kyle at her heels.

I smoothed my hair and followed at a more sedate pace. When I reached the living room David was standing just inside, being introduced to Joyce's boys. "These are the evil twins, Kevin and Kyle. Their mom has a date tonight too, so they're staying with us."

"We're not twins," Kyle said.

"But we are evil," Kevin announced, then collapsed against his brother in a fit of giggles.

"Hello, David."

He looked up at my approach, and his smile was so dazzling I wondered what kind of reaction I could have gotten if I'd elected to show my shoulders *and* cleavage, per Joyce's advice.

"Hrrmph."

I jumped as my mother cleared her throat behind me. "David, this is my mother, Claire Sharpe." I introduced them.

He shook hands. "It's a pleasure to meet you, Ms. Sharpe."

"Please, call me Claire." Mom smiled, showing her dimples. So how insecure was I, to worry that my mother was better-looking than me? "Won't you sit down and visit a minute?"

"We really can't, Mom." I collected my purse and stood by the door. "We have to go."

David took my hint and said goodbye to everyone, including Kevin and Kyle. When we were safely buckled in his car, I let out a sigh. "I hope you didn't think you needed to protect me from your family," he said. "It's been a while, but I've had a little experience in weathering grilling from parents and other relatives."

I laughed. "I wasn't protecting you," I said. "I was protecting *me*. A woman can put up with only so much embarrassment in front of a date."

"I'm sure it wouldn't have been that bad."

"Stick around a while and maybe I'll let you find out. My mother can be unnervingly direct at times." I imagined her asking David what his "intentions" were, or if he practiced safe sex.

"I hope I will 'stick around.'" He offered another killer smile and I sank back in the seat, fretting eased out by something like bliss.

The rest of the evening was something of a blur, outstanding because nothing provoking, worrisome, embarrassing, difficult or problematic occurred. We ate dinner at a Thai restaurant downtown, then cruised Sixth Street, pausing for drinks at a small pub, poking through tacky souvenir shops and stopping to watch a sidewalk artist sketch a woman's portrait.

We talked! Adult conversations about politics and books and music and the world as we knew it. For those few hours I wasn't Trudy's mom or Gil's ex-wife or even Joyce's best friend or Claire's daughter. I was just Grace, a woman on a date with an interesting man.

When we arrived back at my house three hours later, David held my hand as he walked me to the door. "I had a great time tonight," I told him. "Thank you."

"Thank *you*," he said. "I hope it's the first of many wonderful times we'll have together."

Then he kissed me. Or I kissed him. Or maybe we both leaned toward each other at the same moment and the next thing I knew, we were kissing.

We started with just our lips touching, soft and sweet and not nearly enough. David pulled me close, his hands on my waist, and I slid my arms around his shoulders. That didn't seem to be enough either, so I opened my mouth and deepened the kiss.

Everything about the moment was so perfect. We moved together so well, and standing here with his arms around me felt so…right. I was delirious with happiness, dizzy from not breathing and positively giddy with the idea that for once things might be going my way.

About that time the porch light came on. I jumped

back and blinked in the harsh glare. I believe David may have cursed. He glanced toward the small window in the front door. "Was that supposed to be some kind of hint?"

I shook my head, already planning the speech I'd give whoever was on the other side of the door—a speech about respecting my privacy and minding their own business and…

The door opened and my mother stood there. My anger vanished when I saw her face. She was gray, her eyes filled with fear. "I'm sorry to disturb you," she said. "I tried to call earlier but you didn't answer your phone and I didn't know what to do." She burst into tears, covering her face with her hands.

Oh God. Is there anything worse than watching your mother cry? Mothers don't do that sort of thing, at least not in front of their children. And I was still her child, even at thirty-five. "Mom, what's wrong? What's happened?" I gathered her close, smoothing her hair, kissing her forehead.

"It's Trudy! I can't find her. I don't know where she is."

CHAPTER 17

My heart stopped beating for a moment. I swayed, wondering how I could possibly stay on my feet.

Then David was there, propping me up, leading both Mom and me to the sofa in the living room. "Take a deep breath," he commanded, and handed Mom his handkerchief. "And tell us what happened."

Mom sniffed and dabbed at her eyes with the hanky. "The boys were watching a movie in here and Trudy went to her room to do homework. About an hour later, I made popcorn and went to see if she wanted some. She didn't answer when I knocked on the door, so I opened it. And she wasn't there." She shook her head. "I looked everywhere and she wasn't there."

David's eyes met mine. "My son has been known to sneak out of the house to meet friends. Maybe Trudy's done something similar."

"She's never done anything like that before." But the teenage years were all about doing things you hadn't done before, including disobeying your parents and sneaking out of the house.

"I tried to call you." Mom sniffed and gave me an accusing look. "I don't know why you bother with that phone if you're not going to answer it."

"Maybe you had the wrong number." I opened my purse and dug out my phone.

"I checked. I had the right number. You must not have had the phone on."

I stared at the blank screen on the phone, my stomach heavy with guilt. "I…I guess the battery's dead. I meant to plug it into the charger last night, but I forgot." I closed my eyes, unable to push back thoughts of what might have happened if Trudy or my mother had needed me.

But of course, they *had* needed me.

"What time did you first notice her missing?" David asked.

"About nine o'clock."

I checked my watch. "An hour and a half. Did you call Gil?"

Mom shook her head. "Isn't he in Hawaii?"

"He and Mark are at the airport hotel. Their plane leaves in the morning." I looked at my cell phone, debating whether to call him. On one hand, he *was* Trudy's father and deserved to know if something was wrong. On the other hand, I hated to spoil the beginning of his vacation if everything turned out all right. Plus, part of me resisted turning to him in yet another crisis. "I'll call him if we don't find her soon," I said. "Where the *hell* is she?"

"Call her friends' parents," David said. "They might know."

"I'm going to check her room first."

I led the way down the hall to Trudy's bedroom. In typical teenage fashion, it looked as if someone had recently ransacked it. Clothes spilled from open drawers and every flat surface was covered with CDs, books, magazines and half-empty soda cans. Sheets and blankets trailed half-off the bed and no less than six pairs of shoes lay scattered on the floor.

"How can you tell if anything's out of order?" Mom asked, snatching a bra off the back of the desk chair and stuffing it into a drawer.

David walked to the window and shoved it up. "It wasn't locked."

"It's supposed to be." I stood beside him and frowned at the darkness outside. It was a fairly short drop to the ground. Nothing for an active fourteen-year-old. But where had she gone?

I turned to the bed and stared at the litter of books and papers. A sheet of pink cardstock on the pillow caught my eye. I leaned over and snatched it up, relief and anger warring as I read:

Dear Mom,
If you find this I guess I'm in big trouble. Don't be angry. I'm not doing anything bad or anything, I just

had to go out for a little while. I'll be okay, I promise. Don't worry.

Love,
Trudy

"You better believe she's in big trouble. And what is this
crap about not worrying? I've never read anything so ridiculous."

Mom sat on the edge of the bed and shook her head. "I
don't know whether to laugh or cry."

"Laugh?" I glared at her. "Why would you laugh?"

She smiled. "When you were a teenager and gave me
so much grief, I always said if there was any justice in the
world you would have a daughter who was just like you and
then you would understand what I went through."

"Very funny." Of course I knew I'd been a trial to my
parents. It was one reason I tried not to come down too
hard on Trudy now, to give her room to be herself without tying her down too much. And look where all my
leniency led. Maybe if I'd been stricter I'd know where she
was right now.

I went to the bedside table and opened the drawer.

"What are you doing?" Mom asked.

"Trudy has an address book somewhere. I'm going to
find it and call all her friends."

David began sifting through the items on Trudy's desk.
"Wait a minute—what's this?"

He held out a flyer printed on goldenrod paper. "Poetry
Slam, West Lynn Tavern, Friday November eighth," he read.

"That's tonight," I said.

"What's a poetry slam?" Mom craned her neck to read over my shoulder.

"I believe it's where people stand up and perform poetry and the audience critiques the work." David turned to me. "Didn't you say Trudy writes poetry?"

I nodded.

"Do you think she would go to something like this?"

I studied the flyer. "Maybe." She'd certainly been worried about *something* lately. And the budding drama queen in her would probably love to angst on stage like this. "I guess it couldn't hurt to check it out."

He folded the flyer and slipped it into his shirt pocket, then took my arm. "Then let's go."

West Lynn Tavern turned out to be a bungalow in a former residential neighborhood that had become commercial. The craftsman-style home squatted between an Italian restaurant and a Pilates studio, a neon sign hanging from the porch the only outward indication that it was no longer a residence.

The front door was open, the sounds of talking and laughter and the smells of strong coffee and stale beer spilling out across the porch. On shaking legs, I followed David inside, uncertain what to expect. What was a *fourteen-year-old* doing here, alone, on a Friday night?

But then, maybe she wasn't alone. Maybe this was Simon's or some other guy's idea of "cool." I'd thought Trudy

267

immune to that kind of peer pressure but then, that was probably unrealistic, considering her age.

Typical of most places with the word "tavern" in their name, the interior was so dimly lit I couldn't walk two feet without stumbling into someone or something. David managed to find a table to the far left of the stage and we sat down. An older man was on stage, squinting at a torn sheet of notepaper in his hand, his voice droning.

"You look at me and stab me with your eyes.

You want to wound me, but I won't let you.

I should have known I couldn't love a woman

Who owned a cat."

"Oh, my," I whispered to David. "Even Trudy is better than that."

The audience apparently agreed. "Don't quit your day job," one helpful man advised.

"Unmetered and irrelevant" was one more erudite critique.

"What have you got against cats, buddy?" asked a third.

And my daughter wanted to do this? For fun? "I don't know," I said. "I don't think she's here." I turned in my chair, squinting into the dimness, hoping to spot Trudy in the crowd.

"We should find out if there's a backstage area we can check," David said.

Just then I spotted a familiar figure. As the lights came up between performers, I recognized Cal standing to one side, his gaze directed off-stage.

I jumped up and wove through the scattered tables and chairs toward him. When he saw me he hunched over, and looked around for escape.

I grabbed his arm before he could slip away. "Cal? What are you doing here?"

His cheeks looked as if someone had painted on circles of rouge. "Uh, hello Mrs. Greenleigh."

"Is Trudy here with you?" I shook his arm. "Answer me."

David's hand squeezed my shoulder. "Maybe if you let the boy go he'll talk."

I realized that I was holding Cal's arm so tightly he'd probably have a bruise tomorrow. I let him go and stepped back, taking deep, calming breaths.

Except I didn't feel any calmer at all. "You cannot even imagine how terrifying it is to come home and find your daughter gone," I said. "If you know where Trudy is, please tell me."

His eyes widened. "I know she didn't mean to scare you. She said you'd be mad if you found out, because she's supposed to be grounded and all, but we thought we could get back to the house before you came home."

"So you helped her sneak out?" I'd expected something like this from Simon, but Cal? Sweet, ordinary, nice-guy Cal? "Why?"

He had the grace to look guilty. "I didn't really help her. But when she told me she was planning on doing this, I couldn't let her come here by herself."

I wasn't sure if he was being a gentleman, or if he saw

this as an opportunity to make points with his crush's mom, but I decided to give him the benefit of the doubt. "So she sneaked out of the house and met you. Then what? How did you get here?"

"I rode my bike to your house and left it in the hydrangea bushes in the back. Then we walked to the corner and took the bus over here."

"I take it you planned to get home the same way?" David asked.

He nodded. "I brought money for a cab, just in case."

Simon would have never done anything like that, I was sure. I patted Cal's shoulder. "I'm sorry for grabbing you like that earlier. Thanks for looking after Trudy."

He shrugged. "I'm not really looking after her. She's just my friend, you know?"

We could all use more friends like Cal. "Let's go get her and go home," I said.

"You can't do that!" He looked alarmed. "I mean, well, she's supposed to perform pretty soon."

I was torn between dragging Trudy back home immediately, and letting her do this thing that was important to her. In the end, curiosity won out over my need to see her safe. I glanced at David. "Do you mind staying?"

He shook his head. "I'll stay as long as you want."

We returned to our table, Cal in tow. David ordered coffee for the adults and a soda for Cal. I called Mom and let her know we'd found Trudy, that she was safe and we'd be home in a little while. For once she didn't grill me. On the phone she sounded as tired as I was.

We listened while a thin woman with long black hair, dressed all in black, read a tribute to Austin's urban bat colony. "Not bad," was David's assessment. "At least it rhymes."

Other comments were equally as lukewarm. I wrapped both hands around my coffee cup and fought to stay in my chair. I didn't know if I'd be able to sit still if someone openly criticized my baby.

"Look, here she comes." Cal sat up straighter and nodded toward the door behind the stage.

Someone dressed like a gypsy—long skirt, tuniclike blouse, a scarf or veil draped over her hair—walked to the center of the stage. Or should I say tottered. Trudy was wearing platform sandals that had to be at least six inches tall. "Why is she dressed like that?" I whispered to Cal.

He coughed. "Well, you know, you're supposed to be eighteen to be in here, on account of they serve beer. So we both tried to dress older."

For the first time I noticed that Cal was wearing a suit—or at least the coat and pants, without a tie. What I'd mistaken for dirt on his upper lip proved to be a fledgling moustache, which I suspected had been darkened with an eyebrow pencil, or perhaps a brown crayon.

As I watched, he reached up and stroked the lip fuzz. "We found out nobody asks for ID unless you try to order alcohol. Plus it helps that it's dark in here."

I made the mistake of looking at David. He was rubbing his chin, obviously trying very hard not to laugh. I had to bite my lip to keep from joining him.

Trudy hadn't seen us yet. I doubted if she could see much beneath her "veil" which I now recognized as a good silk scarf from my closet. "My name is Trudy Greenleigh, and my poem is called Advice," she said, her voice surprisingly strong and clear. My knees would have been banging together like cymbals if I'd had to stand up there.

She began to read.

"My fortune cookie says today's my lucky day.
The paper tells me 'be prepared for rain.'
My boyfriend wants to go out on the town,
While my teachers stress the need to buckle down.
All good advice, I'm sure,
But what pieces do I take, and which do I leave behind?

"My father says to study hard, be smart,
While preachers say the kindest deed endures.
My mother says 'follow your heart.'
But I wonder if she ever follows hers,
As she does this and runs there, always doing her part
To help, but rarely speaking her mind.

"My grandmother tells me to 'be a good girl.'
It's obvious she taught my mother well.

I want to be like her, because I know she really cares.
But sometimes I wonder if it isn't better to be a little
bad,
If that means following your own dreams
Instead of always helping others to realize theirs."

My eyes stung and my throat ached. I squeezed David's hand so hard I probably left marks, but I had to hold onto something and he was the closest. It was either that or break down in tears. "How am I supposed to be angry enough to punish her now?"

I hadn't realized I'd said the words out loud until she jerked her head in my direction. Her mouth dropped open and she turned pale, then tried to run.

Of course, nobody can run in six-inch platforms. Instead, she tripped and launched herself across the stage. One of the bartenders caught her, and David, Cal and I rushed to her side.

"Mom, what are you doing here?" she wailed. Her gaze darted to David. "Don't tell me you came here on your date?" Her voice let us know she couldn't think of anything less cool.

"We found the note in your bedroom," I said. "And the flyer about this place. Your grandmother was absolutely frantic by the time I got home." *Not to mention the years you took off your mother's life.*

Her face crumpled. "I didn't mean to worry her. I didn't think she'd even find out."

I was too relieved and upset and exhausted to discuss all this right now. I took her hand. "Come on. Let's go home."

David and I didn't talk on the drive home, though I heard Cal and Trudy whispering in the back seat. I thought I heard him say her poem "rocked," and her reply that she wished she'd had a chance to hear what everyone else thought.

Cal walked Trudy to the house while I said goodbye to David at the car. "Do you think we'll ever have a date that doesn't end in some family crisis?" I asked.

"I guess we'll have to keep trying and find out."

"Are you sure you want to keep seeing a woman with such a complicated life?"

He laughed. "Life is complicated." He kissed my cheek. "Let's hang in there and see what happens."

I waved as he drove away, smiling in spite of everything. I liked his philosophy. It was as good advice as any on how to get through anything.

Including the talk I was going to have to have with Trudy.

"Mom, I'm sorry," she said when I came into the living room. She sat on the sofa, arms around my mom, so I assumed the two of them had made their peace.

"Where's Cal?" I asked.

"He got his bike and went home."

"That's good. Where are Kevin and Kyle?"

"Their mother came and got them while you were out

looking for Trudy." Mom stood. "I'd better get home, too. Your father will be wondering what happened to me." She patted Trudy's head, then gave me a hug.

When we were alone, I could feel Trudy watching me. "Mom, say something," she pleaded.

"Let's get some sleep first. We'll talk in the morning."

Maybe by then I'd have thought of the right words to say to her.

CHAPTER 18

When I got up the next morning, Trudy was waiting in the hall outside my bedroom, sitting cross-legged on the floor with her back against the wall. "What are you doing?" I asked.

She shrugged. "Waiting for you."

"How long have you been sitting here?"

Another shrug. "I don't know. A while."

I lowered myself to the floor and sat beside her. I would have preferred to have a cup of coffee first, and maybe something to eat, but kids have their own timetable sometimes and you have to run with it. "Do you have something you want to say?"

"I'm sorry I worried you, and I'm sorry if I messed up your date." She directed the words toward her lap.

"You didn't mess up my date." I suppose I could even say the ordeal had been a kind of a test. David hadn't bolted, which raised his standing with me considerably. "But you did worry me. And you worried your grandmother, too."

"Does Dad know?"

"No. I didn't want to spoil his trip, so I waited to tell him."

"That's good." She sniffed and rubbed at her nose with the side of her hand.

"Is that all you have to say?"

Her eyes met mine. They were red from crying, smeared mascara and eyeliner making dark smudges against her pale skin. "Are you gonna stay mad at me forever?" she asked.

I might have laughed, if not for the anguish in her voice. I put my arm around her shoulders and pulled her close. "Oh, honey, I'm not mad at you. Not much, anyway, and certainly not forever. I'm more disappointed. And confused." I drew back enough to look her in the eye. "Why did you sneak out of the house last night? And why did you go to a bar, of all places?"

"I didn't go there because it was a bar. I went because they were having this poetry slam."

"Okay, fair enough. But you still went there without permission, and without any of us knowing where you were."

"I left you a note telling you I was okay, that you didn't have to worry."

To her fourteen-year-old mind I'm sure it all made perfect sense. I bit the inside of my cheek to keep from telling her that one day she'd see things differently. The speech that formed in my head actually began "Someday you're going to have a daughter just like you and you'll understand...." Boy, didn't that one sound familiar?

And the worst part was, I'd had to admit that Mom was right.

At least I could spare Trudy that indignity. "I'm glad you left the note," I said. "But it doesn't take away from the fact that you went somewhere you weren't supposed to go, behind my back."

"I know." She plucked at imaginary lint at the knee of her jeans. "I just..."

I waited as the silence stretched between us. My stomach rumbled and the beginnings of a caffeine withdrawal headache pounded at the base of my skull. "You just what?" I prompted. "Why was this poetry slam so important to you?"

She tilted her head sideways and slanted a look at me. "Mom, it felt so awesome up there on that stage. I knew it would. I mean, at school nobody much pays attention to me, which is okay and everything. But last night...I mean, people really listened to what I had to say. I could tell. And some of them even applauded. It was so incredibly awesome."

I thought of her poem again. It wasn't great literature, but no one in the room could have doubted that it was heartfelt. Mine probably weren't the only wet eyes in the room. And isn't that the mark of good writing, to be able to move people? To make them laugh, or cry, or rage, or *feel* something?

I took her hands in both of mine. She was wearing navy blue nail polish, chipped at the edges, and the nail on the pinky finger was chewed to the quick. Something I did when I was stressed also. I smiled at the thought.

"Why are you smiling?" she asked.

Instead of telling her, I lined my fingers up against hers. They were almost the same length. "I can remember when your hands weren't even a third as big as mine," I said. "I could cover them both with one of mine."

"That must have been when I was really little."

I nodded. "And you're not little now. I know." I met her gaze. "But you are only fourteen. Not grown by a long shot. And you had no business being in that tavern last night without your father or me with you. If this was so important to you, why didn't you ask one of us to take you?"

She made a face. "I didn't think you would. I'm still grounded for going to the carnival with Simon."

"You could have asked. If you'd made a good case for going, we might have made an exception."

She looked doubtful. "When would you have taken me? You're both so busy lately I hardly see either one of you."

Ouch. "Trudy." I took her chin in my hand and made sure she was looking at me when I spoke. "Yes, your father and I are busy. But we're not too busy for you. You should know that."

"I know, but...maybe part of it was I didn't want to embarrass myself in front of you."

"I thought you did a great job last night," I said. "And the poem made me cry—but in a good way."

She looked pleased. "Not that it's all that hard to make *you* cry."

"You're lucky the poem was good. Before then I was seriously considering locking you in the house until you're eighteen. And if you ever pull a stunt like this again, I just might."

She hung her head. "I know. I'm sorry. I won't do it again."

"You know you're not getting away with this without being punished."

She wrinkled her nose. "I guess not."

"Then what do you think should be your punishment?"

She jerked her head up and stared at me. "You're going to make *me* decide?"

I nodded. This was a trick my mom had played. Only now could I fully appreciate the deviousness—and the wisdom—of this approach. "You choose your punishment, but I get to decide whether or not it's severe enough."

She thumped her head back against the wall. "I don't know. How about...I have to weed all the flower beds. And since I also upset Grandma, I have to weed her flower beds, too."

This was a more severe punishment than I would have handed down. Trudy *hates* to weed flower beds. She didn't inherit my green thumb. "I'm proud of you for remembering you need to make this up to Grandma, too. So weeding flower beds it is." I stood and offered her my hand. "Let's go see about breakfast."

"I'm hungry. Will you make pancakes?"

"Don't push your luck, child."

That afternoon, Trudy presented me with a computer printout of her poem, nicely framed with construction paper. "I was gonna wait until your birthday or something, but I figured it might be better to give this to you now," she said.

"Thanks, honey." I smiled at this peace offering. "I'll hang it in my bedroom, where I'll see it every day."

"So, do you think it would be okay for Cal to come over this afternoon? We're gonna study for the history test tomorrow."

So there was an ulterior motive behind her gift. Why was I not surprised? "Have you ever thought about being a professional diplomat some day?" I asked.

She wrinkled her nose. "Huh? What does that have to do with Cal coming over?"

"So you and Cal are friends now?"

"We've always been friends." She shoved her hands in

her pockets and studied the toes of her shoes. "Now we're just…better friends."

"All right. He can come over. And he can stay for dinner if he likes."

"Thanks, Mom." She whirled around and raced back to her room, presumably to call Cal with the news.

I took the poem to my room. Reading the words again made me choke up. *My mother says "follow your heart." But I wonder if she ever follows hers, As she does this and runs there, always doing her part To help, but rarely speaking her mind.*

Was that really how Trudy saw me? As a slave to what other people wanted? A "good girl" who put others' dreams ahead of my own?

I sank down on the edge of the bed, the impact of the words knocking my legs out from under me. I hadn't exactly set out to cultivate that image. I didn't even particularly *like* that image, flattering as it was in some respects. I didn't want to be a martyr, I just wanted to be an ordinary mother.

No, that was wrong. I wanted more. I wanted to set an example for my daughter, and that did not include giving up my life to the demands of other people. Sure, it was easy to like someone who always did what you wanted, but it was a lot harder to like *yourself* when you were that person.

So if this is what I'd become, what was I going to do about it?

The question still rang loud in my head when I went to bed that night, keeping me awake for hours. By the next morning, I was determined to make some changes in my life. The prospect both excited and terrified me. But I couldn't live with myself any longer if I didn't make them. I didn't have any more room in me to swallow the discontent I'd been feeling for months, even years. Trudy's poem—her vision of me—had given me the kick in the butt I needed to set things right.

As luck would have it, the first person I encountered when I arrived at St. Ed's was Josh. Did he lurk in the parking lot, waiting for me? "Good morning, Grace," he said, striding toward me, a big smile on his face. "You look great this morning."

I thought back to our first encounter, similar to this one. Back then I'd been impressed by Josh's good looks and friendly manner. Now I was suspicious of his motives. "Hi Josh." I greeted him warily. "How's it going?"

"Not too bad. My faculty advisor approved the outline for my paper. He thinks focusing on the sociological impact of married men who 'come out' as gay has a lot of potential."

He grinned at me, obviously expecting congratulations and offers to help him with this project. The "nice girl" part of me was tempted to wish him well and go on. But that wouldn't stop him from trying to wear me down. How many times before had I tried to get out of some unpleasant task by ignoring it or avoiding the subject? And it almost never worked.

Goodbye, good-girl Grace—hello, gutsy-girl Grace. I stopped and faced him. "Look, Josh, the answer is 'no.' No, I don't think your paper topic is a good idea, no you can't use me for research and no, I won't help you with this in any way, shape or form."

"Now, Grace, this will be a good thing, I promise. I won't use your name or anything."

"Josh, I don't care. No!" I glared at him. You know how in cartoons they show angry people with steam coming out of their ears? That's exactly how I felt. "And another thing—I am really pissed off at you for using me this way. You took advantage of our friendship and I don't appreciate it."

He actually took a step back. Talk about power surges! I've never been known for intimidating people, but I could get used to the idea.

"Grace, what's gotten into you? You used to be so sweet."

Guilt pinched hard, but I reminded myself that all that sweetness had gotten me so far was a reputation as a pushover. "And I used to think you weren't such a jerk."

Head high, I marched past him, fighting the urge to look back. Standing up for myself didn't come naturally to me by a long shot, but I hoped with practice it would get easier.

My first stop was the campus bookstore, where I picked out software that promised to make it easy for anyone to balance their checkbook. No more knowing way more than I needed to about Gil's finances. I'd always think of him as a friend, but it was time to step back a little and find a full life for myself without him.

"Hey, I remember you."

I blinked at the bookstore clerk, searching my brain for some clue as to his identity. Was he in one of my classes?

"You came in at the start of the semester with your daughter Truvi."

"Trudy." I remembered now. My smile was positively evil. "She's fourteen."

"Oh." His smile wavered. "Cute girl." He handed me my bag. "Here you go. Have a nice day."

I held back my laughter until I was out the door. Trudy wouldn't have appreciated that but what can I say? I'm still her mother.

I pretty much soared to class on my self-esteem high, and played it cool, pretending not to notice David trying not to notice me. Being a bad girl was turning out to be a kick. When he stopped by my desk after class I took my time putting my books in my backpack, though I couldn't keep back the beginnings of a smile.

"Grace?"

"Yes, Dr. Hauser?" I tried for a demure look, though I felt anything but.

"How was your weekend?"

"It was fine."

"And Trudy? Is she all right?"

"Yes. Trudy's fine, too."

"Do you think we might try again for an uninterrupted evening together?"

His choice of words sent a shiver of anticipation up my spine. Imagine what we could do with a whole uninterrupted evening, alone. "I definitely think we should try again," I said. "I wouldn't want to think you were the type of man to give up easily."

"Oh, no. I'm definitely not a quitter." He leaned toward me, his voice a seductive growl. "When I find something I want, I make it a point to go after it."

I squirmed, resisting the urge to fan myself. I forced my mind back on track. I'd lain awake half the night thinking of what I should say to David and I didn't intend to let my great speech go to waste. "There's just one thing," I said.

He straightened, worry edging out lust in his expression. "What's that?"

I smoothed my hand across the desk. "I need the name of a good economics tutor."

I checked his response through lowered lashes. The glee I felt at his obvious confusion over the swift change of subject shows how far I'd veered from my good girl training. "A tutor?" He cleared his throat. "It just so happens, I'm available."

I laughed and shook my head. "No, I mean a *real* tutor."

He didn't *harrumph*, but he might as well have. "I'm a *professor*. I think I'm competent to tutor a student."

"Of course you're competent to tutor a *student*. But I'd hoped, since we're dating, that I was a little more than that."

"Of course you are. That doesn't mean—"

"Yes it does." I looked him in the eye, making sure he was paying full attention to what I had to say. "In the classroom, you're my professor. Outside the classroom, you're my good friend. I don't want to confuse the two." I smiled. "Besides, how much studying do you really think we'd get done?"

He nodded. "I see your point. All right. Stop by my office tomorrow and I'll have the name of a tutor for you."

"Thanks." I stood and slung my backpack over my shoulder. I was almost to the door when I turned to him again. "David?"

"Yes?"

"Thanks. For everything." I blew him a kiss, then hurried away, feeling equal parts giggly schoolgirl and femme fatale.

Not a bad combination when you think about it.

Half-afraid my newfound determination would wear off overnight, I made it a point to stop by my parents' house on my way home. Though the weekend had given me a new appreciation for what my mom had gone through when I was a teen, I didn't intend to let guilt sway me from my resolve. As soon as she opened the front door, I marched past her into the living room. "Mom, I absolutely cannot look after Fifi while you're gone on vacation," I said.

She stared at me for a long moment, clearly trying to determine if this woman in her living room was really her daughter. "If you can't take care of her, what am I going to do?" she finally asked.

"I don't know. Why don't you take her with you? I'm sure the vet can prescribe some medication for her motion sickness."

"But I thought she'd be happier here at home. She really likes you, you know."

I glanced at the dog, who reclined on the sofa, eyeing me with disdain. "The only person she really likes is *you*," I said. "She'll be happier wherever you are. Besides, don't you think you'll miss her if you're gone three months?"

"I suppose you're right." She sank onto the sofa and reached over to pat the dog.

"Take Fifi with you, Mom. Everyone will be happier if you do."

"All right. I'll think about it. She does like to ride in the car...."

"There you go. She's a natural. You worry over nothing."

She sighed. "It's what mothers do. Don't you know that by now?"

I laughed. "Yeah. I think I'm catching on." We both stood and I gave her a hug. "I'll talk to you later, Mom. And thanks."

"What are you thanking me for?"

"Just for…everything." I shrugged. "I probably don't say that enough."

"You don't. But it's nice to hear it." She patted my arm. "I'm going to miss you, you know."

"I'm going to miss you, too." I gave her another hug. "We'll talk on the phone. I promise."

"You'd better. I want to hear all about you and this professor. I want to know if he's good enough for you."

"I guess we'll find out, won't we? But I'm not rushing into anything, so don't get your hopes up yet."

"That's fine, dear. You have plenty of time."

And to think only a few weeks ago, she'd told me time was running out. I decided not to bring this up. Another thing I was learning is that mothers are always allowed to change their minds.

I headed toward the bank, but halfway there I took a detour to Travis Gardens. "Hey, Grace!" Kimmie said when I came in the door. "What can I do for you today?"

"I want to apply for the manager's job." I nodded to the notice in the window.

I braced myself for laughter. After all, to Kimmie I was just another customer with a green thumb. But instead of laughing, she looked pleased. "Great. I'll tell Gerald."

Gerald Barmus turned out to be the manager of the Travis Gardens in Westlake, a wiry, fiftyish man with Willie Nelson braids and a Do It In the Dirt T-shirt. "I'm pulling double duty until we hire someone here," he said after introducing himself. "Kimmie tells me you're interested in the job."

"Yes. I've been a customer here for years, so I'm familiar with the inventory. I'm an avid gardener and I'm studying horticulture at St. Edward's University."

He nodded. "That's good. Why don't we walk around the place and talk a minute. How do you feel about working weekends?"

"I don't mind. Since I'm in school every morning during the week, weekends are good for me."

"We're only open until two on Sundays, but Saturdays and Sundays are our busiest times. That's been a sticking point for most of the other applicants we've had."

"I don't have a problem working then. But I'd need time off for my classes during the week."

"We can be pretty flexible on your weekday hours." He stopped beside a display of deer-resistant plants. "I had a lady in here earlier who said deer ate every one of her pyra-canthea bushes, thorns and all. Can you imagine?"

"A hungry deer will eat almost anything. She could try planting oleander or something like that. But sometimes the best solution is an electric fence around the bed."

He nods. "What do you know about drip irrigation systems?"

"I've had one for five years now. I think I've figured out all the possible problems and solutions with it."

"Roses?"

"I have those, too." I grinned. "If it has to do with gardening or landscaping, I've probably tried it at one time or another."

"Japanese bonsai?"

"You've got me there. But I know a professor at the college who's won prizes for his bonsai, so I could consult him if someone had a question I couldn't answer."

He turned to me and offered his hand. "The job is yours if you like."

I opened my mouth to say yes, but my no-longer-a-pushover side reminded me I still had business to conduct. "What about pay and benefits?"

"We have medical and dental and a 401K. Nothing fancy but it's decent coverage." He named a salary figure that was a dollar more an hour than I was making at the bank.

I resisted the urge to kiss him. "I'll take it. I have to give notice at the bank first, but their policy is usually to pay two weeks severance and send you packing. I think they're afraid an employee on the way out might be tempted by all that money."

"Are you? Tempted, I mean?"

I shook my head. "You handle money long enough and the first thing that comes to mind isn't wealth, it's how dirty it is and how many germs are on it. Seriously, I go home every afternoon with my hands black from counting money."

He laughed. "Now you can get your hands dirty the old-fashioned way."

I all but skipped out of there. Imagine, being excited about going in to work every day? What a concept! The first thing I was going to do was send Joyce flowers. If I'd listened to her four weeks ago, just think of the hours of drudgery I'd have avoided.

Mr. Addleson was less than thrilled when I gave him the news. "Grace, I think you're making a very big mistake," he said. "If you continue your education, I think you have a solid future in banking."

Funny, he'd gone out of his way to discourage me from going back to college. Now all of a sudden it was a wonderful thing. "I've decided I don't want a future in banking," I said. "I'd much rather work with flowers and plants."

"All these years of loyalty and this is how you repay

me?" He shook his head. "I'm very disappointed in you, Grace."

His words made me a little queasy, but I stood my ground. "I'm sure you'll find someone who's even more capable to take my place," I said. After all, while I'd been good at my job it wasn't something that required genius or above-average skills.

I pulled into the drive of Reagan Junior High School just as Trudy came out of the side door to the band hall, flute case in hand. "Mom, I need a new white T shirt and five dollars for art class," she announced as she slid into the front seat.

"Good afternoon, Trudy. I'm fine, thank you."

She rolled her eyes at me and fastened her seat belt. "How was your day, Mom?"

"My day was great." I put the car in gear and eased into traffic. "I got a new job."

"For real? No more slaving at the drive-through?"

"No more slaving at the drive-through. You're looking at the new manager of Travis Gardens."

"The manager! Mom, that is so cool." She bounced in her seat. "Did you get a big raise?"

"I got a little one. There are no new cars or designer shoes in our future, but we'll still be able to afford macaroni and cheese and mascara."

"Oh, well, in that case, we're on easy street." She grinned at me. "Really, Mom, I think that's cool."

"No more being too busy with other people's dreams to realize my own."

She flushed. "Honest, Mom, I didn't mean to hurt your feelings or anything."

"No, you're right. I was putting everybody else ahead of myself. I was being a 'good girl'—not because I wanted to, or even because I thought it was right, but because it was an easy out. If you always go along and do what people expect, you never have to risk them being upset with you, or having to make hard choices. But no more." I glanced at her. "You've inspired me, Trudy. From now on I'm going to do a better job of taking care of myself and not worry so much about what other people think."

"Go, Mom. We should celebrate."

"I have homework and you do, too. But I could spring for take-out pizza."

"I vote for Thai chicken pizza."

"I thought you were a vegetarian?"

She shrugged. "I was, but you know, I don't like tofu much. And I missed hamburgers. I figure it's okay to change your mind, especially at my age. I mean, that's what being a teenager is about, right? Trying to figure out stuff like whether or not you want to be a vegetarian, and how you feel about nuclear weapons and whether or not rap is better than pop."

"Right. All those important issues."

She frowned. "Are you making fun of me?"

"No." I smiled. "I'll let you in on a secret, though. A lot of us adults don't have those things figured out yet, either."

She did her eye-roll thing and shifted to look out the side window as I turned onto our street. "Why are Joyce and her boys standing in their front yard?" she asked.

"The shoe tree ate my Frisbee," Kevin announced as we emerged from the car.

"Can you believe this?" Joyce brushed her bangs out of her eyes and stared up at the bright green Frisbee, lodged like an errant UFO to the right of the tiger-print platforms.

"I'd leave it up there, except that the boys would tell Peter about it and he'd make it a point to come over and get the thing, just to prove what a man he is and how incompetent I am."

"You're not incompetent." I gave her a hard look. "Why do you care what he thinks?"

She sighed. "Good question. But I do."

"You deserve better."

"I know I do." She looked away. "I'm just scared."

I put my arm around her. "We're all scared. But you've got me, and you've got your boys. Most of all, you have yourself."

"And you think that's enough?" She gave me a shaky smile.

"Of course it is." I punched her shoulder. "If you can transform yourself from matronly schoolmarm to sexy mom and raise two boys and take care of your household by yourself, you can do anything."

"No one ever said I did a good job with the household stuff, and the sexy mom idea is still open for debate." But the life had come back into her eyes, and she was smiling again. She looked up into the tree, then squared her shoulders. "Okay then. I can do this." She jumped up and grabbed onto the lowest branch, then planted her feet against the trunk.

"Mom! What are you doing?" Kyle gaped as she started up the tree.

"I understand the view from up here is incredible," she said, pulling herself onto the first limb. She grinned down at me. "I figure it's time I see for myself."

I laughed, and put one arm around Kyle, and the other around Trudy. We watched as Joyce climbed to the very top of the tree. I felt as triumphant as if I was up there with her. After all, I'd scaled a few heights of my own today. I didn't have everything in life figured out by a long shot. There were still too many things to do each day, and not enough hours to do them. I had yet to settle on a major, and I didn't have a clue where my relationship with David would go, or even where I *wanted* it to go.

But I was making a start. I was finally doing what I'd set out to do months before. I was getting my life out of the ditch I'd been in and moving forward. It was exciting and scary and almost overwhelming.

Deep breath, Grace. You can do this.

After all, if I didn't like the way things turned out this time around, I could give it a new start.

Tomorrow.

REQUEST YOUR FREE BOOKS!

2 FREE NOVELS TO INTRODUCE YOU TO OUR BRAND-NEW LINE!

There's the life you planned. And there's what comes next.

NEXT05TALL

HARLEQUIN®
Next™

Coming this September

In the first of Charlotte Douglas's Maggie Skerritt mysteries, an experienced police detective has to predict a serial killer's next move while charting her course for the future. But will Maggie's longtime friend and confidant add another life-altering event to the mix?

PELICAN BAY
Charlotte Douglas